DEATH
BY
MISADVENTURE

ALSO BY TASHA ALEXANDER

A Cold Highland Wind

Secrets of the Nile

The Dark Heart of Florence

In the Shadow of Vesuvius

Uneasy Lies the Crown

Death in St. Petersburg

A Terrible Beauty

The Adventuress

The Counterfeit Heiress

Behind the Shattered Glass

Death in the Floating City

A Crimson Warning

Dangerous to Know

Tears of Pearl

A Fatal Waltz

A Poisoned Season

And Only to Deceive

Elizabeth: The Golden Age

DEATH
BY
MISADVENTURE

A LADY EMILY MYSTERY

Tasha Alexander

MINOTAUR
BOOKS
NEW YORK

First published in the United States by Minotaur Books, an imprint of St. Martin's Publishing Group

DEATH BY MISADVENTURE. Copyright © 2024 by Tasha Alexander. All rights reserved. Printed in the United States of America. For information, address St. Martin's Publishing Group, 120 Broadway, New York, NY 10271.

www.minotaurbooks.com

Designed by Omar Chapa

Library of Congress Cataloging-in-Publication Data

Names: Alexander, Tasha, 1969– author.
Title: Death by misadventure / Tasha Alexander.
Description: First edition. | New York : Minotaur Books, 2024. | Series: A Lady
     Emily Mystery ; 18 |
Identifiers: LCCN 2024016442 | ISBN 9781250872364 (hardcover) |
     ISBN 9781250872371 (ebook)
Subjects: LCSH: Hargreaves, Emily, Lady (Fictitious character)—Fiction. |
     Murder—Investigation—Fiction. | LCGFT: Detective and mystery fiction. |
     Novels.
Classification: LCC PS3601.L3565 D39 2024 | DDC 813/.6—dc23/eng/20240415
LC record available at https://lccn.loc.gov/2024016442

Our books may be purchased in bulk for promotional, educational, or business use. Please contact your local bookseller or the Macmillan Corporate and Premium Sales Department at 1-800-221-7945, extension 5442, or by email at MacmillanSpecialMarkets@macmillan.com.

First Edition: 2024

10 9 8 7 6 5 4 3 2 1

For Andrew. In one kiss you'll know all I haven't said.

The soul that sees beauty may sometimes walk alone.

—*Johann Wolfgang von Goethe*

DEATH
BY
MISADVENTURE

1

Villa von Düchtel, Bavaria
1906

Far too many—if not most—social gatherings would be immeasurably improved by the strategic removal of a troubling guest. When said individual's behavior is particularly egregious, one may be forgiven for considering murder as an acceptable remedy for the situation. The civilized among us curb this instinct. They may think about it; they may go so far as to indulge in flights of fancy as to the method they would choose; but they don't strike a fatal blow.

It was unclear if such propriety would triumph at the soirée hosted by the Baroness Ursula von Düchtel to celebrate the completion of her striking modern villa. The meticulously designed structure of mosaic glass and concrete was a revelation, a visible reminder of the progressive direction of our still-young century. Bright blue glass tiles above towering entry doors spelled out *Villa von Düchtel*, the words gleaming against the pale wall. Deep eaves jutted from the edges of the roof, creating a strong horizontal line. More tiles, fashioned in geometric designs, decorated the doors and the space between the tall, narrow windows lining the first floor. Below them, near the ground, and above them, approaching the roof, the windows were stained glass, wider and shorter than the rest. More breathtaking than the building were its surroundings. Towering peaks ringed the valley around the grounds, thrusting into the sky. Winter had painted everything a fragile, icy white that pulsed and glowed. Tree limbs hung heavy with snow. Icicles glistened. The air was so cold it looked as if tiny diamonds were floating in it. The baroness's guests were insulated from the chill inside the house, where an unobtrusive staff anticipated one's every whim as they perused their hostess's stunning—and enormous—art gallery.

The guests gathered were an eclectic bunch. Most were far-flung friends and neighbors whose sprawling estates were scattered in the valleys dotted between the mountains. There were dealers and artists from Berlin; a handful of journalists and critics; an Australian who could be heard far across the room praising the virtues of the breed of sheep he favored; a young woman who claimed to have been kidnapped by a band of traveling acrobats as a child; a Sikh poet; and two American sisters, Anna Josephine and Emeline Christine McAndrew, who had traveled to every continent on Earth save Antarctica. They were currently in the midst of organizing an expedition there. Instead of conversing with any of these fascinating individuals—all of whom spoke fluent English peppered with a charming smattering of their native tongues—I'd found myself cornered by the baroness's son-in-law, Kaspar Allerspach. Almost at once I reached the inevitable conclusion that we would never be friends. An aquiline nose, strong jawline, and handsome enough face can only carry one so far. The gentleman—I use the term loosely—was a boor, whose only interests appeared to be congratulating himself for various sporting achievements and criticizing others. He was the sort of man whose loutish behavior might easily lead any number of otherwise civilized

2

individuals to contemplate murder. I'd just started wondering what would be the most satisfying method of eliminating him when his wife, Sigrid, approached, looped her arm through his, and kissed his cheek.

"You know, Lady Emily, this is just the sort of evening *der Mär-chenkönig* would've adored," she said to me. Tall and slim with delicate features, pale blonde hair, and turquoise eyes, she looked like a princess plucked out of a Germanic fairy tale.

"*Der Märchenkönig?*" I asked.

"It means *the fairy-tale king* and is what we locals call Ludwig the Second," she said.

"Mad King Ludwig, who bankrupted himself building ridiculous castles," her husband said, puffing on a Cuban cigar. I knew its origin because he'd spent nearly a quarter of an hour explaining in excruciating detail the lengths—and expense; he was quite specific as to the cost—he went to in order to ensure he smoked nothing but the best. "Fortunately, he had the good sense to kill himself before he entirely destroyed Bavaria. It's a pity he didn't do it before he'd run through his fortune. I certainly could have spent the money better."

"Do not mistake eccentricity for insanity." Sigrid's bright smile and tone, as well as the way she met her husband's eyes, suggested flirtation rather than censure. "Further, he didn't commit suicide. He was murdered."

"The man was a monster. His only generous act was to remove himself from the population." He grabbed a flute of champagne from the tray of a passing footman dressed in colorful livery that looked straight out of sixteenth-century Venice, a nod to the baroness's eclectic tastes. Kaspar's hands were so large it seemed inconceivable that he could hold the delicate crystal without crushing it, but somehow he managed. "He forbad his servants from looking at him and meted out abusive punishments. Ordered one man to wear a mask and another to have sealing wax put on his forehead."

"You're hardly one to criticize anyone's treatment of servants," Sigrid said. "Just because the king's enemies liked spreading those sorts of stories doesn't make them true."

"As always, *mein Schatz*, I bow to your superior knowledge, although one would hope a person of intelligence wouldn't fall for such obvious propaganda. You do consider yourself a person of intelligence, do you not?" He swallowed the wine in a single gulp, bared his teeth—long, yellow teeth—in what I believe was intended as a grin, and tossed his glass onto a gleaming marble-topped table, where it shattered.

"Kaspar often hides his finer qualities," Sigrid said, turning to me as her husband rolled his eyes. "I beg you not to hold it against him. We don't all have spouses as charming as yours. He's promised me a sleigh ride tomorrow, along my favorite loop near the house, so I'll forgive him. It passes the most beautiful frozen waterfall one could ever hope to see. There's no place more magical. You'll have to visit it while you're here."

My husband, Colin Hargreaves, and I had been included in the party at the urging of my dear friend Cécile du Lac, who'd known Sigrid's mother, the baroness, for decades. They'd met at an auction in Paris where they'd each been vying to acquire an early Manet painting. When, at the last minute, a gentleman from Bruges outbid them both, they retired to Cécile's house in the Boulevard Saint-Germain and consoled themselves with what she described as a catastrophic amount of champagne. Their taste in art—and penchant for passionate affairs with artists—cemented their relationship.

The baroness had gathered us all in the villa's long, wide gallery,

which was crammed full of decorative objects. An elaborately en-
graved suit of Renaissance armor occupied a corner, flanked on one
side by a large Fragonard canvas depicting a couple playing blind-
man's bluff and on the other a Klimt portrait whose subject was
no other than Cécile. She sat for it some years ago when we were
both in Vienna and she and the artist were entangled in an affair.
She loved the painting, but, not want it looming over her, had given
it to Ursula. It was hanging slightly off-kilter, so I straightened it.
Fifth-century Greek vases occupied shelves next to a medieval book
of hours. Degas wax models of dancers and horses stood alternating between six Cycladic sculptures that dated from approximately
2500 BC. Paintings, drawings, tapestries, woodcuts, and panels of
stained glass covered every inch of the interior walls. Here, Matisse
was a neighbor of Dürer, André Derain a friend of Rembrandt.
Tall windows on the exterior wall framed a panoramic view of the
mountains. Night drenched the rocky peaks with inky darkness, but
the sky was clear and a bright full moon cast shadows of the tall trees
lining the estate on the snow-covered ground. Faintly visible in the
distance was the glint of the white walls of Schloss Neuschwanstein,
Ludwig's famous castle, which more than justified the king's nickname. Its soaring towers looked straight out of a fairy tale, the sort
of place a princess might be held prisoner, waiting to be rescued by
a handsome prince. Far better, of course, if she rescued herself.

"Ludwig was inspired by Germanic legends, not the Brothers
Grimm," Sigrid said, following my gaze out the window. "Hence his
devotion to Wagner's operas."

"Swan kings and Rhine maidens," Kaspar said. "I never saw
the appeal."

"The music is sublime," I said, "regardless of how one feels
about the stories."

5

"Don't let Sigrid start on Wagner," he said. "She'll become—"

A stunning young lady who moved with the grace of a dancer interrupted him. "Don't let Kaspar start on anything. I'm Birgit Göltling and I already know you're Lady Emily Hargreaves. Who made your dress? It's divine."

The cruel amusement in her pale blue eyes as she spoke betrayed her true feelings. I wasn't surprised. For the occasion, I'd chosen an unusual gown, fashioned from filmy, cream-colored silk chiffon and decorated with bands of deep blue embroidery in the meander pattern, the Greek key. A wide belt with a Swarovski crystal buckle cinched my waist. It was striking, but could not be described as au courant.

"The House of Worth," I said. "I wanted something that celebrated the baroness's collection."

Birgit crinkled her perfect little nose. "Whatever can you mean by that?"

My husband appeared behind me. "The baroness's art collection is wonderfully diverse and includes a significant number of ancient Greek pieces," he said. "Emily's dress is a nod to them."

"I know Worth's not as fashionable as it used to be, but I never dreamed it was that out of date. Ancient Greece, you say?" Birgit's physical beauty was extraordinary. What a pity her brain didn't sparkle as well.

"Yours is by Jeanne Paquin—am I right?" I asked. The red fabric coupled with her daring use of black were instantly recognizable. I had recently acquired several items from her, an innovative woman with one of the finest ateliers in Paris. She despised the currently popular S-bend corset almost as much as I. I adored her empire style, which did not require tight lacing.

"I prefer Poiret, but once in a while I slum with Paquin." She leaned close to me, adopting a pose of obviously false camaraderie. "I figured there'd be no one here among all these fuddy-duddies I should bother to impress." With that, she spun around so that her gauze skirt flared, positioned her hands as if she were dancing with a partner, and waltzed away through the throng of Ursula's friends who filled the room.

"She's got spirit, doesn't she?" Sigrid said. "Endlessly amusing."

Kaspar raised his eyebrows. "If you say so. I'll never understand what my friend Felix sees in her, but if he's happy, what more can I ask? And given that he brought her here, he must be happy. The man's always had appalling taste. Prefers sailing to boxing, if you can imagine." He was squinting and watching the Fräulein as she continued her solo waltz along the windows lining the room. It was an appalling display, manufactured to show off her perfect figure. Kaspar's face colored ever so slightly. "Maybe I do understand, now that I look again."

Sigrid gave him a playful whack on the arm. "You're a brute." I was shocked she took his obvious admiration of another woman so lightly. Colin and I exchanged a discreet glance.

"Yes, but I'm your brute." Kaspar patted his wife on the head as if she were a dog or a small child and grimaced as he saw our hostess walking toward us with Cécile. "I've no interest in speaking to your mother, so you'll have to excuse me." He slunk off, calling for someone to bring him beer.

"You ought to have left him in Munich." The baroness snapped open her fan and waved it, as if it might send her son-in-law far, far away.

"Mama, don't start," Sigrid said. "I know how overbearing he can be, but he adores me and that's all that matters."

"I care about nothing save your happiness and if you insist

you've found it shall have to accept that." Ursula von Düchtel stood half a foot taller than the other ladies in the room. Her height, along with her broad shoulders, shining white hair, and turquoise eyes, conjured the image of an elderly Valkyrie. "What do you think of my little collection, Emily?"

"It's unlike anything I've seen before," I said. "You've managed to curate a display that assaults the senses without overwhelming them. It's a feast."

"Kaspar claims it gives him a headache," Ursula said. Sigrid rolled her eyes, huffed, and stormed away.

"It is, perhaps, better to let some things go unmentioned," Cécile said.

"She should've married Max," the baroness said.

"Max?" Colin asked. "I don't believe I've met him."

"Even if you had, you wouldn't remember," Ursula said. "His special talent is fading into the background. It's not a weakness, but rather a strength. There's not a self-interested bone in his body. He would've been content to stand back and let Sigrid shine." She clapped her hands and called out his name. A nondescript man of average height and build with mousy hair and forgettable features responded to the summons.

"You called, my lady?" He gave a little bow, but the movement, awkward rather than fluid, caused him to lose his balance, and he nearly tripped.

"Max Haller, meet my new friends," she said, and made the requisite introductions.

"What a pleasure," he said. "I understand Sigrid was telling you about Ludwig and rhapsodizing about Wagner. Are you lovers of the opera?"

"As much as anyone," I said.

"A cryptic answer, Lady Emily, but I'll forgive you for it. Not everyone shares my passion."

"I wouldn't say I don't share it, only that—"

"Max is a musical genius, you know." Sigrid returned to our little group the instant she noticed he'd joined us. "Mama's convinced him to stay here, with us, for a few days instead of returning home. He plays the Wagner tuba. If we're very kind to him, we might be able to persuade him to give us a little concert."

"Sigrid, you mustn't suggest any such thing." Max's pale skin turned crimson from his forehead to the tips of his fingers. "Even if I wanted to, I don't have it with me. I—"

"You always travel with your tuba—don't pretend otherwise. I know you too well." She squeezed his arm and met his eyes, pulling back only when a great bear of a man with thick, black hair and a jagged dueling scar on his cheek appeared and stood next to her. "This is Felix Brinkmann, my husband's best friend."

"The only thing about Kaspar worthy of a compliment," Ursula said.

"Mama, stop criticizing him. I cannot—"

Ursula raised a hand to silence her daughter, but before she could speak, a woman rapidly approaching the depths of middle age broke into our circle, clapping her hands.

"Baroness, the evening is a triumph." She moved her hands with an almost violent enthusiasm. Her voice, resonant and rich, fell upon us like drops of pleasant, cool summer rain. She possessed ordinary brown eyes and nondescript features. Her strawberry blonde locks ought have been a striking feature, but she'd styled them with so little care they did nothing for her appearance. She looked like a maladjusted spinster. Until she spoke, that is. Then her face and her body came alive.

"You've an eye for beauty that's rarely seen, and you combine it brilliantly with a nose for significant works. Someone who is entirely ignorant about art will be as enthralled by your collection as a scholar."

Ursula laughed. "This is Liesel Fronberg, an art dealer from Berlin. She's brought two paintings for me to consider purchasing and has evidently decided that flattery might help her get the sale."

"No, I assure you—" She stopped and blinked, then shook her head. "You're jesting. I ought not to be so serious all the time."

"Not jesting, no, only speaking a truth you might not yet have learned yourself," Ursula said. "Come, I will introduce you to some of my guests who will be interested in your gallery. Staying here will only irritate my daughter. She doesn't like me criticizing the boy she married."

"He's not a boy," Sigrid said when they'd gone, her voice signaling long-running frustration. "He's nearly forty years old."

"Your mother likes being hard on Kaspar," Felix said. "I ought to have pointed out to her that he has a collection of watches I've long envied, so perhaps she could add fine taste to his qualities that merit compliments. But don't let yourself believe she was all that insulting. I'm nearly forty-five and wouldn't object to being called a boy."

"Nearly forty-five?" Cécile asked, looking him up and down. "*Intéressant*." He grinned and the skin around his eyes crinkled. His face was golden brown, tanned from the sun, even on this winter day.

"*Charmant*," he said. "You, that is, not I." He kissed her hand, then laughed. "I'm not good at playing the gentleman. Forgive me."

"Then you must learn, Monsieur Brinkmann." Her eyes danced. "And if you'd like to be friends with me, you must learn to choose champagne over whisky."

Felix grinned and opened his mouth to reply, but then Kaspar's voice boomed from the other side of the room, calling for Felix.

"Best not to keep him waiting," Felix said. "One never knows what sort of trouble he might get into. Come with me, Max, will you?"

"Max is a decent boy," Cécile said as they walked away. "He grew up nearby and was always close to Sigrid. I thought they'd marry—she's an unfortunate sort who craves bourgeois respectability—but once she met Kaspar, poor Max stood no chance."

"Kaspar doesn't strike me as much of a catch," I said.

"Not once you know him, no, but Sigrid was bowled over by his handsome face. By the time she realized he was an ignorant boor, it was too late."

"It's the sort of bad decision many people make," Colin said.

"Like Monsieur Brinkmann. Birgit is an appalling creature," Cécile said. "There's something intriguingly untamed about him. He deserves better than her. Further, he's old enough to be interesting."

Old enough, by Cécile's definition, was over forty. "Too old for Birgit," I said.

"Not if she possessed wisdom enough to know what to do with him," Cécile said.

"And what's that?" I asked.

"I strongly suspect Monsieur Brinkmann needs to be schooled in the art of pleasing a woman."

Colin laughed. "I shouldn't think Birgit would have the slightest idea of how to go about such a thing."

"*Bien sûr*, monsieur," Cécile said. "Inexperience is never an asset. It is why one needs a qualified teacher."

Shouts came from the other side of the gallery. Felix and Kaspar were standing opposite each other, gulping large steins of beer. Kaspar finished his before his friend, threw the stein onto the floor, and pulled a cigar out from his jacket pocket.

"You'll never best me, Felix. I'm twice the man you are."

As I said, many parties would be improved by the strategic removal of a troublesome guest, yet tonight, no one had exerted the slightest effort to do so with Kaspar. Perhaps this was due to the extreme measures it would require. An action less violent than murder would have no effect on a man like him.

Or so I thought.

A tall, wiry man approached him, hesitating for a moment before pulling him aside. They spoke. The color drained from Kaspar's face as his obnoxious grin disappeared and the cigar fell from his mouth. Then, he regained his composure, pulled himself to his full height, shouted for silence, and addressed his mother-in-law's guests.

"I didn't realize until this moment that I'm attending my own wake. This late arrival to our gathering was sent to write my obituary."

2

Near Füssen, Bavaria
1868

Niels von Schön's passion for the Bavarian countryside was the essential thread in the tapestry of his existence. Alpine lakes and mountains provided a much-needed escape from the claustrophobia of his family's Munich home, where he was subjected alternately to his mother's cloying adoration and his father's crushing disappointment. Convinced he deserved neither, he couldn't decide which rankled him more.

He had nothing in common with either of his parents. His father was a baron with no interests beyond finance, hiking, and his pack of hunting dogs. Niels loved music, opera in particular. He had a fine, strong voice, and wanted to sing. His father abhorred the very idea. His aristocratic mother's singular obsession was the House of Wittelsbach, Bavaria's royal family. She claimed her friendship with Marie of Prussia, King Ludwig II's mother, was the most important of her life. Disdaining high society, Niels avoided her circles. Far from letting this bother her, she decided it confirmed her belief that her son possessed an enviable intellect, despite his lackluster performance at university. Her compliments made him uncomfortable. Prickled him with guilt. So he stayed away as much as he could, fleeing even in the winter to their summer house in the mountains.

At first, he struggled, alone in the Alps, unsure of what to do with himself other than study music and sing. His sense of self battered by his father's constant criticism, he hadn't the slightest idea what else he wanted from life. His father hunted, hiked through the mountains, and had been a soldier—briefly—in his youth. Slight, with narrow shoulders, one noticeably lower than the other, Niels was built for none of this. So conscious of the lack of symmetry in his body, he never noticed he had a pleasing, handsome face. All he'd been taught to see were flaws.

This was, perhaps, unfair to his mother, but her excessive compliments made him reject her opinions out of hand. Who could believe the sincerity of a person who lauds everything one does? Her bias in favor of him was so complete, she was incapable of seeing him as anything but an idealized version of someone he'd never wanted to be. It was as destructive as his father's censure.

Niels's sole comfort was music. He could play the piano well enough, but his talent lay in his voice, pure with perfect pitch. His range made him a *Jugendlicher Heldentenor*, suited to singing heroic tenor roles that required more lyricism than dramatics. Not that the classification mattered. He sang whatever he desired, things that moved him or gave him a respite from the pain that plagued his psyche. Sometimes that was folk songs. Sometimes it was arias from the operas of Richard Wagner.

It was the latter he was singing the day his life changed.

3

Villa von Düchtel
1906

The party came to a rather crashing halt after Kaspar's announcement. The journalist explained that he'd received a telegram from his editor directing him to Ursula's villa so that he might attend the wake of her son-in-law, whose athletic accomplishments and violent death merited an obituary. Colin and I pressed for more details, but there were none, so we penned a message to the editor, asking for more information. All the guests who weren't staying at the villa scattered. The house echoed with silence after their departure.

"It's more than a little off-putting to be informed that one is dead," Kaspar said, his face still pale, his voice shaking.

"It's obviously a mistake," Sigrid said.

"Or someone playing a joke," Felix said.

Kaspar frowned. "I see no humor in it."

I felt a bit sorry for him. Anyone would be unsettled in the circumstance. My sympathy waned, however, when I woke the next morning to the sound of him and Felix playing a modified version of ice hockey in the corridor outside the bedrooms. The puck, I believe it is called, slammed against the walls over and over, making it impossible to sleep.

"He's an absolute toad," I said. "I don't understand how anyone can tolerate him. If he keeps this up, he will require an obituary."

Colin, who'd stuck his head out the door and got them to stop, hadn't yet bothered to dress. He was stretched out on a settee in front of the windows, wearing only his pajama trousers. "Allerspach is a brute, but a harmless one. Tedious if you're stuck with him and he starts talking about his watches. From what I can tell, they're quite extraordinary, but he has no appreciation for them beyond their being expensive. Not the sort of gentleman capable of charming a lady of refined tastes like yourself, I grant you, but he could be worse. If your interests veered to athletics, you'd feel entirely different about him. Does your irritation stem from him or is it due to your not wanting to ski today?"

"I'd much prefer to stay in and read Homer."

"*Words sweet as honey from his lips distill'd.*" He rose, crossed to me, and took my hands. "Who's worse, Kaspar Allerspach or Birgit Göltling?"

"No one could claim her gifts are mixed with good and evil both."

"She and Liesel Fronberg are quite the contrast. One has all the beauty, the other all the brains."

I raised an eyebrow. "All the beauty?"

"Only that possessed by the two ladies I mentioned, neither of whom interest me in the slightest, not when I have you before me, she who moves a goddess and looks a queen."

"If you keep quoting Homer neither of us will have to go skiing. Shake your ambrosial curls and I'm done for good."

"Will Shakespeare tame you? *'Tis one thing to be tempted . . . another thing to fall.*"

"You want me tamed?"

"Only temporarily."

I stood on my toes and kissed him softly on the lips.

He closed his eyes. "Very temporarily."

I kissed him again. He took my face in his hands, bent over, and after a delicious interval, every atom in my body was left quivering. I buried my face in his chest, then forced myself to pull back.

"We shouldn't miss breakfast, not if you insist on skiing," I said.

"You're going to torment me all day, aren't you?"

"Until we've retired for the evening. At that point, we shall see what happens."

"How I long to hear the nightingale, not the lark." He kissed me again, quickly this time, and retreated to the bathroom to dress. I went down to the dining room.

"You're not planning to ski, are you, Kallista?" Cécile asked, frowning when she saw my heavy woolen suit. She'd called me the nickname since we first met, preferring it to my Christian name. My late first husband had bestowed it on me in the pages of his diary, but never in my presence.

"I thought we'd all been commanded to do so."

"To go out, *oui*, but not to ski. Ursula has ordered a sleigh for anyone who'd prefer a drive."

I was about to express relief and claim a seat in it when Birgit entered the room.

"Don't count me among that number," she said. "I'd much rather ski. It'll be a lark." She, too, had on a woolen suit, but one whose skirt came only a few inches below her knees and whose jacket was so finely tailored I doubted she would be capable of a brisk walk, let

17

alone serious physical exertion, while wearing it. Thick stockings, sturdy boots, and a jaunty red cap completed her ensemble.

"I wouldn't mind trying to ski." Liesel sounded less sure of herself than Birgit. "I'm told Sigrid is quite good at it."

"I'm sure you'll keep to the sleigh, Lady Emily," Birgit said. "The baroness and Madame du Lac are closer to your age, after all. Skiing is difficult for the elderly."

Sigrid was five years younger than I at the most; Cécile and Ursula were of an age with my mother. While I had not even the slightest interest in competing for attention with a girl of Birgit's age, I recognized her motive at once. Gentlemen can be beasts, often treating their female counterparts with disdain and refusing them the respect they deserve. But there are some among the ranks of women who are equally diabolical to their own. Birgit was just such a person. Her sublime beauty hadn't brought her confidence, only cruelty.

"I'm quite desperate to ski, if you must know," I said, filling a plate with steaming hot eggs and buttered toast.

"It's difficult to learn." Birgit opened her eyes wide whenever she spoke. I suspected her tone, high-pitched, almost childlike, was all affectation.

"Beyond difficult," Max said, sitting with a half-finished plate in front of him. "I gave it up as a bad job years ago. That's why I'm staying in this morning. I'll be able to play my tuba without irritating anyone. I prefer snow from a window, not in my boots."

"I adore the snow," I said.

"You'll feel different soon," Birgit said, smirking.

"If I'm left spending the morning crawling in it instead of gliding over it, I'll be entirely content." I would be lightness itself. Nothing would bother me. Certainly not this chit of a girl.

Intentions so rarely bear fruit; it's a crushing disappointment.

Two hours later, I was half-frozen, soaked, and desperate to return to the villa. I like to think I'm fairly coordinated. I've always been an excellent dancer, no matter how difficult the steps. Yet, to call skiing difficult was a catastrophic understatement. How the Scandinavians manage to use it as a method of crossing long distances is wholly beyond me. Birgit was nearly as badly off as I, which I'm not proud to admit provided a measure of comfort. Liesel managed well enough, but gave up when our party reached the top of a small hill. Afraid she would fall and find herself hopelessly tangled if she tried to descend it, she retreated to the sleigh.

Incompetent a skier though I was, I had infinite appreciation for the Bavarian countryside. The jagged, main dolomite and limestone peaks of the Ammergau Alps pierced the sky, where clouds like spun sugar hung above us, heavy with snow. The thick forest, densely packed with snow-covered deciduous and evergreen trees, sparkled with magic. I half expected to see an elf or some other mystical creature emerge from a hidden trail. The beauty of the place was inconceivable, overwhelming. One felt very small in such magnificent surroundings.

Skiing did not daunt Colin; he took to it as if he'd been raised in the mountains, as if he'd worn skis before he could walk. After I'd fallen for the twentieth time, I gave up, sprawled in the snow, and watched as he effortlessly moved across the frozen ground. He cut a dashing figure in slim wool trousers and a fitted jumper. Kaspar, a few yards ahead of him, was concerned only with speed, his self-determined measure of success. He powered along, huffing and puffing, grunting and snorting, no elegance at all in his movements. His friend, Felix, fell somewhere between the other two gentlemen. Before long, he, too, had retired to the sleigh.

I would've liked to do the same, but had collapsed in a tangle of skis and poles on my final fall, and made a mess of it when I tried to stand. Birgit, too, had had enough and called out to Felix.

"Take me back to the house, will you?"

"Get in the sleigh and we'll go."

"I'd rather ski there instead," she said. "It's not that far."

"Sigrid knows the way better than I," he said. "Why don't you catch up and ask her to escort you?" She had kept pace with Colin and Kaspar, who had disappeared into the forest on a trail that ran along the ridgeline.

Birgit growled back at him—words I shall not repeat here—but their argument was interrupted by a piercing scream. Sigrid.

We all snapped to attention. I removed my boots from the leather bindings on my skis, struggled to my feet, and dragged myself to the sleigh, lugging my equipment. Birgit followed not far behind. We climbed in and the driver urged the horses forward in the direction of the sound.

When we reached the others, Kaspar was on the ground, writhing. Colin was holding one of the other man's skis in his hands.

"How the mighty fall!" Felix grinned and leapt out of the sleigh. "You're not invincible after all, Allerspach. It warms my heart to know you're human, like the rest of us."

"I don't know what happened," Kaspar said, grimacing. "One minute I was fine, the next I was in a heap."

"You're lucky you didn't fall in the other direction," I said. I was standing on the ridgeline, gaping at the steep ravine below. If he'd fallen down it, he could've been gravely hurt.

"There was no luck involved, Lady Emily," he said. "I make a point of being acutely aware of my surroundings. Only a fool would

let himself plummet down that cliff." He scowled. "I don't understand how I lost my balance."

Colin held up the ski. "You lost your balance when your boot
came out of its binding."

"Are you calling me incompetent? I fastened it plenty tight."

"Which would have made no difference when the leather strap
split. It's been cut, more than halfway through, with a sharp blade.
The motion of your heel moving tugged at it until it tore the rest of
the way."

"Cut?" Sigrid asked. "Who would do such a thing?"

For an instant—only an instant—I allowed myself the indul-
gence of silently acknowledging that most people who'd met Kaspar
might be tempted to do such a thing. He was fortunate not to be
more seriously injured or, worse, to require the obituary that had
ended the previous evening's festivities. He'd twisted his knee, but
was able to get to his feet without much of a struggle. Colin and Felix
supported him as he limped to the sleigh. Sigrid was right behind
them and sat next to her husband, holding his hand.

"Don't think this counts as our sleigh ride," she said. "I need
you alone for that, and I want to take the loop near the house, the
one that goes past the frozen waterfall." Kaspar pulled his hat down
over his eyes, but did not reply.

Colin and Felix skied back to the house. Liesel, Birgit, and I
did the same. It was a struggle, but we made it. I nearly cried with
relief when I reached the door and vowed I would never again strap
my feet into a pair of skis. By the time we arrived, the others were
already gathered in Ursula's music room, a comfortable space on
the ground floor that contained a grand piano, a harp, and furniture
designed by her architect. Kaspar, on a chair with his leg propped up
on an ottoman, had stripped off his wool sweater and had a bandage

draped around his knee so loosely it couldn't have served any function beyond the theatrical.

"How now, Hargreaves," he said. "Have a cigar, will you? They're Cuban and I rarely share them, but having escaped what could've been a dreadful fall, the occasion seems to call for it."

"Thank you, no." Colin turned to Ursula. "Are the skis put out for us this morning used frequently?"

"No," she said. "They were in the old house, which had to be pulled down to construct this one. I kept them only because I thought the young people might enjoy a winter adventure. The building project took several years, and they wouldn't have been taken out in the interim."

"We'll discuss this further after we've all had a chance to clean up and change our clothes," Colin said. He took me by the hand and led me from the room, but instead of going upstairs, we spoke to a footman about where the skis had been stored. He explained they were kept in the attic and had only been brought out yesterday morning.

"You're certain?" Colin asked.

"Yes, sir. I carried them myself and put them in a room where one of the grooms checked them over and waxed them."

The room in question was in the back of the house and never locked. Anyone—staff, guests, or residents—might have accessed it. After interviewing the servants, who all insisted they saw nothing out of the ordinary, we retrieved Kaspar's broken ski and went to the stables. There, we found the groom, who assured us that the skis had been in perfect working order when he inspected them. An avid skier himself, he had taken particular care when looking over the bindings.

We returned to the house and went straight to our room where, a short time later, a footman brought us a reply from the newspaper editor. He had not ordered his reporter to the villa. Someone else, using his name, had done so. A street boy had delivered the message to the telegram office three days before it was sent. The envelope containing it included instructions that it be held until a precise time.

"Which means any of Ursula's guests could've arranged for its delivery before coming here." I was in the bath, my aching muscles screaming with relief at soaking in the hot water. Everything in the villa was modern and worked flawlessly. The taps filled the tub—enormous and deep—more quickly than I had imagined possible.

"Quite," Colin said, running a hand through his messy curls. "I'd be inclined to dismiss it as a prank if it weren't for things escalating today. Allerspach has made it clear he has no interest in pursuing the matter."

"Neither does the baroness, probably because she's got as much motive for having done it as anyone. She makes no effort to hide her dislike of him and would likely be delighted if she could wrest her daughter away from him," I said, rinsing the soap off my body. It had a delicate rose scent and a marvelous feel on the skin. Ursula had paid careful attention to every detail in her home.

"Yes, but would she adopt such tactics?" Colin asked. "She'd be more likely to put financial pressure on him."

"Unless she simply can't stand the sight of him; but if that were the case, she'd take stronger action. Murder is a much more effective method for removing someone from one's sphere than tampering with his ski."

"I can't say I've the ability to focus on any of it, not with you in the bath. You're thoroughly distracting amid all those soap bubbles."

"Then my plan's working," I said. "I warned you I mean to torment you."

"Only until this evening." His eyes focused on me with a ferocious hunger. It would be no easier for me to wait than him.

4

The Alpsee, near Schloss Hohenschwangau, Bavaria
_1868_

While Niels would never be the outdoorsman his father was, the more time he spent in the Alps, the more fond he became of the trails snaking through the region. The Alpsee, near the royal palace Hohenschwangau, was his favorite spot, a lake rimmed by snowcapped peaks. Its clear, azure water beckoned him like an old friend. He'd taken to spending many an afternoon wandering along the path beside it, singing as he went.

On that day—that critical day, the most important of his life, the day when everything changed—he'd stopped along the shore and climbed onto a rock to watch a swan swimming, its white feathers shimmering in the sun. The creature's movement was pure and majestic; Niels found himself unexpectedly moved. It stretched its long neck and took flight, soaring into the sky. Niels started to sing "Mein lieber Schwan," Lohengrin's Farewell, from Wagner's opera.

> *My thanks to you, dear swan!*
> *Glide back over the wide water to the place*

from which your boat brought me;
return to where alone lies our happiness!
Then will your task be faithfully fulfilled.
Farewell, farewell, beloved swan!

He stopped, then started again, and sang it twice more. He paused, drew a breath, but blew it out. Three times was enough.

"Again, my good man, again." The voice came from behind him, in the trees. For an irrational moment, Niels thought it was his father, but it was nothing like. He turned around and saw a tall, dark-haired young man, handsome, with a noble bearing: Ludwig II, King of Bavaria.

"Your Majesty." Niels bowed low, his heart pounding.

"Rise, rise," the king said. "Your voice . . . sing again."

"I'm no singer, Your Majesty, only—"

"Your king commands it."

Niels fought to control his voice. It was a struggle, but he managed. Ludwig leaned against a tree, his eyes closed, his face a mask of blissful rapture as he listened.

"Who are you?" the king asked when the song ended.

"Niels von Schön, Your Majesty."

"You are Bavarian."

"Yes."

"A subject of mine."

"Yes."

"Something about you is familiar." The king walked closer and studied Niels's face, then waved a hand. "I cannot place you."

They had met before, as boys, brought together by their mothers, but hadn't liked each other. Not at all. Niels because he'd felt uncomfortable in the vast Schloss Nymphenburg, summer residence of the royal family. The day had been unbearably hot. Why Ludwig hadn't taken to his guest, Niels didn't know. It had never bothered him. If anything, he'd been relieved not to be asked back.

His mother was less pleased. She'd hoped the boys would become fast friends, inseparable companions. When that didn't happen, she'd started to tease that if only he'd been a girl, he might have married the crown prince. Spouses, she said, didn't need to like each other. His father never found the joke amusing, but then, he didn't find much amusing. He'd long hoped for another child—another son—but that was never to happen.

"I'd say you're the familiar one," Niels said, deciding not to bring up their previous encounter. "But then, your face is everywhere."

Ludwig narrowed his eyes. "You treat me in a very offhand manner. I think I like it. Come, lunch with me at Hohenschwangau. We will discuss the works of my Friend, my ardently beloved Richard Wagner." *Friend* was capitalized when the king spoke, of that there was no doubt. He turned on his heels and walked away, not waiting for Niels to reply.

What could he do but follow?

5

Villa von Düchtel
1906

After Colin and I dressed, we joined the others in the music room. A footman—not the one who'd answered our questions about the skis—greeted us with a tray of steaming mulled wine. Max was playing the piano, a melody I recognized from *Lohengrin*. Sigrid stood behind him, at the ready to turn the pages of his music. Every few bars she would take a breath and sing, so softly she could barely be heard, only a word or two, and then stop. Kaspar had installed himself on a long settee, stretching out his injured leg. Cécile was sitting near the fire with Felix, who was wearing a bright yellow waistcoat, hovering nearby. They were the only two in the room drinking champagne. Birgit was nowhere to be found. No doubt her toilette was highly complicated and time-consuming. Ursula and Liesel sat across from each other in two of four chairs lined up on either side of a low, narrow table with a mosaic top, perpendicular to the piano.

"You two look engaged in something serious," I said, taking the empty seat next to Liesel.

"The Fräulein has brought two paintings for me to consider pur-

28

chasing," Ursula said. "I mentioned this to you before, did I not, Lady Emily? She's going to reveal them to us tonight."

"What is your gallery's specialty?" I asked.

"Contemporary painting and sculpture," Liesel said. "There are so many talented artists working today, most of them vastly under-appreciated. Are you familiar with Hilma af Klint?"

The question caught Cécile's attention. She came and sat beside Ursula. Felix, trailing her like a puppy, stood near Colin, next to the table. "The Swedish painter," she said, "in possession of a talent *formidable*. I particularly like her plein air works."

"She's become even more interesting of late," Liesel said. "She started experimenting with automatic drawing a decade or so ago."

"Automatic drawing?" Colin asked.

"It's a method of opening up to one's subconscious. Letting the pencil do what it will, rather than deliberately controlling it," Liesel said. "She's recently begun a series of abstract paintings. Their power is extraordinary."

"I'd like to see them," Colin said.

"You don't object to the abstract?" Ursula asked. "I thought you English gentlemen were a hopelessly traditional lot."

"Not all of us, I assure you. I'm fascinated by the notion that art can be separated from obvious representations of the world around us. I read something Maurice Denis said, some years back, about a paint-ing being *a flat surface covered with colors assembled in a certain order*. I may not have the quote precisely right, but the idea stuck with me. Why not, then, free oneself from merely copying objects as we see them?"

"Did I not tell you, Ursula, that he is the most extraordinary gentleman?" Cécile asked. "Handsome and enlightened."

"Enlightened has always tempted me more than handsome," Ursula said. "Handsome rarely leads to anything but trouble."

"*Quelquefois*, but only when it is not accompanied by enlightenment."

"This modern art is a lot of rot," Kaspar said, still sprawled on the couch, a cigar dangling from his mouth. "I don't know why you insist on stuffing your house with it. But it's yours, so I suppose you can do as you like." His rudeness shocked me. I've no fondness for rigid rules of behavior, but to treat his mother-in-law in such a manner was unconscionable.

"Mama has as much ancient art as she does contemporary," Sigrid said. "Don't be unkind."

"I'm a beast, but always willing to admit it," Kaspar said, as if that excused his loutish manners. "I've a tendency to do what I want and to voice my opinions loudly, without considering how doing so makes other people feel. Forgive me. No doubt my thoughtless, dreadful behavior is what inspired someone to cut my binding this morning. Which of you wanted to see me fall?"

His voice was less forceful than I'd heard it before, as if his confidence was shaken. Not much, but enough that it was noticeable.

"You believe one of your friends would do such a thing?" Felix asked.

"I've flaws enough that have plagued you," Kaspar said.

"Remember your Goethe: *Certain flaws are necessary for the whole. It would seem strange if old friends lacked certain quirks.*"

"He doesn't deserve you, Felix," Sigrid said.

"If you talk like that, you'll have me believing you cut my binding, *mein Schatz*." Kaspar gestured for his wife to come to him, but she stayed put.

"You're exactly the man you were when I chose to marry you. How could that be a disappointment? What will be crushing, however, is if I never get my sleigh ride. How many times have I told you I want you all to myself, just for a few hours?"

"Is there anything more boring than married couples fawning over each other?" Birgit refused the mulled wine offered as she entered the room, demanded whisky, and flopped onto a chair.

"You might hold a different opinion once you become a wife," Colin said.

"Heavens no! I'd rather die than dote on my husband. It would be boring beyond belief."

"That depends upon the husband," I said.

Birgit met my gaze and fluttered her eyelashes. "And now we're all meant to exclaim over Herr Hargreaves's Adonis-like features."

"I'd prefer if you all exclaimed over my rugged good looks," Felix said.

"Marred by that ridiculous scar," Birgit said.

"It won't heal because you refuse to kiss it better."

She rolled her eyes. "You had it a lifetime before you met me. Probably before I was born."

"Not quite that long," Felix said, flashing a crooked grin. I started to see why Cécile considered him potentially interesting. There was a certain attractiveness about him. His manner was easy and affable, and he possessed a modesty entirely absent in his friend Kaspar.

"Your scar distresses me, Monsieur Brinkmann. It's difficult to believe you were ever stupid enough to take part in a duel," Cécile said.

"I did nothing of the sort," Felix said. "It was all the rage when I was at university. Everyone who mattered fought and had a scar. I wanted the badge, but had no interest in risking serious injury, so I took care of it myself with a scrupulously clean razor."

"*Non!*" Cécile's eyebrows shot to her hairline. "A very clever strategy, monsieur. Foolish and immature, but clever nonetheless. What did you study?"

"Literature, Goethe to be precise, but, as it turned out, I wasn't suited for university life. I left without completing my degree."

"I shouldn't like you at all if you'd finished," Birgit said. "I despise intellectuals. They're boring beyond belief."

"Is the yellow waistcoat a nod to Goethe?" I asked.

"It is, Lady Emily. I thought yellow trousers would be taking things rather too far, but have made the waistcoat my signature."

"Surely you're too old to still be playing Werther," Sigrid said. Goethe's wildly successful novel *The Sorrows of Young Werther* tells the story of a man destroyed by unrequited love. His chosen uniform was a blue jacket over yellow trousers and a waistcoat identical to Felix's.

"A man is never too old to be guided by passionate emotion," Felix said. "Goethe may have regretted his creation, but I still celebrate it."

"Enough of this book talk," Kaspar said. "I hear you've been questioning the staff about my skiing accident, Hargreaves. Surely it wasn't necessary."

An undercurrent of discomfort shot through the room. "A mere precaution," Colin said.

"Have you any reason to suspect an enemy is trying to harm you?" I asked.

Kaspar laughed, but his wife laughed harder. "Good heavens, no," he said. "I've been subject to a certain amount of jealousy as a result of my athletic accomplishments, but never anything serious. Like it or not, my competitors accept that when I win, it's because I'm better prepared and better trained."

"And more talented," Sigrid said. I couldn't make out whether she was sincere or sarcastic.

"That goes without saying. At any rate, I've no enemies."

Max lifted his hands from the piano, cocked his head, looked rather perplexed, and then started to play another piece, one that rang with anger.

Sigrid laughed again. "Oh, Max, surely not 'Bin ich nun frei?' That's too much." She explained for the rest of us. "It's from Wagner's *Das Rheingold*, the aria the dwarf Alberich sings after his golden ring is stolen. He puts a curse on it, to ensure that everyone who possesses it will be destroyed."

"It's not the precisely right reference," Max said. "Nothing's been stolen, after all, but it will do. Someone is angry enough to lash out at Kaspar. I'd like to know what inspired his notice."

"Not some piddling piece of jewelry, I can assure you of that," Kaspar said.

"None of us would have acted in malice," Birgit said. "We all like each other, well enough. I'm sure it was nothing but a badly planned prank, but whoever's behind it will never admit it now."

"I absolve them," Kaspar said. "There was no serious harm done. As a gesture of my goodwill, I suggest we ask Liesel to unveil the paintings she brought. I vow not to make any ill-mannered comments on them."

"Aren't they in the ballroom?" Birgit asked. "Can you make it up the stairs with your knee?"

"So long as I take my time, I'll manage," he said. "It doesn't hurt much. The truth is, I'm playing it up to get everyone's sympathy."

Ursula led us down the corridor and up two flights of steps to the ballroom.

"It's absurd to have wanted such a thing in the middle of the countryside, but I do adore dancing," she said. The chamber was enormous, far too big given the house's remote location, but the baroness's fortune enabled her to indulge her every whim. The sprung wooden floor gleamed, sunlight filtering through ten-foot-tall windows on two walls. A balcony extended from one of them, offering staggering views of the mountains, and a minstrels' gallery looked down from the opposite end of the room.

The room was empty save for two easels draped in canvas. "Not even a chair for a rest when one becomes winded from waltzing?" I asked.

"The furniture is kept in a storage room through that door," Ursula said, pointing. "I didn't want it cluttering things up when it wasn't needed. Liesel, show us what you've brought for me."

Fräulein Fronberg tugged at the first canvas, revealing a painting approximately three feet square, depicting a young girl in a white dress and bonnet standing next to a sphere that reflected the garden surrounding her.

"It's the work of Paula Modersohn-Becker, an expressionist," Liesel said. "There's always been a hint of scandal connected to her family. Her uncle tried to assassinate King Wilhelm of Prussia."

"That's the sort of scandal that makes moving in society a challenge," Sigrid said.

"She studied in London and Paris. This painting was completed in 1901. Look at the emotion on the child's face. It's so wistful. Her innocence has not yet been destroyed."

"Do we assume it will be?" I asked.

"It happens to us all, does it not?"

The view visible in the garden globe brought to mind an idealized childhood with a cozy house, its windows glowing gold, but the darkness in the trees immediately behind the girl suggested something else was lurking.

"Mama, you must buy it," Sigrid said. "It looks like me as a tiny girl!"

"I can hardly say no if that's how you see it," Ursula said. "What's next, Liesel?"

Intriguing though the first painting was, I preferred the second, by André Derain, a vibrant and fanciful view of the Pyrénées from the French village of Collioure. "If you don't want it, I'll take it," I said, drawn to the bright colors and the movement of the trees in the foreground.

"I'm afraid I've already got a second buyer lined up should that happen," Liesel said. "Derain painted this only last year when he and Matisse summered in France. If you're interested in his work, I can try to track down something else for you."

"I'd like that very much, thank you," I said, "but will always regret having missed out on this one. There's something about it . . ."

"That's how it is with art," Liesel said. "It's not always possible to explain in words why a particular piece tugs at you. All that matters is that it does. I selected this especially for you, Baroness. It told me it was destined for you."

"How can I resist, then?" Ursula took a few steps back, folded her arms across her chest, and studied each painting, one after the other in turn. "I'll live with them for a few days and make my final decision. Now, leave me, all of you. I want to spend some time alone with them. We shall reconvene for supper, when I'll tell you all about our plans for tomorrow. We're going to visit Ludwig's so-called masterpiece, Schloss Neuschwanstein."

"So-called?" Colin asked.

"It's one of my least favorite places on earth. I've never shared the king's taste for fantasy."

6

Schloss Hohenschwangau
1868

Ludwig uttered not a single word as he walked along the path skirting the shore of the Alpsee. Niels trailed behind, every step he took unsteady. If the king noticed, or found it strange that his companion was holding back, he showed no sign. The castle was a kilometer and a half away. Niels had seen it from a distance many times, its yellow ramparts reaching beyond the tops of the trees that surrounded it. Ludwig's father, Maximilian, purchased it when he was crown prince and it was little more than a ruin. Two decades later, Maximilian had restored it to pseudo-medieval glory, and it became one of his official residences.

Ludwig walked quickly, and they reached the castle in little over a quarter of an hour. The guards at the gate bowed as the king strolled through. Niels hesitated when he reached them.

"I—forgive me—His Majesty invited me—I—"

The king spoke without turning to look back. "Come, Schön, we've no time to dally." He stepped through doors held open for him;

Niels followed. "If you keep lingering so far away, you'll be late for luncheon and you don't want that, do you?"

"No, Your Majesty, I don't. I shall endeavor to—"

"Less speaking, more walking. Try to keep up."

The king led him to a large dining room, its ceiling painted sky blue between elaborate white plaster designs. A series of paintings covered much of the pale yellow walls. Niels paused in front of one of them.

"It's the swan knight, Lohengrin," he said.

"Yes, the murals tell the whole story," the king said, gesturing to the panels. "The brave knight arrives on a boat pulled by a swan to aid a desperate duchess on the verge of being forced to marry a man she did not want."

"A man who lied and claimed she'd agreed to the match," Niels said. "Lohengrin challenged him and won."

"Not only the fight but the duchess as well."

"Elsa."

"He made her promise to never ask about his origins or his family," Ludwig said. "For some time, she did his bidding. Until someone goaded her, chastising her because Lohengrin had not proved he was a nobleman."

"It plagued Elsa, and at last she could take it no more," Niels said. "She asked the forbidden question."

"Lohengrin answered. He was the son of Parzival, king of the Grail. God had sent Lohengrin to rescue Elsa, but now, because she broke her promise, he would have to leave. So he left." Ludwig stared into the distance. "On the same vessel pulled by the same swan, who appeared exactly when he was needed."

"Would that we all had such a loyal friend," Niels said.

"The swan, a loyal friend?" Ludwig spun around and looked at him. "Do you say this to mock me?"

"No, Your Majesty. Why would I do such a thing? I've always found the story profoundly moving. Lohengrin made one simple request to the woman who loved him dearly. She agreed, but did not keep her word."

"So he returned to the service of the Grail, a holy and noble calling," the king said.

"And a lonely one, I've always thought."

"I like to think he still had the swan." Ludwig smiled.

"Just what every boy needs."

A woman in her mid-thirties entered the room, her face bright with enthusiasm. Her brown hair, curly and untamed, fell around her shoulders. She had a high forehead and a pleasant enough face, though no one would ever call her a beauty. The gown she wore, white and flowing, reminded Niels of an ancient muse.

"Who is this newcomer, Ludwig?" she asked.

"My new friend, Lohengrin. He was singing a farewell to his swan when I came upon him at the Alpsee."

"I'm Niels von Schön." She hadn't offered her hand to kiss, so he stuck out his, then pulled it back, unsure how to properly greet her. She laughed and shook it.

"Elisabet Ney, court sculptor." Her smile was infectious. "I was summoned to Munich to make a portrait bust of our royal friend, but it proved an unmitigated disaster. Not my work, that is, but dear Ludwig. He was constantly surrounded by ministers and hangers-on. It was impossible for him to concentrate on what he needed to do: sit still."

"I'll brook no criticism from you, Elisabet," Ludwig said. The words might have sounded harsh, but his tone was all teasing and warmth. Niels found himself surprised by it. "You were as distracted as I."

"It's why we came to Hohenschwangau," she said. "It's far more peaceful here. Not that I'm suggesting he's become an obedient model."

"She reads from Goethe's *Iphigenia in Taurus* when I lose focus."

"May I ask if he loses focus frequently, just to hear more of the story?" Niels regretted the words the instant they came out of his mouth. How could he speak with such familiarity about the king? His feet felt like lumps of concrete. His mouth went dry. He wished he could disappear into the floor, unless there was some way to instantly flee to the Alpsee and find a swan waiting with a boat.

Ludwig laughed. "You see why I collected him, now, don't you?"

"We're lunching here, then, with your Lohengrin?" Elisabet asked.

"Where else?"

From that moment, Niels's life bore no resemblance to his former existence. It was inexplicable, really. That Ludwig had found him on the shore of the lake. That Elisabet was waiting for them at the castle. That when the three of them spoke, it was as if they'd been friends for centuries, like knights of the Grail, waiting to be called into service.

Niels could never remember what they ate that afternoon. Nor could he remember how he was persuaded to send for his things and take up residence at Hohenschwangau. When Ludwig was around, magic happened at his bidding. He was a master at getting what he wanted. And so, the rest of the summer was spent not wandering alone through winding forest paths, but instead rejoicing with the dearest friends a man could ever have, all the while learning the sort of man he was destined to be, a man he'd never thought he could accept.

7

Schloss Neuschwanstein
1906

Eager though I was to see the Swan King's fairy-tale creation, I struggled to drag myself out of bed. Colin and I had not retired until horrendously late. Forgive me; that statement is not precisely true. We retired, but did not sleep for some time, and my difficulties stemmed less from exhaustion than from wanting to stay exactly where I was, perfectly comfortable in my husband's arms. However, one may not long indulge in such frivolities when at a house party. Early the next morning, we were in the sleigh, en route to the castle.

Few people have not seen drawings or photographs of Neuschwanstein, its sleek, white towers jutting into the sky from its rocky perch, as sublime, magnificent, and dramatic as the mountains surrounding it. No image can do the structure justice. Some alchemy occurred when it was built, combining the structure and its setting, making it a dream come to life. It's the perfect setting for a little girl who wants to wait for her prince. Or, if she's sensible, the perfect place from whence to summon her prince to do her bidding.

It's where little boys imagine they'll set off on knightly adventures, atop a noble steed, in search of the Holy Grail. It's a spot where even the most cynical adult can remember a time when fantasy meant possibility, not disappointment.

In those days, the castle was not ordinarily open to the public in the winter, but Ursula had arranged for us to be admitted. We'd set off from the villa in multiple sleighs, but, much to my relief, no one liked the idea of exploring the castle as a herd. Instead, we splintered into smaller groups. Sigrid and Max, sharing an interest in both Ludwig II and Wagner, had paired up before we departed the house. Liesel, wanting to avoid any perception that she was trying to pressure Ursula to purchase the paintings she'd brought, asked to join them. Birgit, Felix, and Kaspar—whose knee apparently was no longer bothering him in the slightest—each expressing disinterest in Ludwig and Wagner, went off together, which left Colin and me with Cécile and Ursula.

"I've never liked this place," Ursula said, sniffing discontentedly, after we'd entered the Palas, the castle's main building. "No grown man, let alone a king, should waste his time and money playing with toys."

"It's awfully large for a mere toy, Baroness," Colin said.

"You must stop referring to me by my title. The formality of the previous century has no place in this one. Regardless of size, Neuschwanstein is a toy, and was from the start. Ludwig was a selfish man indulging narcissistic whims."

"It didn't end well for him," Colin said, "if that's any consolation."

"Very slim indeed. The rest of the world thinks it's marvelous, and, as it would be wrong to deny you all the chance to see it, I shall do my best to withhold my opinions on the matter. My family are descended from the Baiovarii, who drove the Romans out of what we now call Bavaria. When one has real history, one need not wallow in the fictional."

"You object to myths and legends?" I asked.

"Not in the slightest," she said, "but fairy tales become dangerous when one is obsessed with futile attempts to make them real. Therein lies a path to ruin."

We were standing in the two-story-high throne room, its dome reminiscent of the one found at Hagia Sophia in Constantinople. An enormous chandelier, Byzantine in style, hung from the ceiling. In 1868, work began on the site, and only a few years later, the Kingdom of Bavaria was incorporated into the newly unified Germany. While Bavaria maintained more independence than many of its neighbors, it no longer was a sovereign state, which was a blow to its king. Yet here was a room, profused with gilt, that shouted the power of the monarch and his divine connection; it was more cathedral than castle. Paintings of the apostles and holy kings decorated the walls of the apse. In this space, Ludwig had made clear his divine right to rule. I said this aloud, but Cécile protested.

"There's no throne," she said.

"Correct." Ursula's voice was clipped. "Ludwig died, and the throne was never built. That's what they say, at least. I can claim no special insight into the man's disturbed thoughts, but I spent enough time with him to find another story more plausible. One of his many obsessions was the Holy Grail. Some believe he intended this room to be its sanctuary. In that case, the cup of Christ, not a throne, would be the intended centerpiece."

"The Grail is lost to history," I said.

"Which explains why the room is empty," Ursula said. "If

Ludwig left it deliberately so to make a point, that may be the only thing about the whole wretched place I can almost appreciate."

"If the story about the king's intentions is true," Colin said.

"When it comes to that, I shall temporarily allow myself to indulge in fantasy."

As we explored the other rooms in the castle's interior, I began to understand Ursula's conflicting feelings about Neuschwanstein. Mine were different from hers, but complicated nonetheless. Beautiful though it all was, there was an undeniable falseness to the place. It was not a medieval castle but rather a nineteenth-century construction. As such, there was a certain sincerity in its artifice; there was no pretending to be something it wasn't. But what was Neuschwanstein? The escapist fantasy of a mad king? A loving homage to a time when honor and chivalry reigned? A celebration of Norse and German legends?

Many of those legends featured in Wagner's operas, and Ludwig's castle included multiple references to them. *Parsifal* tells the story of the man who became Grail King, ruling from the Castle of the Holy Grail, lending credence to Ursula's theory about the throne room. Ludwig's elaborate blue bedroom, full of ornate wood carvings, told the heartbreaking story of Tristan and Isolde, another story brought to life by Wagner. The unresolved chord in its music leaves every listener with an almost unbearable longing that can never be satisfied. It seemed to me an odd choice for a room where one hoped to slumber, but perhaps Ludwig's royal duties, as was the case for many monarchs, kept him from finding love and left him sympathetic to the doomed lovers.

The Wagner connection was most visible in the Singers' Hall, which stretched nearly the entire length of the Palas's fourth floor. Murals on the walls depicted scenes from the life of Parzival, upon

43

which the composer based *Parsifal*. The chamber, with its coffered wooden ceiling, was modeled after two medieval rooms in Wartburg: the Festival and the Singers' halls. It might have been a set for *Tannhäuser*.

"It's spectacular," I said to Colin. "I half expect to find a knight singing to the goddess Venus."

He took me by the arm, led me across the room away from our friends, and leaned so close I could feel his breath on my neck when he spoke. "I didn't realize you'd paid that much attention when we saw the opera."

"You didn't make it easy. If I recall, you were exceedingly distracting that evening."

"We had the box all to ourselves," he said. "What did you expect? *Your sweet charms are the source of all beauty, / and every fair wonder springs from you. / Only he who has known / your ardent embrace knows what love is.*"

"I didn't realize you were so familiar with the libretto."

"Only that particular aria."

Our eyes met and a delicious heat passed between us. Sadly, a piercing, high-pitched squeal extinguished it.

"I'm so pleased to have found you all!" Birgit marched across the room, took Cécile and Ursula by their arms, and dragged them toward us.

"Where are Felix and Kaspar?" I asked.

"I abandoned them," she said. "They decided to hike to the Marienbrücke and I wasn't about to get embroiled in such a ridiculous outing." The steel bridge, built by Ludwig II, spanned the nearby Pöllat Gorge and a spectacular waterfall. It provided breathtaking views of the castle, but I suspected the gentlemen were less interested in that than in pushing through the snow and proving their virility to each other on the slick metal high above the ground. "I hope they fall on the ice and break their heads. I wasn't about to trek through all that snow. I'm tired of this ridiculous place. There must be somewhere comfortable I can sit until it's time to meet up in the courtyard."

"I know just the spot in the king's study and shall take you there," Ursula said, waving at her to come. "We'll see the rest of you at two o'clock. Don't be late. I promised the caretaker we'd be out by then."

"She must be pleased to have an excuse to abandon our tour," I said after they'd left. "It was generous of her to bring us despite despising the place."

"It is very like Ursula," Cécile said. "She's always loved the complicated, the difficult. She despises many things but often pulls them close to her nonetheless. It tells me she does not define *despise* as you and I do."

"When did her husband die?" I asked.

"Eons ago. It was neither a happy marriage nor a long one. They lived separately nearly all of the time. This was frowned upon by their families, *naturellement*, but when one is unhappy . . ." She shrugged. "I never met him."

"Never?" Colin asked.

"Is it so strange that I should not meet a man of so little consequence to my friend? I had no interest in his acquaintance. Understand, I do not suggest he was cruel. The marriage was arranged by their parents, and the couple had nothing in common. Each sought their pleasure elsewhere, in love and in everything else."

"A situation not altogether unusual," Colin said.

"Not everyone has the good fortune to be married to a man like you, Monsieur Hargreaves. It is the tragedy of womanhood."

We meandered through the rest of the handful of rooms that were accessible to the public. Much of the rest of the castle was off-limits; it had never been completed, the project abandoned after Ludwig's death. I wondered what he would think of the bare walls and empty spaces. Would there ever be another person with the passion—and fortune—necessary to restart work? I couldn't imagine it would happen, not given the size of the structure and its location. Merely getting supplies to Neuschwanstein would be a challenge, and to what end? It wasn't a place anyone would want to live. From a distance, it was exquisite, but inside there was no warmth, only cold, impersonal beauty held in check by the lingering and oppressive scent of tragedy.

By the time we made our way back to the ground floor, I was more than ready to leave. I fastened my coat, pulled on my gloves, and secured my hat firmly on my head before we headed for the courtyard to meet the others.

The day was frigid, and clouds had gathered in clumps over the mountains. A bitter wind bit through my clothing. I shivered. My teeth chattered. Then snow began to fall, the most ethereal snow I'd ever seen, and I forgot the cold altogether. The flakes were enormous, but delicate like lace. I tilted my head back, caught one on my tongue, and laughed. Despite its many contradictions and problems, Ludwig had achieved something transcendent in this place. All at once, my uneasiness with it all evaporated and fantasy swirled around me. What was real, what imagined no longer mattered. Neuschwanstein had caught me in its magic.

The spell was broken when Cécile slipped on an icy patch of the courtyard's smooth stones. Colin nimbly caught her before she fell.

"Are you all right?" he asked.

"Perfectly fine, better than before, if you must know," she said. "All you need now is gleaming armor, Monsieur Hargreaves, and you can be my knight."

"He'll also require a noble steed," I said, "preferably white."

We all laughed, but I admit to rather taking to the image of my husband in the guise of medieval warrior, ready to right all the wrongs in the world. I've never fancied being rescued and shall always prefer to take matters into my own hands, but on occasion, one can be seduced by the idea of being swept away by a capable gentleman. A voice shattered my reverie.

"Hargreaves!" Felix shouted from below. "We're in the lower courtyard!"

We started toward the stairs that would take us to them, Colin between Cécile and me, with a firm grip on our arms, but before we took three steps, a gunshot shattered the mystical calm of the snow, clapping against the limestone-clad walls. Someone shouted. Colin dropped our arms and ran to Kaspar, who'd collapsed on the ground in an indecorous heap.

8

Site of Neu Hohenschwangau, Bavaria
1868

The beauty of the jagged Alpine peaks and lakes around Hohenschwangau was profound to the point of being almost spiritual. It was as if God himself had demanded perfection in its beauty, creating a setting that would allow man a sublime glimpse of heaven itself, inspiring him to live in a way that would ensure his place in a blissful afterlife. Ludwig had taken Niels and Elisabet to a steel bridge above a deep gorge, so they could observe a patch of land on the top of steep cliffs.

"In order to build where I want, all of this will have to go," Ludwig said, pointing to a cluster of rocky ruins barely visible in the distance, the remains of a long-since-vanished medieval castle, Vorderhohenschwangau. "It pains me, but what is one to do? My father incorporated ruins into Hohenschwangau. The same will not be possible here. I will have to construct my knight's castle from scratch."

"You'll never be able to get the materials up there," Elisabet said.

"I don't agree," Niels said. "We are living in an age of progress and have options not available to our ancestors. Imagine what a steam crane could do here."

"Quite right. Roads will be put in for better access," Ludwig said. "It will be accomplished, no matter what it takes. I do have a fortune, after all. No expense will be spared. I can accomplish anything I put my mind to. Take this bridge. What do you think of it?"

"It's beautiful," Elisabet said.

Niels gripped the railing. "I'm not interested in what it looks like, only that it doesn't fall."

"You ought to know better." The king gave his friend's arm a playful swat. "Its appearance matters above almost everything. My father had an ugly wooden one built here for my mother, hence the name, Marienbrücke. I suppose it was a present of sorts, so that she could take in the view. She might be sentimental about it, but I couldn't stand the sight of the thing, so I replaced it with this."

"You're a terrible son," Elisabet said.

"She's a terrible mother." Ludwig shuddered. He'd never shared details with Niels, but his friend had heard enough to know that the king's childhood had proved devastating to his soul. It was one of the things that bonded them together: parents who wanted sons they could never be. He suspected Ludwig had been subjected to far more outright cruelty than he had. Cruelty that was unforgivable. "You don't know the half of it. Part of the reason for starting work on the new castle is to get away from her. I love it here, in the Alps, but she insists on summering at Hohenschwangau, and the place isn't big enough for both of us."

"Is Bavaria big enough for both of you?" Niels asked. His eyes crinkled when he smiled. "You might have to consider annexing more land."

"Would that such a thing were possible, but I fear current world politics won't allow it," Ludwig said. "However, as I've no fondness for playing soldier, even if it were, I shouldn't think I'd bother."

"You're a king. Don't you have an army who could take care of it for you?" Elisabet asked, laughing. "Wave your arm and tell them what to do."

"There's no more territory to be had, so I'll make a castle on the top of a mountain my refuge. It shall be an authentic knight's castle, but with all the modern comforts. Neu Hohenschwangau will be a superior place to live, not to mention far more beautiful than Hohenschwangau. I'm going to have it clad in the brightest white limestone. It will shimmer from a distance."

"Will Niels and I have rooms in it?" Elisabet asked.

"Only if your husband doesn't object."

"Edmund doesn't get a say in the matter."

"You're married?" Niels asked. "I had no idea."

"Why should you? It's not relevant to anything in my life. It's my business and no one else's."

Niels hoped he didn't look as shocked as he felt. "And your husband's, I presume."

"Our lives are quite separate. We correspond. Shouldn't that be enough? I've no interest in living in bondage."

"Then why did you marry him?" Niels asked.

"Because she didn't have the sense to emulate me and disentangle herself." Ludwig crossed his arms and looked away. "Come now, let's go explore the site."

The previous autumn, the king had called off his engagement to his cousin Sophie, sister of Sisi, the Empress of Austria and one of the king's closest confidantes. Niels, having surmised this had put a wedge between Ludwig and Sisi, wanted to ask him what happened, but when he turned to his friend, he saw a ruddy darkness on his face. Now was not the time for questions.

The king started to walk and Niels and Elisabet followed, crossing back over the bridge and through the forest, where wildflowers bloomed and birdsong filled the air. When they reached the ruins, Ludwig began pacing out where he planned to build. "We'll start with a gateway building. That, they can build quickly, and I'll live there while they finish the rest. The entire project shall take three years."

Niels's eyebrows shot up. "Surely that's not enough time."

"When men work for their king, God motivates them."

"Of course, of course, you were chosen by the divine master himself," Elisabet said, "a sacred instrument made to reign sovereign over the masses."

"I appreciate most of your jokes, but not this one," Ludwig said. "I am an anointed holy king and, yes, chosen by God. You can understand neither the responsibility nor the difficulties that come with that. I'm not like other men. The two of you are some of my closest friends, but you will never fully comprehend what it means to rule. I am cursed to forever be separate, alone."

"Your cousin might have an inkling as to your struggle," Elisabet said. "She is Empress of Austria."

"Yes, but Sisi doesn't run the empire, her husband does. It's different."

Niels could see the veins in Ludwig's neck starting to bulge. It was time to redirect the conversation from hard subjects to the realm of fantasy. "My liege, noble King of the Grail, tell us more about this wonderful palace to be. Will there be a space for the Grail, somewhere safe for it when, at last, we find it?"

That did the trick. Ludwig grinned. "A sanctuary for the Holy

Grail instead of a throne room, perhaps? Yes, I like that idea very much."

"Will I have a seat at your Round Table?" Elisabet asked.

"Keep your mythology straight, my dear," Ludwig said. "We're Bavarian, not English. There's no Arthur here."

9

Schloss Neuschwanstein
1906

The snow was falling harder now, and the chill in the air was no longer kept at bay by whatever magic Neuschwanstein had temporarily woven. The shot had chased it all away. My heart was pounding. I looked around for the shooter, but saw nothing, so I took Cécile's arm and guided her through the slippery upper courtyard and down the steps that led to where Colin was hunched over Kaspar. Felix had disappeared. Kaspar stood up and pushed Colin away.

"No damage done," he said.

"Someone shot at you," Colin said. He walked methodically up and down the courtyard, then bent down, picked something up, and returned to us. "Here's the bullet. Where's Brinkmann?"

"I'm well aware that someone shot at me." Kaspar took the bullet from Colin. "Felix went in search of whoever did it. This could've killed me. Or him."

"It's a much more pointed effort than tampering with a ski binding," Colin said.

Kaspar swayed, and the color drained from his face, leaving his complexion a dingy gray. He pulled his shoulders back, shook his arms, and smoothed his face in what appeared to be a concerted effort at looking composed, but I could see he was nonplussed. His eyes crinkled and his forehead creased. We heard the clatter of footsteps and a man came running toward us from the gatehouse at the far end of the courtyard.

"What happened here? Where is the baroness?"

"You're the caretaker, I presume?" Colin asked. The man nodded. "Is anyone on the premises other than you and our party?"

"No, sir. I locked the gate behind you all when you came in."

We heard more footsteps, this time accompanied by shouting, coming from the direction of the Palas. Sigrid and Max descended upon us, Ursula, Liesel, and Birgit close behind. Soon thereafter, we heard Felix shouting.

"*Ich habe kein Gewehr gefunden, keinen Einbrecher und nicht eine einzige vermaledeite Spur!*" He was standing on a balcony, high above us. "There's no one here but us. I've found no gun, no intruder, not a bloody thing."

"Come down at once, sir!" the caretaker said. "You're not meant to be rummaging through the place."

"I hardly think rules matter right now," Felix yelled, his voice gruff. "Someone's shot at my best friend."

"That someone must be one of the lot of you." The caretaker's tone was defiant. "Nothing out of line happened until you arrived."

"Is there any way in and out of the castle other than through the main gate?" Colin asked.

"No, everything else is securely locked."

"Would you object to my making a thorough search all the same?" He was employing the tone of voice he used when it was imperative he get what he wanted. Calm, competent, commanding.

"Of course, sir. Anything you need."

"I'm most appreciative," Colin said. "Perhaps you'd be willing to accompany me? You're bound to know every nook and cranny, and that sort of expertise would be invaluable at a time like this." We exchanged a look. He knew I'd take charge of the others.

"The rest of you, let's go back inside so we don't freeze," I said. "I want to speak with each of you in turn, to find out if you noticed anything out of the ordinary while you were exploring the castle."

Because the ground and first floors of the Palas were unfinished and empty, we climbed back up the stairs to the antechamber outside the king's study. "Max, you come with me."

"Are you interviewing as if we're suspects?" Liesel asked. "Surely you don't think one of us—"

"It's simpler to recall details when a crowd isn't talking all at once," I said.

"Couldn't we wait until we're back at the villa?" Ursula asked. "It would be far more comfortable, and I know I could use a brandy."

"Too much time would pass. I want your immediate thoughts."

"I don't see why any of us should tell you anything," Kaspar said.

"Kallista has sent scores of murderers to the gallows." Cécile's voice was imperious and cold. "She's something of an expert when it comes to investigation."

"We've not had a murder," Kaspar said. "I'm sure this is nothing more than another prank. I'm not hurt, so we may as well forget about it."

"Given that you've been the object of so much violent attention, one would think you'd be loath to stand in the way of finding out who was behind it," I said. "Or do you think if slain you'd be forever honored, forever mourned? You're no Hector."

"I can take care of myself."

I ignored him. The trouble with men—one of the many troubles with men—is that they're incorrigible and bullheaded, appalling qualities that do nothing save stand in the way of a multitude of things that need to be done. "Max, come with me now."

He scurried over and I closed the door of the study behind us. I stood in front of the king's desk. "Where were you when the shot was fired?"

"Here, in this room, funnily enough," he said. "Sigrid and I were discussing *Tannhäuser*, scenes from which are depicted in the murals on the walls."

"You're certain? You arrived outside not long after the shot. That would've meant traveling quite a distance—and going down all those stairs—in a remarkably short period of time."

"You're right, of course." He raised his shoulders, then dropped them. "I only meant that this is where we'd been around that time. Liesel had wandered into the grotto next door, but came back in to alert us to the fact that we were in imminent danger of being late to meet the others, so we left posthaste and proceeded to the courtyard as quickly as we could."

"Did you see anyone else on your way out?"

"No. I heard Ursula's voice as we reached the bottom of the steps inside the Palas, but she was some distance behind us."

"So you had no idea something had happened?"

"None at all."

I called for Sigrid next. She confirmed—unprompted—most of Max's story, but insisted that she'd heard the shot.

"Why else would I have rushed down the stairs?"

"Did you say anything about it to Liesel or Max?"

"I can't remember. . . ." She paused. "Yes, yes, I told Liesel."

When I brought in Liesel, however, she did not remember

this. "No, no, Lady Emily. I heard no shot, and I don't see how Sigrid could've either. The study is an interior room. There are no windows."

"You're certain you didn't hear it? The grotto has a window." I'd looked out of it when we'd passed through the room. The view of the mountains was spectacular, so spectacular that I wondered why Ludwig had allowed for any rooms in the castle to have no windows.

"No, I don't believe I did." She chewed on the end of her thumb. "There was a noise—something—something unexpected, but it didn't startle me. At least I don't remember being startled, and a shot would do that, wouldn't it? I'm not sure whether I remember it or am just imposing it on myself after finding out what happened. I'm afraid I'm no help at all."

"When you came back into the study, where were Max and Sigrid standing?" I asked.

She bristled. "Is that important?"

"It might be."

She hesitated. Her lip quivered. She blinked twice. "They were both near the fireplace."

"You're certain?"

She sighed. "I'm not. I do apologize. Let me see. . . . I was in the grotto. What an odd room; who'd want a fake cave in one's house? Ludwig, yes, I know. Royalty aren't like the rest of us, are they? I was thinking what a strange place it is and then I looked at my watch and realized we were going to be late to meet you all. I went into the study. . . ." She closed her eyes and crinkled her brow. "Yes, yes, they were near the fireplace, both of them." Her eyes flew open and she smiled. It brightened her whole face.

The remainder of my interviews weren't any more helpful.

People are notoriously bad at paying attention to their surroundings, which is why eyewitness testimony must always be treated with a heavy dose of skepticism. Birgit insisted she nearly fainted at the sound of the shot, but Ursula, who'd been with her at the time, heard nothing unusual and said that Birgit was prattling on about some new style of gown and never showed the slightest sign of fainting.

"I confess I wasn't paying her close attention," she said. "She's a beautiful girl, but there's no one living in the attic, if you know what I mean. I'm amazed she can string a sentence together."

"Is she a good match for Felix?"

"I don't know the man well. He's not an intellectual, but he has other beguiling qualities. Or so Cécile tells me." Her smile was like a cat's.

"Do you think they'll get married?"

"Cécile will never marry again."

"I meant Birgit."

Ursula laughed. "I know, but I couldn't resist. I don't see a strong enough connection between them and I haven't heard him sneaking along the corridor to her room after everyone's gone to bed. That's never a good sign, especially in the young."

"Felix isn't all that young," I said.

"Birgit is. And men, they never really grow up, do they?"

Cécile came to me when Ursula left. She'd noticed nothing. As I'd been with her, I believed this. I hadn't either.

I spoke to Kaspar next; he was singularly unhelpful. "I've already told you, there's nothing to say. Felix and I were in the courtyard, discussing nothing in particular. A shot rang out. I turned on my heel to see where it came from and slipped on the ice. There's no more to it."

"You recognized the sound?"

"Of course. I'm an expert marksman."

"And you could tell what direction it came from, despite the echo in the courtyard?"

"I'm an expert marksman," he repeated.

Felix was more forthcoming than his friend. "I swear I heard something before the shot. Footsteps. Heavy footsteps. Like that from a hobnailed boot, coming from the direction of the connecting building between the tower and the gatehouse, but that didn't make sense as there wasn't anyone else in the lower courtyard and I'm sure the windows were all shut."

"What happened after the shot?" I asked.

"Kaspar fell and I thought he'd been hit, but I quickly saw he'd only slipped on the ice and was unharmed. We both thought it had come from the connecting building, so I went into it."

"The door was unlocked?"

"No. I ran up the outside stairs to it and broke a window. The caretaker won't be pleased."

"And you found nothing?"

"As I reported, *nicht eine einzige vermaledeite Spur*. I went through the connecting building, the tower, and the Palas."

"Who do you think did it?"

He shifted his weight from one foot to the other. "Kaspar can be something of a beast. He'd be the first to admit that. As a result, he lives in a world of extremes. People love him or hate him."

"Which category does Sigrid fall into?"

"The former, of course. You can't suspect her of wanting to hurt him?"

"At this juncture, I have to suspect everyone."

"Come now, Lady Emily, I appreciate your concern, but surely this is all just a bizarre coincidence or a silly prank. I shouldn't be surprised if it turns out the caretaker fired that shot. He might be unhappy at having visitors poking around when the place is supposed to be closed. On the other hand, it could have been an accident."

"An accident?" I asked. "Are you suggesting the caretaker just happened to be pointing a gun into the courtyard and inadvertently fired? And what about the skis? And the people who hate Kaspar? Tell me more about them."

"There are men he's bested in sport, that's all. That sort of gent isn't going to come all the way out here and torment him."

"Has he crossed anyone in love?"

"Now we're back to Sigrid?" he asked.

"I was thinking more along the lines of jealous husbands."

He laughed. "I can promise you he would never entangle himself with a married woman."

That struck me as odd. From what I'd heard from my childhood friend Jeremy—the Duke of Bainbridge and a most reliable source when it came to inappropriate relationships—a gentleman in search of female companionship often preferred married women; they weren't looking for commitment. "What about you, Felix? Do you love or hate him?"

"He's the best friend I've ever had. I love him and hate him equally."

10

Schloss Hohenschwangau
1868

Upon returning to Hohenschwangau from the building site, Elisabet retreated into her studio. Ludwig and Niels retired to the *Hohenstaufenzimmer*, the music room, where Richard Wagner played the piano on his visits to the king. Ordinarily, Ludwig commented on this whenever he passed the instrument. He'd rhapsodize about his memories of the composer, a man he loved above all others, sometimes going on for nearly half an hour, repeating stories Niels had heard before, stories that had taken on the tone of great legends, as if Ludwig were Agamemnon and Wagner Achilles. Except that Ludwig would never, ever cross Wagner. Today, however, the king was focused on something else. He touched the piano gently, with reverence, as he walked by, but he continued without comment to a telescope he'd set up at one of the windows.

"It's visible from here," he said, "Neu Hohenschwangau. Can you conjure, even in theory, a more perfect location for a castle?"

"I cannot," Niels said, peering into the eyepiece. He couldn't get it to come into focus, but that didn't matter. There was nothing yet to see. Not that he'd say as much to Ludwig. Better to let him enjoy his enthusiasm. Niels waited for a while before asking the question that had been nagging at him for hours. "What exactly happened between you and Sophie? I didn't want to ask in front of Elisabet."

"Whyever not?" Ludwig flung himself onto a settee. "Pour us some brandy, will you?"

Niels picked up the crystal decanter standing on a table against the wall and pulled out its stopper. "I—I suppose I thought she might be jealous."

Ludwig laughed. Ferociously. With his whole body. Relief surged through Niels. He still wasn't entirely comfortable with their friendship. Couldn't believe he'd become so close to the king. Couldn't believe he was hiding it from his mother. From everyone. Not that there were many others. His father wouldn't care, and he'd not stayed in touch with many of his friends from school.

"What's so funny?" he asked.

"Elisabet is not in love with me, nor I with her."

"Are you sure?"

"I think I'd know, wouldn't I?" He took the snifter Niels held out to him. "I'm exceedingly observant, you know, but even if I weren't, it's not too difficult to recognize when someone is in love with you. I saw it in Sophie. That's why I had to end it."

"She loved you." Niels stated it as a fact, but a fact he'd not expected. Royal marriages and love, so far as he knew, did not often mingle.

"Why wouldn't she? I'm handsome, charming, and endlessly entertaining when I want to be."

"The last is the closest to being true."

"This is why I like you, Niels," Ludwig said. "You speak without the slightest thought for how it will make me feel. I do, however, object to your not praising my good looks. I'm inarguably handsome. Even so, I prefer you to nearly anyone else. I'm used to sycophants and hangers-on and I despise them all. I want something real, and you give me that."

"I'm flattered."

"Don't be. I'm sure to tire of you before long."

Niels felt his face flush.

"You're too easy to goad." The king took a slug of brandy. "But to return to the subject of Sophie. You'd like her very much and would probably be much happier with her than I was. Of course, she requires a husband of higher rank, so you need not fear that I'll force you into the match."

"She loved you and you didn't love her."

"Not at all. I loved her—and still do—very much. She admires my Dearest Friend nearly as much as I. It's what bonded us, our appreciation for his music. We would sit for hours discussing it. Reminiscing about productions we'd seen. Reading librettos to each other. I showed her the letters he's written me. You do know I'm financing his work?"

"I didn't."

"You don't pay much attention to the papers, do you?" Ludwig asked. "I'm told what I'm doing is a scandal."

"I'm not much interested in the world."

"Another reason I like you."

Niels smiled. "So given all that—mutual love and shared interests—why didn't you marry her?"

"The love was not entirely mutual, not as to its kind, that is. I had no proper affection for her. Couldn't bear to kiss her. Her lips . . ." He shuddered. "She's a dear girl, very dear, but she could never be more than a sister to me."

"Many marriages are built on shakier foundations."

"You're quite right, of course, but her feelings for me were something else altogether. She wanted more, and I would never be capable of giving it to her. It would've been wrong to trap her in a relationship that could bring nothing but pain and disappointment."

"A noble reason to throw her over, Your Majesty."

Ludwig tilted the now-empty snifter in his hand back and forth, staring at it. "I doubt she saw it that way."

"You're a monarch. You've no choice but to marry, eventually, and provide your kingdom with an heir. Perhaps you could find a way to forge a life with her. It might not be too late."

"Don't start pressing me on the subject of marriage or I'll fling you out and never let you back in. The hurt's already done; she wouldn't have me back, even if she weren't marrying someone else. Further, there's more to it than simply Sophie. Her sister Sisi has been the person closest to me from almost the moment of my birth. I've always been honest with her, and she with me. There's no one I've ever spoken to so freely. She's more guarded with me now, and that is a wound that causes existential pain, but it will not always be this way, precisely because I ended the engagement. Had I married Sophie and destroyed her chance at happiness, that would've been a betrayal from which Sisi and I might never have recovered."

"Why did you agree to it in the first place?" Niels asked.

"I thought I should try to make it work. Marriage is expected of a monarch, and I assumed Sophie would be very like her sister. Unfortunately, she isn't."

They sat in silence for nearly a quarter of an hour after that. It was a comfortable silence, the kind that can be shared only by those who, on some fundamental level, understand each other. Then, at last, the king spoke.

"Sing for me, my friend. Something from *Lohengrin*, but not the Bridal Chorus. Anything but that."

11

Villa von Düchtel
1906

We were all rather subdued upon returning to Ursula's house after the incident at Neuschwanstein. The snow was falling harder now, and the villa, rather than enveloping me in warmth, added to the chill that had taken hold in my bones. Everything seemed off-kilter, out of balance. The sparely furnished rooms were cold and every sound echoed ominously through the place. Our hostess went up to the ballroom to contemplate the paintings Liesel had brought. Birgit went to her room for a bath and a nap. Max shut himself in the music room, refusing to allow Sigrid to go with him. Kaspar and Felix, adopting a posture of being aggressively undaunted, announced they were going for a ski. Kaspar, pointing out that he'd had no trouble with the stairs at Neuschwanstein, insisted his knee was fine. Liesel asked to accompany them.

"Are you quite sure you want to?" Felix asked. "Kaspar slows down for no one."

"I shan't try to keep up with you, only follow in the tracks you lay down. I enjoyed it more than I expected yesterday, but am terribly bad at it and don't think I'd like breaking through the fresh snow on my own."

"Suit yourself," Kaspar said. "We're leaving as soon as possible in order to return before sundown."

"I'll change in a flash." She raced off in the direction of the stairs.

"Does this mean you're coming as well?" Kaspar asked his wife.

"Absolutely not," Sigrid said. "As you well know, I'd prefer a sleigh ride."

"We've discussed this ad nauseam. Not today."

"It will have to come, sooner or later. You cannot avoid it forever." She patted his cheek, then went upstairs. As it was abundantly evident the sleigh ride in question was not merely a sleigh ride, I wondered what she meant; but before I could give it much thought, Liesel reappeared, and the skiers set off, leaving Colin, Cécile, and me on our own.

"It is something of a relief, is it not, Kallista?" We'd gone into the gallery, where my friend summoned a footman to bring us champagne. Still cold, I asked for mulled wine instead. He reappeared with it all in short order. Cécile shrugged. "Such an ungainly group of people, and so many of them."

"Each of them more challenging than one would hope," Colin said.

"Indeed. It surprises me that Ursula gathered these particular individuals together. She's usually much better at planning a party."

"I imagine she wanted to include her daughter, which necessitates Kaspar's presence," I said.

"Yes, and then he insisted on Felix, who in turn insisted on Birgit. More champagne, I beg you, Monsieur Hargreaves."

Colin retrieved the bottle from the ice-filled bucket left by the footman and refilled her glass. "You insisted on us."

"Kallista had to see Ursula's ancient art!"

"Quite," I said, wrapping my hands around the hot mug of glüh-wein. "I'm impressed with the manner in which she's displayed her collection. In the context of this gallery, one might be forgiven for thinking the Cycladic pieces are modern. But as for the way the guest list came together, you and Sigrid are the only two people here Ursula really wanted to see."

"Don't forget Liesel and Max," Cécile said.

"Liesel was a necessary addition for the paintings, so it's no surprise she was summoned," Colin said. "I do feel for the poor woman. She's doing her best to fit in, but she's got as much of a chance at succeeding as the Spartans did at Thermopylae."

"I disagree entirely," I said. "They faced far better odds and held off the enemy much longer than she could ever hope to. What about Max, Cécile? Why's he here? He lives close enough that there's no reason for him to have stayed after the initial soirée."

"This is where it is *nécessaire* to consider Ursula as the expert ma-nipulator she is," Cécile said. "Do not think I judge her for this. It is an art, an art she has perfected over a lifetime, and an art she never uses for ill purpose. She knows her daughter is unhappy and is trying to move her in the direction of a little joy."

"By prodding her into an affair?" Colin asked. "Aside from the dubious morality of the whole thing, shouldn't Sigrid be free to choose her own lover?"

Cécile shrugged. "Consider whom she picked when she had the opportunity."

"Consider the baroness's own unhappiness in her arranged mar-riage," Colin said. "Is this so different from what her parents did?"

"It's certainly not the same," I said. "Max and Sigrid have loads in common and they've been fast friends since childhood."

"Rather like you and a certain Duke of Bainbridge, but no one would suggest the two of you should be thrown together romantically," Colin said.

"Jeremy? Perish the thought! I'd sooner be at Thermopylae fighting the Persians."

"I'm glad to hear it," Colin said, touching my arm just for a second. "If Sigrid wanted Max, she would've married him."

"Much though it pains me to disagree with you, Monsieur Hargreaves, I must. You did not know Sigrid before she met Kaspar. There was no soul in Bavaria who didn't expect her to marry Max. The cows in every Alpine valley were aware of the deep connection between them."

"Are we to believe that the lure of Allerspach's charm was too much for her to resist?"

"That's inconceivable," I said. "The man is a boor. Jeremy would make for a better choice of husband."

"Kaspar has not been on his best behavior," Cécile said. "However, he is a decent-looking man, and when he wants to be charismatic, he's more than capable of it. He's strong and fit and full of passion. He can swim across the Alpsee and climb a mountain immediately thereafter. Max is earnest and sincere and gets winded even looking at a lake. His idea of climbing is a musical scale. I do not suggest he is inadequate in any way, only that Kaspar is so visibly different. It is not surprising he turned Sigrid's head."

"Homer tells us love deceives the best of womankind. Were they happy, at first?" I asked.

"*Bien sûr.* The attraction between them was very strong. That it did not last came as no surprise to anyone."

"Did Ursula try to dissuade her from the marriage?" I asked.

"She did."

"Yet the expert manipulator failed," Colin said.

"It was an error she will not repeat," Cécile said. "She abandoned subtlety in exchange for relentless pressure, something that rarely proves effective."

"Why would she adopt such a strategy when she's so proficient at manipulation?" I asked.

"Because she was terrified, terrified of seeing her only child trapped in a marriage as disastrous as her own had been. Desperation leads to bad decisions."

"And brought exactly what she feared," I said. "It's rather sad."

"In a way, I suppose." Colin drew his brows together and ran a hand through his tousled curls before putting down his empty champagne flute. "She shouldn't have been meddling in the first place. Given space and time, her daughter might have realized her choice was a poor one before the wedding."

"Perhaps, but not likely in this case. Sigrid was governed by a grand passion. Who can resist such a thing? You did not, Monsieur Hargreaves."

"Yes, but, fortunately for us all, my grand passion resulted in a disgracefully happy marriage." His eyes met mine and my cheeks flushed crimson.

"Forgive me for interrupting." It was Liesel, still wearing the heavy boots and the thick loden jacket she'd put on to ski. Snow was melting on her wool hat. "Would any of you have a headache powder? I seem to have overtaxed myself and am in more pain than I should ever have thought feasible."

"I'm afraid I don't," I said.

"Nor do I, but Ursula always keeps some on hand," Cécile said. "I'll fetch some from her."

"That's very kind of you. I'm most grateful—" She swayed just a bit, then her head rocked back and forth, her knees buckled, and she fell on the floor. Try though we might, we couldn't rouse her, and none of us was in possession of smelling salts. I object to them entirely. Years of observation have taught me that fainting is the result of affectation or too-tight stays. I would've expected either from Birgit, but not from the sensible Liesel. Colin shot to his feet, scooped her up, and carried her to her room.

The commotion brought Sigrid, whose eyes looked red and puffy, from her room. Shortly thereafter, we heard Ursula's heels clattering on the marble stairs that led to the ballroom. Neither of them had any smelling salts, so I knocked on Birgit's door. It took rather a lot of banging to rouse her, but at last I succeeded.

"Dear me, Lady Emily, what's this all about? Can't a girl get a little rest before the evening's entertainment? Do tell me there will be entertainment. I can't bear another dull night." She looked exhausted, but then one often does when awakened from a deep sleep. Her pillow had left a line across her cheek. I stated my purpose. She did, of course, carry smelling salts. "One never knows when a faint might prove convenient," she said, a wicked smile on her face.

"Isn't it preferable for someone else to have them on hand to revive you?"

"Certainly, but it's less and less common to find someone with them these days, so I make sure they're ready to spill out of my reticule on my way to the ground. Otherwise you run the risk of an overeager rescuer giving you a good slap."

I did not comment on this inanity. "I'll return them as soon as possible."

"That's not necessary. I've got a spare."

She followed me across the corridor and Ursula waved them under Liesel's nose. She started, coughed, shook her head, and started to sit up. Ursula gently pushed her back against the pillows. "Not yet, my dear. You ought to rest."

"My head . . ." Her breath was labored. "I get headaches frequently but the pain has never been quite this excruciating."

"I'll get you a powder that will offer relief and another that will help you sleep," Ursula said. "Don't even think of coming down for dinner. We can have a tray sent up when you're awake."

"You're kindness itself, Baroness. I hate to impose upon you like this."

"It's no imposition at all. Now keep still and don't try to talk. Hargreaves, pull the curtains so the light doesn't bother her. I'll be back before you know it with those powders. The rest of you, go downstairs and leave the poor woman in peace."

We all did as directed, more or less. The others went downstairs, but Colin pulled me into our room.

"I wish this were a romantic assignation, but I suspect you've something else on your mind," I said.

"Quite." He closed and locked the door behind us. "What do you think is going on here?"

"Kaspar's been attacked twice and Liesel fainted. Perhaps something other than overexertion caused her headache."

He shook his head. "That's unlikely. What does anyone want from her? A lower price for the paintings?"

"My mind's running in an altogether different direction. She was in the grotto before we were to meet in the courtyard. Max and Sigrid were next door, in the king's study. When she noticed the time, she went to fetch them. I asked her where exactly they were standing and she hesitated ever so slightly before answering. I had the feeling she wasn't telling me everything."

"What are you suggesting?" he asked.

"She might have caught them in flagrante delicto, perhaps sharing a passionate kiss inspired by some of the racier moments in *Tannhäuser. Only he who has known / your ardent embrace knows what love is* and all that. Sigrid's marriage isn't a happy one, but that doesn't mean she wants her husband to know she's . . ."

"Quite." Colin tugged off his jacket and flung it toward a chair. It landed on the floor. He eyed it suspiciously and unknotted his cravat. "If they're entangled in some sort of affair, her mother has put her in an awkward position having both gentlemen in the house at the same time."

"If they're involved romantically, Max would have ample motivation to want Kaspar entirely out of the picture."

"He doesn't strike me as the murderous type."

"Precisely," I said, "and if he's responsible for the attacks on Kaspar, he's demonstrated that he's not particularly capable, either. He may, however, eventually get the hang of it."

"Unlikely, but possible."

"He could try something easier. Poison, for example."

"That's not what I meant." He started to pace, up and down, in front of the windows. The snow had not stopped, but it was lighter now, and the mountains were visible once again in the distance. "What if these incidents are intended to scare Kaspar, not to harm him? The shot today had a better chance of causing serious injury—"

"Or death," I interrupted.

"Or death, yes, than the cut ski binding, but whoever fired failed to hit his mark. Allerspach was more or less standing still, and there are plenty of vantage points from the windows around the courtyard that would have provided a clear shot. Either the shooter is incompetent or he never meant to injure the man."

"If the shot was deliberately fired to scare him, what's the shooter's goal?" I asked.

"I've not the slightest idea."

I sank into a chair opposite the windows from where I could see both the mountains and my husband. "Max couldn't believe it's possible to frighten Kaspar into leaving his wife. If he's behind the incident, the shot missed its target due to incompetence."

"I agree. So who among Ursula and her guests would want to scare Allerspach and to what end?"

"If Kaspar were a superstitious sort of man, he could perhaps be persuaded that if he doesn't start treating his wife better, he'll suffer an ignominious fate."

"First, although he's not the sort of chap I'd choose to spend much time with, he's not the worst husband I've ever met. He and Sigrid give every appearance of getting along well enough."

"*Appearance* is the crucial word," I said.

"Yes, but until we have firm evidence to the contrary, we've no reason to believe their marriage is in dire straits. Second, is there anyone present in this house whom you believe seeks to bring the couple closer together? We've nothing but our own speculation to support any of these theories."

"It's early days, my dear man, the stage of investigation where fiction is our friend, where flights of fancy may lead us to the truth."

"I'm not sure I can subscribe to that idea," he said. "Still, something isn't right and I'm deeply concerned that if we don't figure out who's behind these incidents, Allerspach could find himself in a most thankless situation."

"I believe *dead* is the word you're looking for. You're in safe company, darling; there's no need for euphemisms with me."

12

The Alpsee
1868

All the glories of the world converged in the Alps that summer. Cascades of colorful wildflowers covered mountainsides below rocky peaks. Snowmelt swelled lakes and streams and converted waterfalls into spectacular playgrounds fit for long-forgotten ancient gods. Ludwig refused to sit for Elisabet's sculpture, instead commanding that the friends explore their environs. They read Byron aloud. Raced through verdant meadows. Dragged themselves to the highest points they could find. Twice, Niels's father ordered him to Munich; his son ignored the directives. Active pursuits filled his days, pursuits of which his father would've approved, but Niels no longer cared about trying to impress him. He'd rather impress the king.

"You're a vision, the both of you," Elisabet said one day as they rode three of Ludwig's finest steeds along the trails surrounding Hohenschwangau. "The Mongolian horseman of ages past would weep at the sight of you. Such fine posture, such expert skill."

"Such well-fitted trousers," Ludwig said. "On me, at least. Niels, your wardrobe is something of a crushing disappointment. As soon as we return to the castle, I shall send for my tailor and have him see to it."

"My wardrobe is perfectly adequate," Niels said.

"Adequate? Do you not understand me in the slightest, man? You know I've no tolerance for anything short of perfection. What use is the world without beauty? What use am I if I don't insist upon it wherever I go?"

"I don't think my trousers have anything to do with it."

"Nor do I," Elisabet said, "but I wouldn't object to a few new gowns of my own."

"I shall arrange it. I'll send for Worth as well. He dresses my cousin."

"I can't afford Worth," she said, laughing, "and have no intention of letting you pay. It's one thing for you to take care of Niels. That won't cause any gossip, but when it comes to a lady, things are altogether different."

"When did you start concerning yourself with gossip?" Ludwig said.

"I'm not concerning myself with it, not exactly, but every once in a while I think I should make a half-hearted gesture in the direction of propriety."

"Madame, I hardly know you!" The king spurred his horse on and soon left his friends behind. No one could match his speed, not through the dense forest along twisting paths. He had no fear, not even a momentary hesitation, only confidence. God had anointed him and would never let him come to any harm. This knowledge, more certain to him than anything, carried him through his life; and on days like this—magnificent summer days spent on the back of a fine horse—he felt it in the depths of his soul.

When he reached the shore of the Alpsee, he dismounted, tied his horse to a convenient tree, and stretched out on a rock in the sun. Sweat drenched him, but he didn't care. Nearly three-quarters of an hour passed before he heard the others approach. He'd been keeping track, pulling his watch out at regular intervals. Every minute that passed confirmed his God-given superiority. They would never be half as fast as he.

"You can't avoid catastrophe forever, you know," Elisabet said. "Riding like the devil himself is chasing you will catch up with you eventually."

"Don't blaspheme. God will always protect his favorite son," Niels said, grinning.

Ludwig turned to him, his eyes wide. "What did you say?"

"God will always protect his favorite son. Why?"

Ludwig sat up, met his eyes, and stepped down from the rock. "There are times it is as if you can read my thoughts."

"It's not so hard, my friend. You're rather predictable."

"Too right," Elisabet said, sliding down from her saddle. "We know all about your holy anointing. I find it rather tedious, if you must know. This heat is unbearable, is it not?"

"Come closer to the water," Ludwig said. "Even proximity to it is cooling."

"Proximity can only go so far." She untied the ribbons securing the hat under her chin, then pulled out two long pins, removed it from her head, tossed it on the ground, and turned to Niels. "Unbutton me, will you?"

"Unbutton you? Good heavens, no!"

"Oh, don't be such a prude. I shan't reveal any more than a bathing costume would."

"Come here," Ludwig said. "I'll do it."

And he did.

"Now unlace my corset. You're a king, so I've no doubt you've a certain amount of experience when it comes to such things. Men in power do whatever they want."

Ludwig grunted and did as ordered. When he'd finished, Elisabet stepped out of her dress, untied her petticoats, tugged at her corset until it came off, kicked off her shoes, and rolled the stockings from her legs. Then, wearing only her chemise, she stepped into the cool water of the lake.

"It's divine," she said, not looking back at her friends. "You must come in."

"I can't claim expert knowledge, but I fear she's revealed far more than a bathing costume would," Niels said.

"It doesn't matter, does it? We'd never take advantage of her nor would we dream of spreading gossip. We're on a royal estate. No one else can see us." Ludwig removed his jacket and tie and unbuttoned his shirt. "I shall take things a step further than she did, however, as I've no interest in putting dry clothes over wet ones. I suggest you follow suit." He stripped off the rest of his clothes and plunged into the water, his slim body white in the sun.

Niels wanted to point out that they weren't all that far from the spot where he'd first met Ludwig, and that wasn't part of the royal estate, but he, too, was uncomfortably warm after their ride. So he did as Ludwig bade him. The rocks on the shore bit sharply into his feet, but once he'd slipped into the water, the cool, clear water, he had no memory of the pain. Elisabet had swum out some distance, but the water wasn't above her head.

"It's heaven, isn't it?" she called.

Ludwig, having gone considerably farther into the lake, was swimming a pace Niels could hardly believe. "Heaven indeed," he said, wading toward the sculptor. "Where's he off to?"

"He's going all the way across."

"That must be a mile."

"It's not the first time he's done it," she said.

They were standing so close to each other now that Niels felt suddenly self-conscious about his nakedness. He turned around so he wasn't facing her. She laughed.

"My dear boy, I'm an artist. You've nothing I haven't seen before."

"That may be so, but have you given any thought to what I've seen before?"

"Oh, do turn around," she said. "I'm not going to speak to the back of your head." He did as she asked. She met his eyes, cocked her head, and laughed. "You haven't seen anything before, have you?"

"That's none of your concern." He splashed water at her. She splashed back, and soon they were engaged in an epic battle that ended only when Elisabet disappeared underwater, grabbed his ankles, and pulled him off his feet. When he rose to the surface, sputtering, he could hardly stop laughing.

"We ought to find our royal friend," she said. "He'll want his clothes and is used to having his needs anticipated. We can take the horses." She made her way back to the shore.

Niels followed, confidence surging in him. He had no doubt it was a momentary aberration, but decided to revel in it while it lasted. He walked past her, then turned to face her as he dressed, unconscious of his body.

Not that she noticed. She was more concerned with her own problems. "I've no desire to put my corset on over a wet chemise, but I'll not be able to fasten my dress without it. Will you assist me?"

"If you'll be so good as to allow me to clothe myself first."

She laughed, and the sound of silvery bells bounced across the lake. "I'm sure Lord Byron was no stranger to this sort of thing. *What men call gallantry, and gods adultery, / Is much more common where the climate's sultry.*"

Niels's muscles clenched and he forced a laugh. "There's no adultery here, not so far as I know."

"No, of course not, but the climate is sultry, at least for now. It's the best I could do. Hurry up. We don't want Ludwig skulking around forever on the other side of the lake. He's ghastly when he's kept waiting."

The corset was more difficult to wrangle than Niels had imagined, although he'd no factual basis for forming expectations when it came to ladies' undergarments. The curves of her body beneath the wet chemise stirred something in him, an appreciation for beauty, more clinical than passionate, but perhaps that was due only to his inexperience.

Once they were dressed, they mounted their horses and, keeping ahold of the king's, made their way around the shore of the lake until they came upon him, stretched out on a rock, his naked body gleaming in the sun.

"The sun will burn you, you fool." Elisabet flung Ludwig's clothes at him.

"Neither of you is impressed with my physical appearance? With my strength? My lean muscles, perfectly formed, like those of a Greek god? What a crushing disappointment." He pulled his shirt over his head. "Hoi polloi, the both of you."

"Praxiteles would pull out his chisel if he were here, but he's been dead for thousands of years," Elisabet said. "Hurry up. I'm ravenous."

"You're quiet, Niels," the king said, turning to his friend. "Our antics haven't offended you, I hope."

"Not at all," Niels said. "Quite the contrary. I've never before in my life tasted freedom like this. It's heaven." For that day, at least, they were like ancient gods, feasting on nectar and ambrosia, concerned with nothing but pleasure.

Such delights can never last.

13

Villa von Düchtel
1906

Colin and I continued our discussion—our sadly fruitless discussion—while we dressed for dinner. By the time the gong sounded, I was attired in a slim, high-waisted gown of the finest ice blue silk decorated with silver lace around the cuffs and the plunging neckline. The color brought out my eyes. Diamonds and Kashmir sapphires mounted in platinum settings so delicate they looked more like lace than metal dangled from my ears. I handed my husband the box containing the matching necklace and bracelet so that he might assist me with the clasps.

"You're glittering, my dear," he said. "I hadn't expected that at a mountain retreat."

"I always like to have something violently fashionable on hand, just in case one finds oneself in company that requires it."

"The baroness certainly doesn't require any such thing. You're still smarting from Birgit's ill-mannered comment about your Greek key gown, aren't you?"

"Yes, and I despise myself for it. I ought not let her get to me."

"She's young and beautiful and frightfully insecure, which makes her vicious. And unbearable."

"Beautiful? You think she's beautiful?"

"It's nothing more than a dispassionate observation," he said, coming around to my front after securing the necklace. "Hold up your wrist. She dislikes you because you make her feel even more insignificant than she already does."

"I've been nothing but kind to her."

He fastened the bracelet. "You've been tolerant."

"I've been—"

"Tolerant, and she deserves no more. You, my darling love, walk *in beauty, like the night / Of cloudless climes and starry skies*, and when you speak, your intelligence shines brighter than all the diamonds mined since the beginning of time. She can never compete with that and she's all too aware of it. She's not entirely stupid. Vapid, yes, but smart enough to know she'll never have your brilliance." He placed one finger on my lips and fixed his dark eyes on mine. "She'll never know love like that we share, because such a thing requires a partnership of equals."

My breath stilled. I could hardly see. Hardly breathe. I knew if I did not extricate myself from his gaze, we'd never make it to dinner. With considerable effort, I stepped back and we headed downstairs.

Liesel, much improved after sleeping for several hours, joined us all at the table, but it was evident she was still not feeling well. The conversation was strangely inconsequential. No one addressed the gunshot at Neuschwanstein. Instead, there was discussion of the weather, an earthquake in Ecuador, and a figure skating competition in Switzerland. It was as if we'd never visited Ludwig's castle. I was astonished. Dumbstruck. Unable to comprehend how such a monumental event could be willfully ignored. After a dessert of

Bratäpfel—baked apples drenched in rum, butter, and a divine blend of spices—served with smooth vanilla custard and a sublime Eis-wein, we retired to the music room for coffee. Birgit, dressed in a rose-colored gown so pale it was nearly white, sat at the piano and poked at the keys in what, so far as I could tell, was an entirely ran-dom manner, the sound incongruent with her perfect appearance. Her light hair, expertly styled, shone like a crown over her glowing, heart-shaped face, with its rosy cheeks and pouty lips.

"I'm bored beyond belief," she said. "Max, come up here and play something so we can dance."

"Dance?" Cécile nearly dropped the glass of champagne in her hand. "This is no time for dancing. Is no one going to address the extraordinary events of the day? It is, to me, *incroyable* that you all can act as if nothing happened."

"What would you have us do?" Birgit asked. "Your detective friends have already interrogated us all and for what? So far as I can tell, they accomplished nothing except to make us feel like common criminals."

"That was not our intent," I said.

"No one's interested in your intent, Lady Emily." She spat the words.

Max replaced Birgit at the piano and started to play a Chopin étude softly, so that the notes sounded as if they were coming from somewhere far away. No one spoke, but the tension in the room pulsed so strongly it had a physical presence.

"Tomorrow might be a good day for ice skating," Birgit said.

Sigrid narrowed her eyes. "I'd agree if there's some way to en-sure no one will attack my husband while he's doing it."

"No one wants to see him attacked." Birgit's voice went up an octave.

"Yet no one is discussing how to keep him safe," Sigrid said.

Birgit huffed. "I don't see you offering any suggestions."

"How many times do I have to point out that no harm's been done?" Kaspar said, his voice sluggish as he rose to his feet. "I—"

Before he could finish the sentence, there was a loud crash as he toppled over and fell onto the floor, his coffee cup shattering when it hit the edge of the mosaic table in front of where he'd been standing.

Birgit shrieked and collapsed in a faint. Assuming this was staged for effect, I ignored her and rushed to Kaspar. Sigrid was already kneeling next to him. He blinked his eyes and his head lolled. Then he turned onto his side and went limp.

"He's dead." The color drained from Sigrid's face and she gulped back a sob.

I felt for a pulse in his neck. "He's not dead. His heart's still beating." I shook him, but he was nonresponsive. "I think he's asleep."

"Asleep? Don't be absurd," Sigrid said. "No one falls asleep mid-sentence. We need a doctor."

I walked over to Birgit and, as expected, found her spare container of smelling salts next to her. She didn't stir. I picked them up, returned to Kaspar, and waved them under his nose. He startled, his eyes blinked rapidly, and he raised himself up on his elbows.

"What happened?" he asked, the words slurred.

"You've been the victim of a third attack," Colin said. "This one more innocuous than the last but worrisome all the same." He reached down for a piece of the broken porcelain. "My guess is that someone put laudanum in your cup. It's long enough since you started to drink your coffee for it to have taken effect."

"Someone send for a doctor," Sigrid said.

Kaspar scowled. "I don't need a doctor. I'm all right. Fatigued, but all right." He tried to sit up, but struggled. "I'm getting tired of these pranks."

"It's time we face the possibility that they're something more nefarious," Colin said.

"There's no need to get carried away," Kaspar said. "Felix, *mein Freund*, are you behind all this? I've never meant you any ill will, but I've tormented you often enough in the past that I deserve whatever you decide to give me."

"Me?" Felix grunted. "You're frequently infuriating, but none of your pranks would induce me to shoot at you. Besides, I was standing right next to you when it happened. You might not be the sharpest of my acquaintances, but even you would notice if I were holding a gun."

"You're right on that count." Kaspar's head bobbed.

"Let's get him up to bed so he can sleep," Colin said. "He'll be fine in the morning."

"I'd prefer that he saw a doctor," Sigrid said.

"Enough!" Kaspar raised his hand. It looked as if he was about to strike his wife, but instead, he brought it down hard upon his own leg. "I'm exhausted from the drug, but nothing more."

"Perhaps we should all go to bed," Ursula said. "Behind locked doors. I don't like any of this."

"You're not suggesting we're in danger, are you?" Birgit asked, miraculously sitting up without the aid of smelling salts.

"I've no idea what to think," Ursula said, "but I don't want any more accidents or pranks or badly executed attacks. Or public arguments." She glared at her son-in-law.

Birgit's eyes widened. "The next one might not be badly executed. I can only speak for myself, but I can't get out of this house soon enough. The whole situation is unsettling. This is not the sort of house party I enjoy."

"There are no trains at this time of night. We can discuss it further in the morning, when we're all less on edge," Ursula said. "Now, though, Kaspar needs his rest and the rest of us could stand some as well." She rang for a footman and ordered him to clean up the mess, then held open the door and shooed us all out.

Felix helped his friend up the stairs. The rest of us followed, lagging behind, calling good night as we reached our rooms. No sooner had Colin closed our door, than a knock sounded. It was Felix.

"Forgive me for disturbing you, but I'm concerned about my friend. I believe the safest course of action is for me to sleep in the corridor outside his and Sigrid's room."

"That's a reasonable enough precaution in the circumstances," Colin said, ushering him in.

Felix shifted his weight from one foot to the other. He was a large man, but not an oaf; the movement might not have been graceful, but it was forceful and strong. He laid a hand on Colin's arm. "Does that mean you think someone is trying to kill him? I confess I'd come here hoping you'd tell me I'm overreacting."

"The actions taken against Allerspach have caused no significant harm," Colin said. "That may indicate that the perpetrator has no intention of escalating things, but we have no way of knowing for sure. I never object to measured caution."

"I hardly know what to think." Felix crossed his legs and pushed his hands into his jacket pockets. "Anyone half capable could've killed him today with that shot."

"Or put poison instead of laudanum in his coffee," I said. "You told me this afternoon you couldn't think of anyone who'd want to harm him. Do you still feel that way now?"

He shook his head and sat down. "I've been mulling it over, and there's only one possibility that merits any credence, but it's too outrageous."

"It's better to say it than not." Colin was leaning against the wall between two windows.

Felix tipped his head back until it hit the top of the chair. He pulled his hands out of his pockets. He sighed. He returned his hands to his pockets. "The baroness. She's never liked him and thinks her daughter could do better elsewhere. Always did. She's a bit of a snob, you know, with her art collection and her new villa, designed by a lauded architect in the latest style. The ordinary has never been good enough for her, and ordinary is exactly what Kaspar is. He may be a superior athlete, but that's not something she values."

"Does Sigrid agree that she could do better?" I asked.

"If she did, I don't believe she would've married him," Felix said. "They adored each other in the beginning. The attraction was instantaneous. But . . ." He sighed again.

"*Violent fires soon burn out themselves*," I said.

"Precisely. You've a way with words, Lady Emily."

"All credit goes to Shakespeare."

"The baroness not only views Kaspar as inferior to her daughter, she also can't bear the thought of him having access to Sigrid's money," he said. "It's no fortune, mind you. The girl has hardly any capital; they rely on an allowance from her mother. But when the baroness dies, the inheritance will be significant. I've no doubt she would be delighted if he could be removed from her daughter's life before it's too late."

"It takes no leap of imagination to accept the logic of your conclusions, but how do they tie into what's happened?" Colin asked, crossing his arms. "Do you suggest she's tormenting Kaspar in the hope that it will inspire him to leave his marriage of his own accord? I don't find that credible."

"Nor would I, if that's all it was," Felix said. "But what if this is only the beginning of her scheme? What if she continues her campaign of harassment until he's half-mad with anxiety? No one can go on unaffected endlessly when there are constant attempts on his life."

"What would her goal be?" I asked.

"To drive him to suicide."

"It doesn't seem a reliable method of getting what she wants, assuming that is what she wants," Colin said.

"Kaspar has struggled with melancholy in the past," Felix said. "It's been years since he had an episode, but it could always happen again. That makes him more vulnerable."

"The baroness is aware of this?" Colin asked.

"She is. She paid for his treatment last time. I'm not claiming it's the most sound of theories, just that it's something you should consider. Attempting to exploit his weakness may not be an efficient way of eliminating him, but would keep her from having to get her hands dirty."

"I still think it's unlikely, but we shall keep it in mind," Colin said.

"That's all I can ask. If you need me, I'll be sitting against Kaspar's door. No one can get past me. That will keep him safe overnight."

I'd listened to everything he said about Ursula, but something wouldn't stop nagging at me. Kaspar might be safe for the night, so long as his attacker was coming from the outside. The same would not be true if the person wanting rid of him wasn't his mother-in-law but his wife. It's often those closest to us who prove the most dangerous.

14

Schloss Hohenschwangau
1868

Dreams kept Niels up half the night after their swim in the Alpsee. In some, he was buoyed by warm, gentle waves. In others, he was half-drowned in a cataclysmic storm. In all of them, there was a steady background of screams, both screams of pleasure and screams of pain, with no order or sense to either. After each one, he awakened and paced his room in the castle, disturbed and afraid to go back to sleep. Then, when he was too exhausted to remain upright, he'd stagger to his bed, only to be roused again by another nocturnal disruption. He longed to see the rosy light of dawn, soft against the mountains, knowing he'd suffer no more watery images, at least not until night fell again.

Unlike Niels, Ludwig was in fine form at breakfast. His face glowed from the previous day's sun, and he had dressed with even more care than usual. His hair was perfectly smoothed and he was humming a melody from *Tannhäuser* as he smeared mustard on a large pretzel, a deviation from his standard breakfast fare. "Today we shall picnic at the site of my new castle."

"Not me," Elisabet said. "I need time in the studio if I'm ever going to finish my wretched sculpture of you. Profligate kings don't have to be concerned with such things, but it's not so easy for the working class."

"I'll pay you double if you abandon the project," Ludwig said.

"I wouldn't want to deprive the world of this eternal image of such a beautiful monarch in the prime of his youth only to benefit my own financial gain."

He tore off a hunk of the pretzel and threw it at her. "You should do as I ask. I'm your king."

"You're *a* king, but as to whether you're mine is debatable." She picked up the improvised projectile from the table and popped it in her mouth. "You'll have to soldier on without me. I'm staying here to work. There's nothing more to be said on the subject."

"What about you, young Lohengrin? You look half dead. I do hope that doesn't mean you, too, intend to abandon me?"

Niels yawned. "I didn't sleep well."

"Is that to be your excuse?" The king's tone took a dark turn.

"Don't be absurd. If I were to make an excuse, it would be something far more fantastical. I'd claim that someone had stolen my ring and that I'd have no time for picnics until I'd recovered it."

As quickly as Ludwig had started to anger, the mood passed. He grinned. "You're a good man. We'll leave in half an hour. I want plenty of time for us to explore the ruins before luncheon."

Niels didn't relish the thought of another bumpy drive to the building site, nor the steep climb that they'd have to make on foot to cover the final distance, but he wasn't about to deny his friend any pleasure. Without Ludwig, he'd be back in Munich, daily disappointing his parents. No life could be entirely without strife, and if his was limited to exhausting himself trekking through the mountains, his plight was not so bad.

Once they'd made the climb and the servants had lugged the baskets of food to the shaded spot the king had selected, Ludwig ordered them to go back down to the bottom of the mountain and wait until he summoned them.

"I can't stand having them lurking around," he said, watching them wind down the narrow path. "I've so little privacy and it's all I crave. Well, nearly all I crave. One can't do without staff, of course, but they're always there. Listening. Judging."

"I doubt they judge," Niels said, lowering himself onto a rock. "You treat them well enough, most of the time."

"You're still cross with me for getting rid of the ugly one last week. I'm exceedingly sensitive. The world should be beautiful, all of it. Every place, every person."

"It never shall be."

"Unfortunately, you're correct, but as king, I have control over my immediate environs. Is it so wrong that I choose to be surrounded by beauty? It's not as if I sent the man off with nothing. He'll be paid for the rest of the month and my housekeeper will help him secure another position with a less discerning employer."

"There's so much good in you, so much light, and then you go and say things like that and I wonder how I can tolerate your company for more than half an hour." He kept his tone light, so Ludwig would consider this a jest, but it wasn't, and knowing that made Niels uneasy. He abhorred dishonesty. He rose, walked toward the king, who was leaning against a tree, and stood directly in front of him.

"That's a rather serious expression," Ludwig said.

"You've plucked me from a life of diffuse misery. I was comfortable enough, but never happy. I felt I couldn't speak my mind or pursue any of my own interests. I wanted nothing to do with my mother's society friends—"

"Who include my own wretched mother."

"Indeed." Niels smiled. "We've quite a bit in common, don't we? Being in the presence of my father means suffering a constant barrage of criticism. I want to sing, but he'd prefer that I concern myself with increasing the family fortune and finding a wife."

"You don't need a wife."

"I agree, but that's not what I'm driving at. You, Ludwig, let me sing. You let me wander aimlessly through your magnificent grounds in search of swans, and you ask nothing in return but honest friendship. That's why I shall always tell you when your actions make me cringe. Watching you get rid of a servant because his looks don't please you sits uneasily with me. You're a better man than that."

The king stiffened and took a few steps away from Niels. "I don't like your tone or your words. You've no right to speak to me that way, especially after all I've done for you."

"You're correct on that count, but I shall say it anyway, because I care for you so much that I'd rather put my own happiness at risk than sit back and let you take actions that lead people to see you as someone you're not."

"What if they're seeing me as I am? You may not agree with my methods, but I cannot tolerate ugliness. If the world wants to cast aspersions on me as a result, so be it. I'm a king and can ignore them."

"Yes, that's true, but . . ." He bit his lower lip, frustrated. "I'm not explaining myself well. I suppose it's that I want people to know you the way I do. To see the good as well as the flaws."

"I'm not like other people, Niels. I think differently. If you consider that as a flaw—" He stopped and looked away. "I value your friendship, but if you can't accept me as I am, there can be nothing between us."

Niels looked at him, at his handsome face, normally full of youthful vigor, but now clouded with doubt. "Friendship requires acceptance. Acceptance of everything, good and bad. I may tell you when I don't agree with you, but I'll never hold it against you when you choose a course of action I wouldn't."

"Do you mean that?"

"I do."

A broad smile softened Ludwig's face. "Then kneel and pledge your loyalty to me, like a knight in days of old." He threw back his head and laughed. "If only I had a sword, I'd make you a knight. Christen you Lohengrin."

"And order me to save a desperate duchess?"

"No, I've very little interest in duchesses, desperate or otherwise." He drew his brows together and reached for Niels's hand. "I'm grateful for your words. I shall hold them in my soul, always, even when you infuriate me."

Niels was vaguely aware of a surge of emotion in his body, but could feel nothing but the king's hand, warm and smooth, on his. He met Ludwig's gaze and his heart pounded. He couldn't move, couldn't speak.

"There's nothing more important than acceptance, especially when it comes from someone who knows you fully, who doesn't reject you because of the bad or the inconvenient. I shall always be the same with you," Ludwig said. "From today, you're my brother. You must never leave me."

That broke the strange spell; Niels was no longer paralyzed. He threw back his head and laughed. "Leave you and go where? Back to Munich?"

"Back to your family's house near Füssen. You were happy enough there before you met me."

"I was bored beyond measure, unsure of what to do with myself. Now, all I want is to help you plan this magnificent castle." He started to sing.

In fernem Land, unnahbar euren Schritten,
Liegt eine Burg, die Monsalvat genannt;
Ein lichter Tempel stehet dort inmitten,
So kostbar als auf Erden nichts bekannt.

[Far and away, unapproachable to your steps,
There is a castle called Montsalvat;
In the middle there stands a luminous temple,
As precious as nothing else on earth is known.]

Ludwig closed his eyes as he listened. "Ah, your voice is divine, but I've mixed feelings about your choice of song. It's the beginning of the end, after all, when Elsa has asked the forbidden question and betrayed Lohengrin."

"Today we shall let ourselves take it out of context, while we stand here on the site of another castle, unapproachable and luminous, as precious as nothing else on earth is known."

"You understand me like no one else ever has," Ludwig said. They looked out from the promontory, taking in the view of the lakes far below and the circle of mountains around them. They were standing so close together that for a moment—only a moment—their hands brushed together and another something charged through Niels, something he could not begin to understand, except to know that his life had profoundly changed once again.

15

Villa von Düchtel
1906

None of us slept well after Kaspar's collapse in the music room, except the victim, of course, whose slumber was drug induced. The next morning, Cécile and Ursula, exhausted, took breakfast in their rooms. When Felix, who'd sat in front of his friend's door all night, entered the dining room, there were dark circles under his bloodshot eyes.

"Did you manage to get any rest?" I asked.

"Very little, but I ought not to have dozed at all," he said, piling eggs and sausages on a plate. "Fortunately, there were no disturbances."

"Obviously," Kaspar said. He looked particularly bright. "I've given the matter considerable thought and cannot conjure any reason that someone might wish to do me serious harm. These pranks—for that's what they must be—are nothing but mere annoyances, and I won't stand for our plans being disrupted by them. If we ignore the miscreant, he'll grow tired of his antics. Birgit, was it you who mentioned ice skating last night? Let's do it today."

"Not before our sleigh ride," Sigrid said. "You've not yet seen the waterfall. It's the most beautiful spot in Bavaria."

"No, not before that." He took her hand. "You've been more than patient, *mein Schatz*. We'll go as soon as I've finished breakfast."

I glanced across the table and caught Colin's eye. He shrugged, then applied himself to the enormous heap of food on his plate. Breakfast had always been his preferred meal. "I'm not comfortable with any of this," I said. "You've been repeatedly attacked, Kaspar. A wiser course of action—"

"Would be what? To lock myself away against some imaginary foe who can't be bothered to aim a gun properly? Am I to spend the rest of my life in hiding? That's contrary to my nature and I refuse to do it. Further, I put you all on notice: I'll tolerate no more discussion of the subject. It's tedious in the extreme."

"That's the first sensible comment I've heard in I don't know how long," Birgit said. "It's all boring beyond belief."

Liesel shifted uncomfortably in her seat. "Surely boring is better than dangerous?"

Kaspar glared at her. "No further discussion, Fräulein. Period."

"I agree," Colin said. "Not with your decision, but I acknowledge that it's yours to take. As you've clearly made up your mind, there's no need for further conversation. You're the only one who's been targeted, so there's no reason to conclude you're putting anyone else in harm's way. You can do what you like."

"I'm hardly going to thank you for stating something so obvious." He wiped his mouth roughly with a napkin. "If you'll all excuse me, I've promised my wife a sleigh ride." Sigrid's plate was still half full, but he grabbed her by the hand and pulled her away from the table.

When they were gone, Birgit rolled her eyes. "That woman has a way of always getting what she wants. Some people are lucky that way." I was on the verge of an unkind retort, but before I could speak, she continued. "What's that appalling noise?"

Liesel perked up. "It's Max practicing his tuba. Isn't it marvelous?"

"Marvelous? More like a dying cow." She pulled a face. "I'm not even hungry. I don't know why I bothered to come downstairs. I'll see you all for ice skating. Until then, I'll be in my room."

"She's so beautiful, yet so unhappy," Liesel said. "I wonder if she has any artistic talent. She certainly has the temperament for it."

This made us all laugh and the tension that had filled the room dissipated. Felix roared the loudest. "Don't think me unkind, but I have to tolerate more from her than any of the rest of you. There are times one can do nothing but hope for a reason to laugh."

"How long have you been courting her?" I asked.

"I wouldn't call it courting, Lady Emily. When she's not in a foul mood, she's a lark, and we have loads of fun. It's nothing more than that, though. We've no understanding. It's just that I don't like tagging along with Kaspar and Sigrid on my own. It's better if I bring someone with me."

"Is it?" Liesel asked. "Forgive me, I ought not be so forward. It's just that"—she paused—"you're something of a catch, Herr Brinkmann. My uneducated opinion is that you could do better."

This surprised me. Aside from his interest in Goethe—which, so far as I could tell, survived only in the form of occasional quotes and his yellow waistcoats—he had little interest in high culture.

"Someday, Fräulein Fronberg, I may want to, and when I do, perhaps I shall make the journey to Berlin."

Liesel's mouth dropped open. "Oh, no, sir, you misunderstand, I had no intention of leading you to believe . . . that is . . . it's only that . . . well, you see—"

"Now it's I who must beg forgiveness," Felix said. "I'm only teasing. I've no interest in art and you've none in sailing. We've nothing in common. Which is not to suggest that Birgit and I do, either, but . . ." He stared down at his large hands.

"But she's beautiful and I'm not." Liesel managed a half-hearted smile.

Felix stammered. "That's not at all what I was driving at."

"It's a simple misunderstanding, nothing more," Colin said.

Felix grimaced. "You must believe me, Fräulein—"

"Please, there's no need. I'm not offended in the least. Do excuse me. I'll be in the gallery if anyone needs me. I promised Ursula I'd help inventory her collection."

She was obviously upset. I waited a few minutes, to give her time to compose herself, then went after her.

"Men are beasts," I said. "I'm sure he meant nothing, but he should've stopped to think what it sounded like."

"I know he intended no harm. People like him—and Sigrid and Kaspar and, most of all, Birgit—view people like me as beneath contempt. I've nothing to offer them. It doesn't trouble me. They've nothing to offer me, either. I'm not made for places like this, fancy houses where the wealthy play. The things I care about are a million miles from here."

"Have you lived in Berlin long?"

"Yes. I was born there."

"And you own a gallery? That's no small accomplishment."

"I've had it for nearly five years. My parents were both artists; my mother, a painter; my father, a sculptor. She was far more talented than he, but he was the better parent. As you can imagine, there was never enough money. We didn't live in abject poverty, but the romantic notion of a cozy garret apartment is rather different from the reality. Which isn't to say it was all bleak. There were times when my mother would sell a painting for more than we expected and the celebration would last for days. In many ways, it was a magical childhood."

"Do you paint?"

"My father taught me to sculpt, but I've no talent for it. I do, however, have a good head for business, and it's much more lucrative to sell art than to make it." She winced, then closed her eyes. "I can feel another headache coming on."

"Would you like me to ring for some tea?"

"That would be most helpful. Could you have it sent to my room? And, if it's not too much to ask, would you see if the baroness has more of that headache powder?" She pressed her palm to her temple. "Perhaps Herr Brinkmann upset me more than I let on. None of us likes to be reminded of our shortcomings."

"Let me walk you upstairs."

"No, no, I'll be all right. All I need is a bit of rest in the dark."

"I'll ask for the tea and fetch the powder," I said.

She squeezed my hand. "Thank you, Lady Emily. I appreciate your kindness."

I collected the medicine from Ursula, who insisted that I take some for sleeping, too. Liesel had already drawn the heavy curtains in her room when I arrived, shortly after a maid had placed a steaming cup of tea on the bedside table next to a pitcher of water with a matching glass and a spoon.

She didn't open her eyes. "Would you mind mixing the powder for me?"

I did as she asked, then helped her sit up so she could drink the mixture. "Do you want the sleeping powder, too?" I asked.

"It proved effective last time." I prepared it and handed it to her. She put it on the table and dropped back onto the pillows. "Thank you. Can I beg one further favor? I know it's an imposition, but would you mind dreadfully coming back in an hour with another cup of tea? If I'm asleep, leave it on the table. I find that a hot drink is the only thing that offers relief in these circumstances. If I wake up, even for a minute or two, I'd like to have one at the ready."

"It's no trouble at all," I said. "I'll come every hour until you're feeling better so the tea has a chance of staying reasonably warm."

"I'm more than grateful." I closed the door quietly behind me and went downstairs. Colin had planned to ski after breakfast. I found him in the entryway to the villa, pulling on his gloves and a wool hat.

He asked after Liesel. "It's good of you to look after her."

"It gives me an excellent excuse to avoid skiing and read Homer instead. I can't have my Greek getting rusty."

"I shan't be gone long," he said. "It's snowing hard and I don't want to get caught in a storm."

"Which trail will you take?""

He pointed out the window. "That one, which goes behind the house and leads in the opposite direction of Allerspach and his wife. I have a suspicion that a sleigh ride is the only way they could get enough privacy to have some sort of difficult conversation."

"Hence Kaspar avoiding it as long as he could."

"Precisely," he said. "You'll skate with me later, won't you?"

"If the storm doesn't make it impossible."

He gave me a kiss and set off. I watched him strap himself into his skis and swoosh off into the woods, then went in search of Cécile, who was with Ursula in the gallery.

"Poor Liesel," the baroness said when she saw me. "How's she doing?"

"Resting as comfortably as possible," I said. "She'll be back to herself in a few hours. Have you made a decision about her paintings?"

"I'm going to buy them both. She has a good eye and understands my taste. A trip to her gallery may be in order. She has a significant number of works by female artists who are underappreciated."

"As they all are," I said.

"That is sadly true. She earns her living selling pieces like those she brought here, by better-known individuals, but I want to discover new talent, to support women striving to make a name for themselves."

"I don't know that you have room for further acquisitions, *chérie*," Cécile said. "The walls are already covered."

"It works, though, doesn't it?" Ursula looked around the room, smug satisfaction on her face. "Everyone told me it wouldn't, that it would end up nothing but a cluttered mess."

"They were wrong," I said. "It's magnificent, truly. You've managed to drive home the point that there's a universality to all art, no matter when it's from."

"Everything in our world is linked. Places, history, people, values. No matter where we're from or when we live, we're not so different."

"Yet our art is," Cécile said. "*Oui*, these pieces complement each other, but their styles are strikingly dissimilar."

"At the same time, they express ideas and emotions that span cultures and centuries," Ursula said. "That's where the universality comes in. Let me show you a charming object from the jungles of South America that was likely carved before the Pyramids were built in Egypt."

We spent a pleasant hour exploring Ursula's collection. The more one looked, the more one found. It could not be denied that she'd accomplished something unique and curated a space that inspired deep, creative thinking.

I heard the clock in the corridor chime and glanced at the watch pinned to my bodice. It was nearly time to check on Liesel. I left my friends and, after passing Felix on his way into the gallery, I went to the kitchen to collect a cup of tea. The cook was not altogether pleased to see me, but when I explained what I was after, she agreed that coming myself was more efficient than ringing for a maid. When the tea was brewed, she put it on a little silver tray and covered it with a knitted cozy. I carried it carefully up the stairs to Liesel's room.

It took some time for my eyes to adjust to the darkness when I stepped inside. Liesel was asleep, her long, strawberry blonde hair spilling over the pillows and the thick down comforter. I put the fresh tea on the table, careful not to disturb her, and slipped out of the room. I then dipped into my own, collected my copy of the *Iliad* and my lexicon of Homeric dialect, and went in search of a comfortable, quiet place to read.

Max was still playing his tuba. I could hear it from where I was in the sitting room across the hall, but the sound was mellow and pleasant. I situated myself at a table near a window, where I could watch the snow whenever I needed a break from a particularly challenging bit of grammar. After an hour passed, I left another cup of tea on Liesel's table—she was still sound asleep and hadn't drunk the first—and returned to my sanctuary.

I can't recall when I've spent such a pleasant interlude. The setting was idyllic, with snow falling on the trees outside, the mountains visible in the distance. The comfort of the room was superior, from the chairs to the enormous ceramic stove that kept it perfectly cozy. Even the light, streaming in through the window, was soft and bright rather than harsh and blinding.

Then Birgit interrupted me.

"What are you doing?" she asked, poking her head through the doorway.

"Reading." I hardly looked up from the book.

"Anything good?"

"Homer's *Iliad*, an epic poem about the Trojan War."

"Sounds boring beyond belief."

As I'd already determined that many, if not most, things sounded boring beyond belief to Birgit, I didn't bother to argue. I hoped this would inspire her to go away, but alas, it didn't. She came into the room and stood looking over my shoulder.

"It's not even in English. How can you make any sense of it? It looks like random marks on the page. There aren't any letters."

"It's ancient Greek," I said. "I've been studying the language for more than fifteen years."

She snorted. "However did you manage to catch a husband as good-looking as yours? I always heard bluestockings attracted nothing but the most hideous sort of men."

"Evidently your sources are not entirely reliable," I said. "I've always found the best sort of gentlemen prefer ladies who are their intellectual equals."

She crinkled her perfect little nose and sat down at the table across from me. "I wouldn't want any part of that. I do like your gown, though. It's Paquin, isn't it?"

"Yes." It was one of my favorite afternoon dresses, sky blue silk—apparently I'd been in the mood for blue when I'd directed the packing of my trunk—with an embroidered bodice trimmed in dark blue velvet. Fine embroidered tulle covered the sleeves, and the slim skirt skimmed my hips beneath a wide velvet belt.

She leaned back in her chair. "You don't like me, do you? Is it because you're reminded of a younger version of yourself when you look at me?'

"Good heavens, no. What a thing to say! I hardly know you. We've had no meaningful conversation since we met."

"No, you're correct, we haven't. It's the type of thing I like to avoid. I never know what to say. My mother taught me that it's best for a lady to leave serious topics to the gentlemen. We're not meant for such things. It's more important to be decorous." She giggled. "For many years, I thought that she meant *decor*, so I focused on my appearance. My manners may have suffered, but I've turned out well enough."

This tugged at me. The poor girl, instructed to be vapid. Her experience wasn't altogether different from mine in that regard, and I felt a deep empathy for her. I've long said an appreciation for high fashion does not preclude the possession of common sense. Perhaps I could help her, teach her that there was more to life than gowns and hairstyles, perfume and jewelry. Diverting though they are, they're not enough on their own to make for a truly satisfying life.

Which is not to say I was about to suggest she take up the study of Greek. In fact, I didn't suggest anything. Before I could, a commotion from the front of the house put a sudden end to our conversation. At first, we could make out no words, only the sound of shouts, loud, desperate, and raw. We went into the corridor and ran to the front door of the house, which was flung open, letting snow blow into the entrance hall. Kaspar was standing there, covered in blood.

"Dead. She's dead. What have I done?" He sank to his knees, buried his head in his hands, and wept.

16

Schloss Hohenschwangau
1868

Profound change can lead to disappointment. That was not something Niels had anticipated. At the time, he wasn't to know whether it was permanent or part of the transition. He only knew how it felt, and he hated it.

When he and Ludwig returned from their picnic, it was as if they shared a single soul. Their conversation had taken up the entire afternoon, as they discussed how the new castle should be furnished and the subjects for its murals. Niels had sung arias from *Lohengrin* and *Tannhäuser*. Ludwig recited poetry. Byron, mainly. The time passed in a blaze, and they both wished for more.

When they first returned to Hohenschwangau, there had been no shift in the atmosphere between them. They dined with Elisabet, who was in a fine mood after a productive day of work. She'd been delighted by their banter, charged with wit and mutual appreciation. After eating, they wandered through the castle grounds, carrying with them lanterns rendered unnecessary by the silvery light of a full moon. They sat by the Alpsee and Niels sang "Höchstes

Vertrau'n," Lohengrin's declaration of love, while Elisabet mimed the part of Elsa. There, by the shores of the lake, all was right with the world. The problems didn't come until the next morning.

Niels slept so deeply that when he woke he half wondered if he'd been dead. Refreshed and energized, he went down to breakfast. Ludwig was nowhere to be found.

"He's in a mood and stormed off outside," Elisabet said. "I wouldn't go after him. It's better to let him sort it out himself and come round when he's ready."

"Did something happen?"

She shrugged. "You know how he gets. Today he's consumed with melancholy and has retreated into himself. Tomorrow he'll want to be back basking in the moonlight by the Alpsee."

Niels had witnessed this many times over the past few months, but on this occasion it felt different. More personal, like a raw wound from a jagged blade wielded by someone you'd thought was close to you. He drank a cup of coffee, but didn't eat anything. Then he went back to his room, changed into sturdier boots, and did exactly what Elisabet had advised against: embark on a search for Ludwig.

It didn't take all that long to find him. Niels started by checking the stables. The king's horse was there, so wherever he was, he'd gone on foot. Niels knew Ludwig's favorite paths through the woods and came upon him in under half an hour.

"You don't want to be here right now." Ludwig was sitting on the ground, his back against a tree.

"I can think of more comfortable places, but beauty sometimes requires pain. The view is magnificent." They were in a valley filled with a riot of colorful wildflowers.

"I'm no mood for it."

"How did that come to be?"

"Sometimes, Niels, there are no answers to questions. Sometimes, we must suffer through things alone."

"Why?"

"Why?" Irritation crept into the king's voice.

"There's never a reason to be alone, not when you have friends who love you, as Elisabet and I do."

"Yesterday, I would've believed that. Today, I'm more realistic. A man like me can't have everything he wants. I was reminded of that this morning."

"By whom?"

"My conscience."

"Have you done something wrong?"

"There are times when merely contemplating an action is enough to conjure images of fire and brimstone." He pressed his palm into his forehead. "Leave. I've nothing more to say. Don't bother me again."

Niels remained there, standing, watching his friend, wishing he knew what was troubling him, but he could find no words of comfort. He turned around and walked away, repeating lines from Byron silently to himself, feeling a sadness deeper than any he could remember.

> . . . *time strips our illusions of their hue,*
> *And one by one in turn, some grand mistake*
> *Casts off its bright skin yearly like the snake.*

17

Villa von Düchtel
1906

"Dead? Sigrid's dead?" Birgit swayed on her feet. It looked as if she were about to embark on another of her feigned faints. Her arms went limp and her eyelids fluttered, but then she stopped and pulled herself up straight. "Kaspar, you're covered in blood. Is that her blood? Has there been an accident?"

"An accident, yes, an accident." He rose back onto his feet, still unsteady, his eyes unfocused.

I heard heels clicking on the marble floor. Cécile, Felix, and Ursula ran toward us.

"Good heavens," Ursula said. "What's happened? Where's my daughter?" Cécile, no stranger to tragic death, read the situation and put a firm arm around her friend's shoulder. Felix hung back, pale as the snow despite his tanned face.

Kaspar's eyes were wild as he stepped toward his mother-in-law. "She's dead. Dead. I don't know how it happened. There was a shot, and—" He started to sob. Ursula wrenched herself away from

Cécile, grabbed his wrist, and slapped him across the face, her hand leaving an imprint nearly as red as Sigrid's blood.

"Hysterics won't help," she said.

"What's going on?" Max was running toward us. He stopped when he saw Kaspar. "No. No. No. Where is she?"

Two things struck me. First, although it was reasonable to draw the conclusion that Sigrid was dead, given she was the one who'd left with her husband, it was as if they'd all anticipated such an outcome. Second, it was clear that someone needed to take charge of the situation.

"Felix, Colin's gone skiing. He took the trail that goes behind the house. He's bound to be well on his way back by now, so it will be easy enough for you to find him and tell him what's happened." He obeyed without question. I turned to Birgit. "Go upstairs and make sure Liesel is all right. Wake her if she's still sleeping. Max, telephone the police in Füssen."

"Is that necessary?" Birgit asked. "Surely it's all just another accident."

"None of this has been accidental," I said. "Cécile, take Ursula somewhere to sit down and give her some brandy. Kaspar, I need you to lead me to Sigrid."

"I'm coming, too," Ursula said.

"No." My voice was strong and commanding. Not so strong and commanding as Colin's, but the effect was the same. Ursula did not protest.

I called for two drivers and a sleigh. Kaspar had walked from wherever he'd abandoned the one in which he'd driven his wife. He told the men how to get where we were going, then sat opposite me, facing away from the direction of travel, and refused to tuck the fur blanket around himself.

"I shouldn't have left her here alone," he said, as the sleigh slowed and stopped. "She wouldn't have liked that."

The scene was less gruesome than I'd expected. There was no doubt Sigrid was dead, shot through the head with a single bullet. Her body was laid out neatly on the bench of the sleigh, her hands folded across her chest. Her husband hung back, averting his eyes.

"I couldn't leave her there in a heap. I wanted her to have some dignity."

"Did you see anyone during your ride?" I asked.

"Not a soul," he said. "No skiers, no one else in a sleigh. Given how isolated the house is, that's not much of a surprise."

I started to examine the scene. There was a riot of footprints in the snow between the road and the forest that lined it. The snow was still coming down hard, but I could make out enough detail in those under the trees to see that they'd all been made by a single person.

"The shot came from above," he said. "Whoever killed her was hiding in a tree."

"In a tree?" I asked.

"Yes, a tree in that direction." He gestured toward the footprints. "I tried to find the bastard who fired on us, but he was already gone by the time I got there. I didn't want to leave her until I was sure. . . ."

"Of course." I gave his arm a little squeeze. "Why don't you go back to the other sleigh and try to keep warm? There's nothing more you need do here."

I searched the area thoroughly, but initially found nothing that could be construed as a clue. No broken branches, no footprints leading away from where Kaspar was convinced the shooter had been. Then, I saw a dark patch in the snow. Sunk down at least eight inches was a heavy pistol. I picked it up, wrapped it in a handkerchief, and returned to the sleigh.

"We'll head back to the house now," I said to Kaspar, who was half-catatonic, sitting in the snow next to the sleigh. "One of the drivers will bring Sigrid, too. Would you like to ride with her?"

"No, I couldn't bear it, couldn't bear to see her like that again, covered in blood, all the life drained out of her." His whole body was shaking violently. "This is all my fault. Whoever did it was after me, not her, and the idiot wasn't a good enough shot to hit his target when it was moving. Why, oh why, didn't I listen to reason and take better care? I never thought she'd come to harm. You must believe that, Lady Emily. I never wanted that. Never."

"Don't upset yourself any further. This is not your fault. We will discover who did this and he will be brought to justice. For now, though, I need you to get back in the sleigh so we can return to the house."

He didn't stir from his spot in the snow. In the end, I had to ask the drivers to physically move him. The return trip to the house felt like it took an eternity. Colin was waiting at the door when we arrived. He told Kaspar to go to his room and bathe, then ordered the drivers to take the body to the stables, where it could be kept cold.

"The police aren't coming," he said. "The storm's getting worse and the roads from Füssen aren't passable. The others are all inside. I've spoken to them each to get their alibis."

"Do they all have them?"

"Not ones that can be corroborated. Max was alone in the music room and Liesel was sleeping in her room."

"I heard him playing and can confirm that she was in bed. I went up there twice with tea."

"Cécile and Ursula were in the gallery, where Felix joined them," he said.

"Yes, I passed him on his way in."

"Birgit was in her room and then with you. No one saw her there, but I presume you know the approximate time she was with you."

"Of course," I said. "I wish we had a doctor who could confirm time of death. Kaspar says it was noon, but he's in such a state I'm not certain his testimony is reliable."

"They weren't gone long enough that it matters all that much. We know, more or less, when it happened." His countenance was serious, his eyes darker than usual. "What we don't know is whether there was an altercation between husband and wife before she was killed. I'll have to examine her body. It's a skill I never would've thought I'd learn, but my work . . ."

His work for the Crown in matters requiring more than a modicum of discretion had often been a bone of contention between us, but for now, I could only be grateful that he was capable of performing the task.

"I'll go with you," I said.

"No, it's better that you go inside. Talk to them. Then we can compare stories and see if anyone's altered what they told me."

"Did anyone in particular arouse your suspicion?"

"I'll tell you later. I don't want to color your own impressions." He took my hand, raised it to his lips, and went off in the direction of the stables.

A footman opened the door for me, took my coat, hat, gloves, and scarf. I switched my boots for a pair of dry shoes and followed the sound of voices to the room Ursula used as a study.

It was a pleasant space, with low bookcases lining two of the walls, a long fireplace on the third, and a great expanse of glass windows on the fourth. Two sofas covered in dark green velvet faced each other, perpendicular to the fire, with two chairs, a small table between them, parallel to the fire. Cécile and Birgit were on one sofa, Felix and Max on the other. Liesel, her skin clammy and gray, was bundled in a shawl and sitting in one of the chairs. Instead of a desk, a large table sat in front of the windows, with the chair positioned to face the view. Ursula was sitting in it, but leapt up and ran over to me when I entered the room.

"What can you tell us?" she asked, gripping my hand.

"It's as Kaspar said. They were attacked by a gunman during their sleigh ride. Sigrid was hit and did not survive. I'm so very sorry."

"She's gone, then." Her voice quavered as she raised her hand to her neck, tears brimming in her eyes. "It's hard to believe. I want to see her."

"Not now. Colin's with her, examining the body. When he's done, he'll make her ready for you. You can see her then."

"I don't want to wait. I want to see what that man has done to her."

"That man?" Birgit's voice rose in pitch. "Do you mean Kaspar? We don't know he did it."

"No one else was with them," Ursula said, "and we were all here, in the house."

"Until we have firm evidence, we won't know what happened." I took her by the arm and led her back to her chair, which I turned so it was facing into the room. "I know you've all spoken to my husband, but I'd like to hear from you, too, not individually, but as a group. We were all having a quiet morning, but did anyone notice anything out of the ordinary?"

"It was not a quiet morning," Birgit said, "not with Max blowing on that ridiculous instrument."

"You'd gone up to your room after breakfast, hadn't you?" I asked her. "You were tired."

"Aggravated, more like. I should never have come to this awful place."

"That's quite enough," Felix said. "We all know you're bored."

"Bored beyond belief." She spat the words. "Not that you care."

"Did you take a nap when you got upstairs?" I asked.

"No. I went through some of my gowns to try to decide what to wear for dinner this evening."

"Which one did you select?" I asked.

"Does it matter?" Max asked, the veins in his neck bulging. "Sigrid is dead. What difference does some chit of a girl's dinner dress make?"

"The dress doesn't make a difference, but what each of us was doing and what we may have observed while we were doing it might."

"I didn't pick one," Birgit said. "Nothing was quite right. That's why I went downstairs and talked to you, Lady Emily."

"I was playing my tuba all morning," Max said. "I'll regret it to my dying day. I couldn't hear anything else."

"Don't be so dramatic," Felix snapped. "What could any of us have heard, regardless? The murder took place miles from here."

"How do you know where the murder took place?" Liesel asked, looking more than a little alarmed.

"Obviously, I don't know exactly where, but they were in a sleigh and had been gone for hours." Felix chewed on his bottom lip. "Or at least an hour. I'm not sure how long it was. How could I forget something like that?"

"At the time, you had no reason to be paying attention," I said.

"We all should've been paying attention," Max said.

"I heard you playing," I said to him. "You're very talented. Did any of you go outside after breakfast? Colin went for a ski, but so far as I know, no one else did."

"Where did he ski?" Ursula asked.

"On the trail behind the house."

"Did he see anything strange?"

"Not so far as I know," I said. "He'd gone in the opposite direction from Kaspar and Sigrid's sleigh."

"Are you sure?"

"Ursula, *chérie*, I can promise you Monsieur Hargreaves had nothing to do with Sigrid's death."

Her shoulders drooped. "Of course. Forgive me. I'm just . . . I'm desperate. I want to know who did this to her."

"I feel completely useless for having been asleep," Liesel said, balling her hands into tight fists. "I half heard you come in once, Lady Emily, and leave tea, at least I think I did. Twice, maybe."

"I could barely wake you up when I came in," Birgit said. "I think we'll all need some of that sleeping powder tonight."

"I went outside after breakfast," Felix said. "Not to ski, but for a little walk. I didn't see anyone else. The snow was too deep, so I came back inside. That's when I went to the gallery."

"He was with Ursula and me until Kaspar returned," Cécile said.

"What do we do now?" Birgit asked.

"Nothing," I said. "The roads aren't passable, which means the police can't get here and we can't leave."

"So we're supposed to just stay here, with a murderer, and wait for him to kill again?"

"You can't possibly think one of us killed Sigrid," Max said. "It must have been some maniac, skulking around the woods."

"You think there might be a madman in the vicinity?" Felix asked.

"Not since Ludwig died," Kaspar said. I hadn't noticed him enter the room. His face was drawn and pale, but he looked better than he had when we'd returned to the house. "I only mention it to invite the pain that comes from knowing Sigrid is not here to defend her favorite king."

"Ludwig the Second was no madman," Liesel said.

"I didn't know you had an opinion about him," Kaspar said.

Her voice was low and soft. "I don't, but I heard enough banter between the two of you to know that's what she'd say. I thought it might bring a slim measure of comfort."

"I don't know that it does, but I appreciate the effort nonetheless." He buried his face in his hands. "I shan't ever forgive myself. This very morning I refused to take seriously the threats against me. I could hardly fathom that they were anything more than a prank, but clearly they were. Felix, you know me better than anyone. Who hates me enough to want me dead?"

18

Near Füssen
1868

Niels did not go back to the castle. Instead, he walked until he'd left the grounds and reached a public boathouse on the shore of the Alpsee. He rented a skiff, slipped it into the water, and rowed across the lake. When he reached the other side, he rowed back. He repeated this until his shoulders ached and the sunburn on his neck and face and hands started to make him nauseous. He returned the boat and, only half realizing what he was doing, started along the path that would lead him to his family's mountain retreat.

He knew, from his father's letters, that his parents were not in residence. His father preferred the place in the autumn; his mother, almost never. The servants, who hadn't expected him, started to bustle about, uncovering furniture and polishing wood, but he told them to stop. He wanted to be alone, and ordered them to leave the grounds and not return until morning. He went into the drawing room in the back of the house, opened all the windows, and lowered himself onto the settee in front of one of them, staring blankly at the view.

Ludwig's words had stung, but Niels understood why they'd

been inevitable. Some friendships burned unacceptably bright. Yesterday, he'd hoped—believed, even—that things might be different.

The sun sank behind the mountains; its absence cooled the air. He didn't close the windows. He didn't light a fire or a lamp. The sky turned inky and then black. The moon rose and the stars dimmed next to its brightness.

He didn't hear anyone arrive at the house. The drive was on the opposite side of the building. He didn't hear anyone bang on the door, or open it, or begin to search the ground floor. He was aware of nothing save a silence broken only by the occasional gust of wind that rustled the curtains and chilled his soul. He didn't notice soft footsteps on the carpet, approaching him from behind. And then, he startled when a warm hand came to rest on his shoulder.

"Don't turn around. Don't look at me. I couldn't bear it, not right now." It was Ludwig. "When you didn't return to Hohenschwangau, I was furious and convinced I would never forgive you. It was only yesterday that you promised you'd never leave. What could I conclude except that to you my friendship was not worth even twenty-four hours? Elisabet ignored my rage for a while, but then grew tired of it. She reminded me that this is what I do, pull people close and then push them away. She's good for me." He sat on the settee next to him. The room was dark and cold and all Niels could feel was warmth emanating from his friend's body.

"Am I good for you?" Niels asked.

"You're the best and the worst."

"But not your only." He spoke so quietly his voice was barely audible.

"Not the first. That's all I'll admit," Ludwig said. "Ring for a servant, will you? I drove over in my phaeton and need my horses tended to."

"I sent them away."

"All of them?"

"All of them."

"There's no one here but us?" Ludwig asked. "Until when?"

"Until morning." They held each other's gaze and the king took Niels's hand. Morning was a lifetime away.

19

Villa von Düchtel
1906

Felix grimaced at Kaspar's question. "How many people hate you enough to want you dead? I imagine half the people in this room could be included in the number," he said. Cold stares from nearly everyone met his answer. "Forgive me. I meant to lighten the mood."

"It's not appropriate," Birgit said.

"Who do you think hates you enough to want you dead, Kaspar?" I asked.

"I'd rather not discuss it publicly."

Ursula scowled. "Are you admitting you knew you have enemies and still refused to take any precautions—"

"Slinging accusations at each other isn't going to help anything," I said. "Kaspar, you and Felix come with me. We'll go somewhere more private to talk."

A murmur of discontent rippled through the room, but no one objected outright. I led the gentlemen to the sitting room, where my copy of the *Iliad* and my lexicon were still lying open on the table in front of the windows. None of us sat down.

"Tell me what you didn't want anyone else to hear," I said.

"It's nothing, really," Kaspar said. "I'd just prefer not to go through the sordid details of my life in front of a crowd."

"Fair enough," I said. "Continue."

"You asked about enemies and the truth is, I'm racking my brain and cannot think of a single person. I admit I'm neither especially kind nor easy to get along with, so while I have scores of acquaintances, I have few close friends."

"I'd say I'm the only one," Felix said softly.

"That's probably true," Kaspar said. "It could be claimed that I'm excessively competitive and that, as a result, I sometimes cross the bounds of propriety when I want to win something."

"Such as?"

"There may have been occasions on which I've encouraged my rivals to drink rather too much the night before a fight."

"Boxing?" I asked. He nodded.

"*Encouraged* might not be the right word," Felix said. "More like tricked, but even so, none of them was angry enough to want you dead."

"Most of them never knew I did it."

"Quite right," Felix said. "You're capable of discretion when you think it's necessary."

It was an interesting choice of words. "What about matters of business?"

"I don't work, of course, but do have some modest financial interests; and when my investments are going well, I sometimes lord the fact over my acquaintances, but that's hardly grounds for murder." He tugged at his collar. "I've lost my wife and can no longer hide from any ugly truths about myself. Even so, I cannot give you a single name. I don't know anyone who wants me dead. If I did, I'd tell you.

My wife has been murdered and though I didn't pull the trigger, I'm as responsible as the man who did."

"I'm sorry for your loss," I said, "and sorry that you had to witness such a violent act. What happens now that Sigrid's gone? You'll inherit her fortune, will you not?"

"Such as it is," he said. "She had a small amount of capital, but the bulk of her money came from an allowance given by her mother. I won't be better off with her dead, if that's what you're asking."

"Were you in love with your wife?"

"What's that to do with anything?" Felix asked, taking a step toward me.

"His relationship with Sigrid could prove central to what happened."

"I didn't kill her," Kaspar said.

"I'm not suggesting you did. However, if your marriage wasn't a happy one, either of you might have become entangled with other individuals."

Felix stepped back. "And those individuals could've decided they'd prefer a world where Kaspar and Sigrid were no longer married."

"Precisely," I said.

"I'm not having an affair," Kaspar said. "As for Sigrid, I haven't the slightest idea whether she was or wasn't. It didn't matter to me one way or another. We weren't so passionately in love as we were at the beginning of our marriage, but we'd reached a comfortable place together. There was no trouble between us."

While Kaspar spoke, I watched Felix's face. He was looking at the ground, clenching his jaw. I turned back to Kaspar. "What did the two of you discuss in the sleigh?"

"Nothing of consequence."

"Sigrid was quite fixated on the excursion," I said. "It was clear she was after more than a pleasure ride."

"We bantered about our differing opinions of mad King Ludwig."

I didn't believe him. "Nothing else?"

"Nothing else."

"If you withhold facts, it will be all the harder for my husband and me to bring the killer to justice. I need you to promise to tell me anything you remember that might be pertinent."

"Of course," he mumbled.

"Anything. No matter how embarrassing or shocking."

"I will. You can count on that."

I doubted very much I could count on Kaspar, but for now, I didn't believe there was more to get out of him. I let him and Felix go and set my sights on someone else: Max. Ursula and Cécile were still in the study, but the others had dispersed. A footman told me Max had gone to his room. I climbed the stairs and knocked on his door.

"Oh, Lady Emily," he said, shock writ on his face. "I wasn't expecting you."

"Were you expecting someone else?"

"No, no, it's just that I'm not in the habit of entertaining ladies in my room."

"We can go somewhere else if you'd be more comfortable," I said, "although staying here is bound to afford the most privacy."

"Of course. Do come in."

His room was considerably smaller than mine and Colin's, and while thoughtfully furnished, was significantly less luxurious. His tuba, in its case, was on the bed, along with a pile of sheet music. A notebook lay open on the desk, a pen on top of it.

"You've been close to Sigrid your entire life," I said. "I'm more sorry than I can say that you've lost her. I've not known you long, nor her, but even brief observation told me that you two shared a treasured friendship."

"Losing her is a blow from which I shall never recover. She was my dearest friend, my confidante, my supporter."

"Your lover?" I asked.

"Lady Emily, I—"

"I apologize for being so blunt, but there's no point skirting the issue. Everyone expected the two of you to marry until she met Kaspar. From what I understand, she was caught up by his superficial charm."

"I hear the doubt in your voice," he said, giving a little laugh. "You've not seen him deploy his charm, but I assure you he can. He's a handsome man, charismatic and strong, full of energy and bluster. She was infatuated. I thought it would pass, but it didn't, at least not soon enough. They married and I was relegated to the background."

"For how long?"

"I was never going to return to the forefront. Sigrid's mother may have bohemian tendencies, but her daughter is far more traditional. She'd made a commitment to her husband and never would have left him, even if she realized she'd made a mistake. The scandal would be too great. People can't just go around getting divorced; it's uncivilized. It's part of the reason so many conventional marriages leave room for, er, close friendships with other people."

"Did she believe she'd made a mistake?"

"Without question."

"Were you content with having only a close friendship with her?"

"I had no choice in the matter," he said, "but it suited me well enough. I've always been a bit of a solitary soul. I love music and can better disappear into it when I'm on my own."

"You might find a partner whose love for it mirrors your own and come to see that sharing it can bring even deeper pleasure."

"It's not so easy as you make it sound. I grew up not far from here and spent my childhood climbing mountains and swimming in lakes, but wasn't much good at either. I've no love for physical exertion, can't figure out how to use a compass, and would likely drown if I tried to cross the Alpsee. Music is the only thing at which I excel. My family's fortune is nothing like Ursula's. I've got a crumbling pile of a house. The repairs it needs would drain all my resources. Which is all to say that I'm not sought after on the marriage market."

"Sigrid didn't need to marry for money."

"If I may use the same bluntness you did earlier, Sigrid married for lust, the one thing that spurs people more fiercely than money. I knew her infatuation wouldn't last and was more than content to wait for her to return to me."

"Was Kaspar aware of the connection the two of you shared?"

"It went further than a mere connection, but Kaspar wouldn't have cared if Sigrid had a stable full of lovers. He had his fun with her and when it cooled, he still had her money."

"But only an allowance," I said.

"A generous allowance, with significant capital to come when the baroness dies." He shifted uncomfortably. "Even if Kaspar were jealous of my relationship with Sigrid, he never would've harmed her. He'll gain nothing from her death and lose a steady supply of monthly cash. It's ironic, isn't it? He's the one who ignored what was happening around him. Couldn't imagine someone was trying to kill him. It's not surprising. He's not the sort of man who would ever acknowledge his own faults. Now his lifestyle will suffer from his inaction."

"Does he have money of his own?" I asked.

"Enough, at least to my way of thinking, but my guess is that a person used to a certain level of luxury will never be content with less."

"He doesn't sound like a pleasant man."

"You've spent enough time with him to know that's the case."

"It must infuriate you," I said. "He treats the woman you love badly, but she refuses to do anything about it."

"What could I do except respect her choices?"

I didn't answer his question, just held his gaze and let silence do its work.

"Surely you don't think I killed Sigrid? I'd never hurt her."

"You might've missed your intended target."

"That's an outrageous accusation!" He'd turned bright red. "If I wanted Kaspar dead—and I'm not saying I did—I'd never have done it in a way that might have harmed her. Further, I wouldn't have wanted her to witness such a violent spectacle. And then there's the matter of getting caught, which I'm told murderers always do. What good would come from eliminating him if it resulted in my rotting in prison until I was hanged?" His voice was measured and calm enough, but worry showed in his eyes.

"Did you and Sigrid discuss the incidents that occurred here?" I asked. "Was she concerned?"

"I met her last night. We went for a walk in the snow and when it was too cold to stay outside, took shelter in the stable. We talked about it, naturally, how could we not? I didn't think she was in the slightest danger. It would be hypocritical for me to criticize Kaspar's reaction to what was happening."

"Did Sigrid believe she was in danger?"

His brow crinkled. "No, quite the contrary. In private, with me, she found the whole thing rather amusing. She enjoyed seeing Kaspar squirm."

"When did he squirm?" I asked.

"Never in front of the others, but with her, he was unguarded. Worried, even. She laughed it off and encouraged him to do the same. I know, because she told me."

"It's sounds like they were closer than I would've expected."

"They were married."

"Yes, but not in love with each other," I said. "Were they friends?"

"She didn't despise him, if that's what you mean. They were bound to each other and accepted that. Neither wanted it any other way."

"How did that make you feel?"

"My feelings, Lady Emily, were irrelevant. A marriage can't have three people in it."

When I left his room, Colin was waiting for me in the corridor, his handsome countenance somber. We retreated to our room. "There wasn't much to learn from the body. No signs of struggle, no bruises, no ripped clothing. Given the angle at which the bullet entered her skull, I can confirm it was fired from above."

"From a tree?" I asked.

"It's certainly possible. It's also possible that she was sitting while the shooter stood over her on the bench of the sleigh."

"Which Kaspar could've done."

"Yes," he said. He was pacing, as he always did when under pressure, stressed, or contemplating a difficult issue.

"I spoke to Kaspar. He denies that he's involved with anyone else, claims to have no knowledge of whether Sigrid was having an affair, and explained that he'll see no financial benefit from her death."

"Do you believe him?" Colin asked.

"I talked to Max immediately thereafter. He said the same about the money, but he also admitted that he and Sigrid had a deep, intimate relationship. Kaspar claims he didn't care if she was involved with someone else, but he doesn't strike me as the kind of man who would sit back calmly and accept his wife having a lover."

"Quite the contrary, particularly a lover he views as inferior to himself. Betrayal is a powerful motive. He wouldn't be the first husband to murder a straying wife."

20

Near Füssen
1868

Niels didn't much enjoy tending to the horses. Ludwig directed him as best he could, and while the grooms would've done a far better job, the animals were at least fed and watered and safe for the night. Ludwig had decided it was too late to return to Hohenschwangau. Too late, too dark, too cold. They both knew this was a lie. The king was no stranger to nocturnal drives. The truth was, he'd never had so much privacy as he did just then. No servants, no family, only him and his friend.

They went back to the sitting room. Ludwig closed and fastened the windows while Niels lit a fire that took the chill out of the air. They sat on the floor in front of it, relishing the heat.

"We ought to eat something. I haven't had a morsel since dinner last night," Niels said.

"My poor man. I've tormented you, haven't I? I don't suppose you know how to cook?"

"I assume that's a jest."

They went down to the kitchen, where they found a loaf of bread.

There was cheese and butter in the pantry and they picked a bottle of wine from the cellar. Niels gathered it all into a basket, along with plates, linen napkins, glasses, and a corkscrew, then headed for the stairs. Ludwig stopped him.

"Do you know, I've never before seen a kitchen. It's a rather fascinating place. I've not the slightest idea what half these things are."

"What, like the stove?" Niels asked, laughing.

"That I'm capable of identifying," Ludwig said. "It's a strange thing to be in this part of a house. It's an entirely separate world from upstairs, a world whose residents slip in and out of mine at will, but a world where I'm not welcome."

"More like a world where you wouldn't ordinarily bother to go. I'm not convinced the average kitchen maid would meet your standards of beauty."

"I hadn't considered that. It's an excellent point." He shuddered and headed for the stairs.

They returned to the sitting room and ate in front of the fire, as if they were picnicking outside. Niels couldn't recall a time he'd seen Ludwig so relaxed, so content. He told him as much.

"I hardly recognize you," he said.

"To know that there's no one here save the two of us gives me the most extraordinary feeling of freedom."

"What are you going to do with your newfound freedom?"

"Sleep," the king said.

"Sleep?"

Their eyes met. Neither spoke for what, to Niels, felt like an eternity. Then Ludwig broke the silence.

"Only sleep, but I shall do it beside you, undisturbed until the lark sings in the morning."

21

Villa von Düchtel
1906

The only physical evidence we had was the gun I'd found at the site of the murder; we showed it to everyone in the house, but no one admitted to recognizing it. Ursula's gamekeeper explained that the baroness wasn't keen on shooting, but that they kept guns in a room in the stable for those times when she might host visitors who enjoyed the sport. He swore that there was nothing like the pistol that had killed Sigrid among them.

"That suggests the murderer wasn't taking advantage of opportunity, but had planned his crime," I said, after Colin and I had searched the gun room. "Uncovering his motive will be the most efficient way to find him."

"I agree," Colin said. "Given the weather and the subsequent impassability of the roads, it's either one of the servants or one of our party. I searched the area around the house for footprints before I examined Frau Allerspach's body. Aside from mine—and the tracks of my skis—I only saw one other set, leaving from the front of the house, going halfway down the drive, and back again."

"Felix told me he went for a walk after breakfast. What about skis?" I asked. "Could someone have skied to the location of the murder?"

"Did you see any tracks near there?"

I shook my head. "Only a riot of footprints, but they all matched Kaspar's boots. Could someone have skied behind the sleigh?"

"It's conceivable," he said, "but a skier couldn't have kept pace with the horses. No one else took out a sleigh or a horse this morning."

"So if Kaspar didn't kill his wife, the murderer would've had to leave the house in time to reach the spot before the sleigh and lie in wait until it arrived. Sigrid mentioned the route she wanted to take—past the waterfall—multiple times. Anyone listening would've known where to find them," he said. "Let's interview all the servants again. It's unlikely one of them had motive to want Allerspach dead, but we need to be sure."

We rang for the butler, an efficient man of approximately fifty, with silver hair and an expression that told me he would brook no nonsense. He arranged for us to see each of the servants in succession in his sitting room belowstairs.

"They'll be more likely to speak freely if none of their colleagues is nearby," he said. Once he'd installed us there—and supplied us with pencils and a notebook—he sat down. "You might as well start with me."

"Are you aware of any reason a person might wish to see Herr Allerspach dead?" Colin asked.

The butler looked confused. "Don't you mean Frau Allerspach?"

"Her husband was the object of a series of attacks before his wife's death."

"Do you believe he was the intended target of the murderer?" His face clouded. "Such a tragedy. Frau Allerspach was a lovely woman.

That her death is nothing more than an accident makes it hurt all the more. Her husband was not the easiest of men, but he was more bluster than bite. I never had a problem with him, nor has anyone else in the household made me aware of issues concerning him."

"Have you noticed anything unusual going on in the house?" I asked.

"Things are always a bit off-kilter when there are visitors," he said, "and on this occasion we had the added complication of the party to celebrate the baroness's art collection. The logistics were something of a challenge, but nothing we couldn't manage. There were any number of people in and out of the villa during the preparations for it—we had extra deliveries of food and supplies— and the musicians who played were all strangers to me. Beyond that, the household staff took care of everything. None of the overnight guests traveled with servants, so we've had no one new staying be- lowstairs. The maids, naturally, are pulling extra duty, dealing with you ladies' hair and dressing requirements, but no one is terribly overworked."

"Have any of the guests come belowstairs?" Colin asked.

"Only your wife, sir, to get tea for Fräulein Fronberg when she was indisposed with a headache."

"Have any of them made unusual requests?" I asked.

"Before he goes to sleep, Herr Allerspach likes to have a glass of beer with two raw eggs cracked in it. I believe an American friend told him it's quite the thing for building strength; and as Herr Aller- spach is something of an athlete, he's concerned with such things. Aside from that, we've been asked to do nothing out of the ordi- nary."

"Have you noticed anyone moving around the house at unusual times of the day or night?" Colin asked.

"No, sir, no one has been keeping strange hours."

For the next two hours, we questioned the rest of the servants. When we came to a pretty young maid called Gerda, she asked to speak to me privately.

"I don't mean to be awkward," she said, twisting a handkerchief in her lap, "but if you're willing, I'd be most grateful."

"It's no problem in the slightest," Colin said. "I'll wait in the servants' hall until you're done, so you need not worry that I'm lurking outside the door listening."

"He's a kind man," she said, after he'd left. "I do appreciate it. There are some things a girl doesn't like to talk about in front of a gentleman. Or any man, for that matter."

"Of course," I said.

"It's just that . . . well, it's more than a little embarrassing, but Herr Allerspach can be a bit free with his hands, if you know what I mean."

"Free with his hands?" I asked.

She nodded. "It happened back in the old house, which was here before the villa was built, and at the baroness's residence in Munich. I warn all the new girls about him. You have to be careful not to be alone in a room with him or you'll find yourself getting pinched and groped in places you don't want anyone touching."

"That's horrible, Gerda," I said. "No one should have to tolerate that sort of behavior. Have you spoken to anyone about it?"

"Only so as to warn the other girls. I don't want to cause trouble, madam. That's a surefire way to lose a position, isn't it, and I need this job."

"You've done nothing wrong. Your job wouldn't be at risk. If anything, the baroness would thank you for alerting her to the situation."

"That sounds nice, but the fact is, it's not how things work. I apologize for contradicting you, but I've seen it all too many times. Make an accusation like that against a fine gentleman, and all you'll get is a reputation for causing trouble. No one's going to believe me over him. He'll say I was the one doing the harassing and the next thing you know, I'll be thrown out with no character."

"That would be utterly unacceptable," I said. "Please, you must let me help you."

"If you want to help, you'll keep quiet. I'm only telling you so that you know Herr Allerspach is that sort of man, and a man who'd do that might have a lot of other bad qualities. I don't know who he might have angered, only that if he made someone mad enough to want him dead, it wouldn't surprise me."

"Do you have a sweetheart, Gerda?" I asked.

"I do, madam. Hans, one of the grooms. He's ever so good with horses."

"Does he know what Herr Allerspach has done to you?"

"I told him, yes."

"What was his reaction?"

"He was mad enough to spit, but warned me against saying any-thing about it. Not just to the baroness but to the other girls working with me. He said I couldn't know if they were trustworthy. One of them might decide she could get ahead by making me look bad. He's a little overprotective, my Hans, but he means well."

"What did he do when he learned you told the other girls?"

"He wasn't upset with me. Said what's done is done and that we'd have to hope nothing bad came from it. Nothing has, so far, and it's been long enough that I don't think anything will."

I thanked her for her candor and promised I wouldn't mention

Herr Allerspach's inappropriate predilection to the baroness. Before it was time to speak to Hans, however, I gave Colin a full report. We decided that he would interview Hans without me, and do it after we'd finished with all the other servants.

When he was done, Colin met me in our room, where I'd started to dress for dinner. "He gives every appearance of being a good lad," he said, buttoning up the back of my dress. "Loves the girl, of that there's no doubt, and is rightly furious with Allerspach."

"Furious enough to have wanted to kill him?" I asked.

"There's no doubt he'd be pleased to see the man dead."

"It would've been easy enough for him to tamper with the ski binding."

"That's true, and he might have believed there was a decent chance it would've sent Allerspach tumbling down a ravine." He disappeared into the bathroom to submerge himself in the tub.

"Maybe at first he thought injury would be enough to satisfy his desire for revenge," I called to him, "but then, when he saw that Kaspar was barely hurt, he got even more angry."

"And followed us to Neuschwanstein?" He'd left the door open, so I could hear him. "It's theoretically possible but unlikely."

"Why? If he killed Kaspar away from the house, when he was supposed to be working, he'd be less likely to be suspected, so long as no one noticed he was gone. He may have thought he was capable of hitting his target but overestimated his skill. But then there's also the laudanum," I said, twisting my hair into a pompadour. It took a catastrophic number of pins to secure it, but I managed. It didn't look nearly so bad as it might have. "He doesn't work in the main house, so it would've been difficult for him to slip it into Kaspar's coffee."

"Not if Gerda is his accomplice, an accomplice who hadn't the slightest idea of how much laudanum it would take to kill a grown man."

"She's resigned to what happened with Kaspar, not angry about it. Given how worried she was about losing her job, I can't imagine she'd involve herself in a plot to murder someone."

"We must consider even the unlikely," Colin said. I heard a gush of water; he was out of the tub and appeared, shortly thereafter, with a thick towel wrapped around his waist, his curls wet.

"You're right, of course."

"I agree, however, that it's more likely one of Ursula's guests is behind the crime, but there is one question Hans didn't answer in a satisfactory manner. There's a bruise on his left cheek. He says he got it when one of the horses startled in its stall. Such things happen, but he went into such overwrought detail when he described the incident that it didn't sound like a credible explanation."

"He might have got it if the force of the pistol's recoil knocked him against the tree."

"That's precisely what I was thinking. It keeps him a potential suspect." He pulled a starched evening shirt from the wardrobe. "Do you find it slightly absurd that we're dressing for dinner hours after a murder?"

"I asked Ursula if she'd prefer to have a tray sent to her room, but she refused. She said she wants to be able to observe everyone."

"She, too, thinks one of us did it."

"Not you and I, and not Cécile."

"Allerspach, I assume," he said, slipping into the shirt and fastening its studs.

"Who else would she be likely to suspect? It's no secret she despises him."

"If he's guilty, he might have gone through the pantomime of making everyone think someone was out to harm him in order to disguise the fact that it was Sigrid, not him, who was in danger."

"I almost wonder if he was pretending his knee was hurt. He had no trouble getting around at Neuschwanstein and was skiing not long after. Could he have fired the shot himself?" I asked, fixing a diamond comb into my hair to hold back some unruly strands.

"Only if his friend was in on it, too. Cécile's spent more time with Brinkmann than we have. Let's find out what she knows about him." He pulled on a pair of trousers.

"Liesel's got no obvious involvement whatsoever, which makes me automatically suspicious."

"What if she's Allerspach's lover?" he asked, fastening suspenders to his waistband. "Perhaps that's how she wound up in contact with the baroness."

"When she came here and saw him with his wife, she could've realized he'd never leave his marriage."

"So she took matters into her own hands and eliminated her rival."

"There's also Max," I asked. "He's got clear motive to want Kaspar dead."

"Yes, but I can't see him doing anything that might have harmed her." He was tying his cravat, but stopped. "What if we're dealing with two people? One—possibly Max—who's responsible for the incidents targeting Allerspach, and another—who could be anyone in the house—who thought those incidents gave the perfect entrée to murder?"

"And that second person just happens to carry a pistol around with him?" I asked.

"It's not impossible."

"It's unlikely," I said. "We agreed the pistol not coming from the gun room suggests that the murderer planned the crime in advance. He must have brought the weapon with him. It's the three attacks on Kaspar that don't fit neatly into any narrative that winds up with Sigrid dead. We've got to find the connection. If the killer wants Kaspar dead, he's going to strike again."

22

Near Füssen
1868

Sleep was what Ludwig wanted, so sleep was what he would get. Niels led him upstairs, but hours passed before the king succumbed to slumber. Niels, basking in the pleasure of their entwined bodies, didn't so much as close his eyes. Sleep, to him, would be a waste of this precious time. Before morning dawned, he shook Ludwig awake. The servants would return soon, to prepare breakfast.

"You shouldn't be here when they arrive," he said. "Better that they find me alone. I can walk back to Hohenschwangau."

"I could lurk on the road, far enough away that they won't see, and drive you," Ludwig said.

"It would, perhaps, be better if we didn't arrive at the castle together."

Ludwig grinned. "There's something ever so titillating about this subterfuge."

Niels didn't agree, but he didn't argue. Instead, he helped the king hitch his horses to the phaeton. Then he returned to his room, crawled into bed, and fell fast asleep, waking only when he heard a tapping at his door. A maid had brought breakfast. He ate, splashed water on his face, pulled on the jacket he'd worn the day before, and headed off on the path that would lead him to Hohenschwangau.

He couldn't remember a time he'd felt happier, more peaceful, less conflicted. He wasn't naïve enough to believe he and Ludwig could maintain the sort of friendship they both craved. The world would never allow that, but at least they each knew how the other felt. Every color around him, from the grass to the flowers to the slate blue mountains, shone brighter that day.

He took a deliberately circuitous route to the castle, desperate to cling to the feeling as long as possible. Yes, he wanted to see Ludwig, but he knew it would not be the same as it had been the previous night. It would never be the same. So he meandered, along lake shores and forest paths, half aimless, half with purpose. Before he reached the gates of the royal estate, he saw a solitary figure sitting in the grass. Elisabet. She rose when she caught sight of him and waved.

"Come and walk with me before you disappear back into the king's magic realm."

"Is he angry that I didn't come back yesterday?"

"You know perfectly well he's not."

"You've spoken to him?" Niels asked.

"Enough to know that, for a few hours, at least, he's the happiest of men."

"Why are you lurking about, waiting for me?"

"I was worried about you. I've been around him long enough to see that he comprehends the difficulties—" She stopped and looked at him, then rested her palm against his cheek. "You know it won't last, don't you?"

"I'm all too well aware."

"I don't wish to bring you any discomfort. I've never seen him quite so blissful, but the reality is—"

"You've seen him blissful?"

"Jealousy doesn't become you," she said. "He's a king and will do what he likes whenever he likes. That can be no surprise to you. I'm not here to warn you off, only to beg you to be mindful of keeping your expectations in check."

His heart started to beat too fast. "You misunderstand. It's not like that. We're—"

"I know exactly what you are to each other. I spoke to him at length when he returned this morning. I told him that God has made you both as you are. You did not create yourselves. As such, you ought to be allowed to freely admit who you are. It may last longer than a single season, but it shan't be permanent. Not in the way either of you would like."

"You think I don't know that?"

"Of course you know that. It doesn't mean I shouldn't remind you to keep on guard. Hold back a little piece of your heart, so that when it all comes crashing down, you'll have something left untouched, something yours and only yours."

"That's all I've had my entire life," Niels said, "my heart, kept for myself. I don't want it anymore."

23

Villa von Düchtel
1906

When Colin and I arrived downstairs, a footman directed us to the gallery, where aperitifs were being served. I accepted a glass of schnapps as we entered the room. Ursula was dressed in white from head to toe. Her eyes, red rimmed, were the only sign of her grief.

"White is the color of mourning in Asia," she said. "It's all I shall wear until I learn the identity of the individual who snuffed out my daughter's life."

"I'm so very sorry," Colin said. "It's a dreadful thing for a parent to lose a child, completely beyond the natural order of things. I promise we shall do all we can to find the perpetrator as quickly as possible."

I looked around, and, seeing that Liesel had not yet appeared, asked Ursula how they'd met. It was time to consider everyone's history with the others in the house.

"I go to Paris twice a year to look for art," she said. "A friend there, who's aware of my interest in collecting pieces created by women, told me about Liesel's gallery in Berlin. I wasn't planning

DEATH BY MISADVENTURE

any more travel in the upcoming months—I wanted to enjoy my house now that it's finished—so I wrote her a letter, explaining my interests and asking what she had that she thought I might like. She replied and offered to bring two paintings, wherever I desired. I invited her to come for the party and stay on a few days thereafter while I decided if I wanted them."

"Is it unusual in the art world to have paintings brought to your house for consideration?" Colin asked.

"Your wife is a collector," Ursula said. "Does she spend inordinate amounts of time going from gallery to gallery?"

"A not insignificant amount of time," he said, "but she does have relationships with several dealers who contact her when they acquire objects they believe meet her taste. I can't recall a time they've brought them to her, however."

"It would've been simpler to have her come to me in Munich, but I wanted to see the paintings here, where I'd display them. I'm rich enough and eccentric enough to get what I want, so she agreed. At first, she planned to deliver them and return after a week, so that I wouldn't feel any pressure while deciding whether I wanted to purchase them, but once she arrived and I saw how sharp she is, I asked her to stay on to catalog my collection. She's been an enormous help."

"Had you no catalog before then?" I asked.

"No. I collect for myself and remember what I have. However, I realized it would be wise to have a more formal accounting of what I own. Naturally, I have records of all my purchases, but that's not the same as a catalog. Sigrid gave me the idea."

"Did she share your interest in art?" Colin asked.

"Not at all," Ursula said. "I suspected it was so she'd know what she'd inherit when I die. One can't blame her."

"What will happen to your estate now?" he asked. "Forgive the

145

crassness of the question, but it's essential to consider who benefits from the crime."

"I've no other family and haven't ever given the matter much thought. Perhaps I'll arrange to turn my house into a museum. There could be a small number of tickets available each day, tickets that would include luncheon, so that the visitors would have the opportunity to get a sense of what it is to live with art, not to pass by it in a rush."

I left Colin talking to her, grabbed a glass of champagne, and intercepted Cécile as she entered the room. "Here," I said, passing the wine to her. "I was hoping we could have a little chat about Felix. You know him better than I—"

"I don't know that I'd go that far, *chérie*. We've conversed here and there, but not in a fashion one could call *très proche*."

"Could you try to change that?" I asked.

"I do not involve myself with gentlemen who are already committed to someone else. So long as Mademoiselle Göltling has his attention, he shall have to do without mine."

"I didn't mean to suggest anything outside the bonds of propriety. Just get to know him so that we can determine whether he's likely to have had anything to do with Sigrid's death."

"That, Kallista, I can manage. I've been embroiled in enough of your investigations that I consider myself almost fully qualified as a detective. I should, perhaps, offer my services to la Sûreté upon returning to Paris." She looked around, spotted Felix, and called across the room. "Monsieur Brinkmann! Do come here. I've some questions for you."

He was at her side in no time, kissed her hand and then mine before giving us a little bow. "Anything for two such lovely ladies. I'm at your service."

"That is a relief *profonde*, monsieur," she said. "Our situation is *difficile, n'est-ce pas?* Sigrid's murder has shocked us all to the core, but the police cannot reach us in this isolated location during a blizzard, which means we're all trapped with the murderer. How is one to bear it?"

"It may not be so bad as all that," he said. "First, there's no blizzard, just an ordinary storm. The roads will be passable again before you know it. Further, it may be that the killer is not—and never has been—in the house. He may have a base of some sort nearby. A mountain hut or some sort of thing. I understand Mahler had several which he used for composing."

"I fear your optimism is unfounded, monsieur. Monsieur Mahler, whom I know well, utilizes his huts only in the warmer months, which, if one were in possession of a hut, is what would be necessary here, as well. I fear there's no logic that suggests the murderer isn't among us. But I did not draw you to my side to speak of such things. What I need is distraction, Monsieur Brinkmann. Tell me about your boat. Where you've traveled in it. The people you've met along the way."

"You'd be interested in all that?"

"*Alors*, monsieur, have I not just made that clear?"

"My experience is that most people who aren't nautical have an aversion to such details."

"I am not most people." She bestowed upon him a glittering smile and held up her empty flute so a footman passing by with a bottle of champagne could refill it.

Seeing she had the matter well in hand, I looked around the room. Liesel had arrived and was sitting by herself on a bench at the far end, beneath an elaborate medieval tapestry.

"May I join you?" I asked.

Her countenance brightened. "If you'd like, I'd be delighted."

"How's your headache?"

"Much better, thank you," she said. "The baroness's powders work a trick. I try to always bring some of my own when I travel but left them out of my case this time. I often go months without an attack. When you aren't having them, you half expect they will never return. Wishful thinking."

"Not a terrible quality," I said.

"Please don't feel obligated to sit here with me. You should go and be with your friends. What happened today is so awful. You all need each other. I'm nothing more than an intruder who's outlasted my usefulness."

"Not in the least. My husband and I knew none of the other guests save Madame du Lac when we arrived. We're as much strangers to the others as you are."

"I hadn't realized that. Frau du Lac and the baroness have obviously been close for ages and the two couples must spend a great deal of time together. It's always uncomfortable to arrive somewhere and find everyone else paired off. Not that it troubled me initially. I wasn't here to socialize but rather to sell my paintings. When the baroness asked me to catalog her collection, I almost refused, but the temptation of spending more time in this magnificent gallery was too great. Then came the attacks on Herr Allerspach and the death of his wife, which made me more aware of my isolation from the rest of you than I'd been before. I find myself all alone."

"That's understandable," I said. "Do remember, though, that Max is here on his own as well."

"Forgive me for speaking so bluntly, Lady Emily, but I think we all know that's not strictly true. Or wasn't true before the sad events of this morning. Please don't think I mean to complain. I've never before been in a situation like this and haven't any idea of how to behave. It's rather like being trapped in the midst of a swarm of bees. Terrifying and painful."

"An accurate analogy," I said.

"Is there anything I can do to help? I hate being useless and am conscious of not having known Frau Allerspach well enough to have the right to mourn her. I'm continuing my cataloging work, but it's not all-consuming. If you and your husband require anything from me, I'm more than happy to assist in any way you'd like."

"That's a very kind offer. I shall keep it in mind."

She closed her eyes for just a moment and then gave a little laugh. "As if I've any qualifications for being able to help. Whatever can I be thinking? I'd best stick to my art. I understand you're a collector. Tell me about your interests."

"Ancient art," I said, "specifically fifth century BC Greek pottery and sculpture." We spent a pleasant half hour discussing the subject, on which she was reasonably well informed, more so than I would've expected for someone focused on contemporary works.

When the gong sounded, we filed into the dining room. The first course was *Flädlesuppe*, rich beef broth filled with leeks and delicate ribbons of savory pancakes. Kaspar, who'd loitered behind the rest of us on the way in, took his seat and whipped the linen napkin off the table and into his lap just as a footman appeared behind him with a steaming bowl of the soup. A slip of paper fluttered to the ground.

"What's this?" Kaspar asked, reaching down for it. He looked at it and frowned. *"Don't rest easy. Next time I won't miss."*

"Where did that come from?" Ursula asked.

"It was under my napkin."

A place card on a sterling silver holder marked each seat; anyone could've known where Kaspar would sit. "May I see it?" I asked. He passed it to me. There was nothing noteworthy about the paper itself and the text was typed.

"Give it to me." Ursula rose from her chair and held out her hand. I brought it to her. "It was done with my typewriter. The *m* always mis-strikes a bit and leaves off the serif on the far right."

"You mean this is not all over?" Birgit's voice rose in frustration. Her face was white as porcelain and her hands shook. "This is too much to bear." She stood up, knocking over her chair, and flew to the door. Then she stopped, a picture of confusion, tears streaming down her face.

Cécile went to her and took her hands. "There's no call for hysterics. They won't help anything."

"Are we to face more violence? Sigrid's death wasn't enough? I'm not going to sit here at a table with a murderer and wait to be poisoned." She sniffed. "Unless my room isn't any safer. Do you think it's more dangerous there? How are any of us to know what to do?"

Colin was more than capable of taking matters in hand in the dining room, so I left the table and crossed to Cécile and Birgit. "We'll take you upstairs." I looped an arm through Birgit's and guided her to her room, Cécile following after she'd instructed a footman to send up tea for our distressed companion.

Birgit regained her composure with astonishing speed once she'd closed and locked the door behind us. "I'll not leave it open again," she said. "I've half a mind to refuse to come out until I can make the trip back to Munich. The servants could leave food for me outside the door. Although that could be poisoned, too, couldn't it?" Her face was ghost white. Her eyes darted around the room, frantic. "I don't know why I ever agreed to come to this wretched place. There's nothing in it for me, which is not at all how it was presented."

"How was it presented?" I asked.

"As a little romantic escape."

"Is Monsieur Brinkmann a romantic sort?" Cécile asked. "He does not strike me as so."

"I haven't the slightest idea and I don't care."

"Is there no understanding between you?" I asked. Felix had told me as much, but I knew better than to rely solely on the opinion of a gentleman when it came to such things.

"Understanding? As in a promise to marry? Good heavens, no. I can hardly stand the man."

"Then why travel with him?" I asked.

She flopped onto her bed, lying flat with her arms stretched out. "It's all going to come out anyway, so I might as well tell you everything. First, though, you must know that I never liked the idea."

"What idea?"

"Coming here and pretending to be mad for him."

"Was that your object?" Cécile was nonplussed. "I never would have drawn such a conclusion."

"I'm no actress nor is Felix much of an actor. None of us thought anyone would notice. I came here to be near Kaspar, of course, but you've probably figured that out already. It's the way he looks at me; it's intoxicating. No girl in her right mind could resist the man. He couldn't stand the thought of being trapped out in the wilderness with no one but his wife to amuse him for a whole week, so he told Sigrid he wanted to bring Felix and that Felix wanted to bring me."

"Kaspar is your lover?" Cécile was nearly bowled over with astonishment.

"Is that so surprising?" Birgit's eyelashes fluttered. "He's the most handsome man I've ever seen and so strong he can do nearly anything. Once he carried me all the way across the English Garden in

Munich. Well, perhaps not *all* the way across, but a very long distance all the same."

"How long has this been going on between you?" I asked.

"Eons," she said.

I was shocked. "Could you be more specific?"

"Longer than I can remember."

"That's not helpful, Birgit," I said. "How long."

"It will be two years this spring. Practically my entire life."

It didn't require an affinity for mathematics to recognize the inanity of this statement.

"It is not right for you to trifle with a married man," Cécile said, "and it is not right for a married man to trifle with anyone, particularly an unattached young lady."

"He wasn't trifling with me, nor I with him," Birgit said. "He loves me and I adore him."

"Be that as it may, he's married," I said. "There can be no future for the two of you."

"I probably ought not point out the obvious fact that he's no longer married. It's bound to give you the wrong idea. Regardless of the events of this morning, you're both too old to see that the world has changed. He was going to leave Sigrid. They could barely tolerate being around each other. We were arranging everything so she could have Max and Kaspar could have me."

"What did Sigrid have to say about all of this?" Cécile asked.

"We hadn't told her yet," Birgit said. "Kaspar meant to do it before the party in the gallery. We both thought that would be a good time, because if Sigrid was upset—not that she would've been; she didn't care one fig for him—she'd have to contain her emotion in front of her mother's guests. Neither of us wanted a scene."

I already knew Kaspar was a boor, but I couldn't imagine even him agreeing to such a scheme. "If that was your plan, why didn't he tell her before the party?"

"They'd got in an argument about some minuscule thing when they were dressing and he didn't want her to think he was leaving because of that. Instead, he decided to tell her on their sleigh ride."

"Wasn't the sleigh ride Sigrid's idea?" I asked.

"It was," she said. "She was driving him half mad over it. Kaspar told me he was worried she wanted to speak with him about something serious and was using it as a pretext to get him alone. She's disgracefully manipulative. In the end, it didn't matter, though. He told her about us before she could bring up whatever it is she wanted to talk about with him. She wasn't even upset and told him she hoped he would be happy with me. She realized she'd never made him happy. And then, not five minutes after all that happened, a shot rang out and she was dead. I feel a bit sorry for her, of course, but it does make things far easier for everyone involved, doesn't it? Sometimes, fate knows exactly what it's doing. The world is a glorious place, even when it seems like things are going terribly wrong."

24

Schloss Hohenschwangau
1868

How many blissful weeks passed after that Niels didn't know. He didn't care. All he wanted was for it to go on forever, but Elisabet wouldn't let him consider that a possibility even for a second. She was like the slave who stood behind a victorious Roman leader at his triumph, holding the crown over his head and reminding him he was no god, whispering *Respice post te! Hominem te esse memento! Look behind you. Remember you are a man.*

Summer turned to autumn and the leaves fell from trees, shimmering on their way to the dappled ground. Another reminder that beauty cannot last forever. Niels understood that, deep in his soul, but as the air grew chilly and gray clouds over the mountains hinted at snow, he almost came to believe his happiness might prove eternal.

Ludwig could not remain indefinitely holed up with his friends in the countryside. He had to make relatively frequent trips to Munich to tend to his royal responsibilities. At first, Niels was at a loss during those times, unsure what to do with himself. Elisabet had her art, so he decided to focus on his vocal work. He never sang anything but Wagner when Ludwig was in residence, so he took the opportunity to rehearse other composers.

"He didn't like me when we first met," Elisabet told Niels one day when he'd come to her studio after giving up on trying to master Verdi's "Di quella pira." She was working on the plaster model that would serve as the basis for her sculpture of the king that, when finished, would stand nearly seven feet tall. "I badgered him to win the commission to sculpt him. Sent so many letters begging him for an audience I'm surprised I wasn't arrested."

"Why did you want to do it?" Niels asked.

"He struck me as the sort of man who would make an excellent patron. He's got a keen sense of the aesthetic, an understanding of artists, and an enormous fortune." She laughed. "Not that I was being mercenary. I heard much about him when he was crown prince and I was a student."

"Where did you study?"

"I wanted to go Berlin, so that Christian Daniel Rauch might train me. He's the best in all of Europe. My parents objected, claiming my aspirations were indecent. I am, as you may have noticed, a female."

"Did you persuade them in the end?" Niels asked.

"Not even a hunger strike moved them. I did manage to convince them to let me go to Munich and stay with respectable family friends. I had to hire a private tutor as the Academy of Art refused to admit me."

"On what grounds? Your talent is evident."

"As is my sex," she said. "They thought I would distract the male students. After some months passed, I applied again. This time, they agreed to let me attend classes, but only as a trial. Eventually, they recognized my skill and allowed me to officially enroll. No woman had been allowed the honor before."

"I don't know which is more impressive, your sculptures or your persistence."

"One requires the other. I went to Berlin after that and was tutored by Rauch. He taught me how to work with live models, but not before I proved to him that I could make exact copies of Greek sculptures. He instilled in me a devotion to accuracy."

"Is that why Ludwig hired you?"

"He never told me his reasons," she said. "I'd like to believe it was because of my dogged insistence on getting the job."

Niels had been sprawled on a settee, but got up and moved closer so that he could better examine her work. "It's masterful. Obviously him—the hair is flawless, and the eyes, they're perfect—but it's him even more so, if that makes sense."

"It's him, but without the black moods and doubt. That's why he likes it."

"If we could only help him avoid them both."

"If only we could stay here forever, pretending the rest of the world doesn't exist."

This pricked him like a knifepoint. "What would you do in my place?" Niels asked. "I agree this can't last, but would you accept that without so much as trying?"

"If it were me, I would chloroform him, tie him up, fling him onto a ship to South America, and live out the rest of my life with him in the jungle."

"He wouldn't like the jungle."

"No, but he likes you. He could learn to deal with the jungle."

Niels smiled. "I'm not sure I could."

Her words made him uncomfortable for the next week. He lay

in bed for endless hours, contemplating them. Was there something lacking in his feelings for his friend? Was he not devoted enough? Unwilling to suffer? Incapable of dedication? He didn't know. But one thing was clear. When Ludwig returned from Munich, he would find Niels consumed with melancholy.

25

Villa von Düchtel
1906

"Appalling, appalling, appalling, appalling." Cécile and I had stayed with Birgit for nearly two hours and now, back in my room, I flung myself onto the bed. "The girl has no sense of decorum, no sense of decency. It's shocking that anyone could be so callous."

"Surely *appalling* is the mildest criticism one could lob at her," Colin said, sitting on the edge of the mattress. "One hardly knows where to start when there's such meet food to feed it."

"I wanted to go straight to Kaspar and ask if he told Sigrid he was leaving her for Birgit. I cannot imagine he did."

"Of course he didn't. His wife is dead and his mistress distraught, so he told Birgit what she wanted to hear. The truth is irrelevant because the only other witness to it will remain forever silent."

"Dreadful man. Reprobate." The words were too weak. I turned my mind to Shakespeare and searched for the worst insult I could remember. "*Beetle-headed flap-ear'd knave.*"

"*A boil, a plague sore.*"

"*Lump of foul deformity.*"

"No, I shan't stand for that," Colin said. "Richard the Third was twice the man as Allerspach."

I pushed myself up on my elbows. "It does change the shape of things, knowing he's been embroiled in a long-running affair."

"It certainly gives him a strong motive for wanting his wife dead. The fact that he didn't stand to gain financially from her demise would've otherwise suggested he's innocent."

"He and Birgit could have orchestrated every incident before the murder to make it look like Kaspar was the one in danger," I said.

"And he could've easily shot Sigrid in the sleigh."

"Kaspar's awful, but would he really murder his wife to pave the way for a lifetime with Birgit?"

"Men have had stupider desires," Colin said, "but I do find it hard to believe. He's a man who likes the trappings of luxury. Think of his Cuban cigars and fine watches. It's unusual for a man to leave his wife, no matter how much he dislikes her. Letting Birgit believe he planned to do so was cruel."

"We have no evidence Kaspar actually disliked Sigrid," I said. "We do, however, have ample examples of Birgit's narcissism. Further, she's unmarried. Jeremy always tells me he prefers married ladies because they've already got husbands and don't want to disturb their status quo. There's much to criticize about the nature of marriage in our society, but it has evolved in a way that provides discreet opportunities for those who wedded for reasons other than love."

"When matches are based on titles and fortunes, such a system cannot be avoided. You're quite right about unmarried ladies. They're best avoided."

I raised an eyebrow. "Are they, now?"

"Unless one plans to marry them, of course. The, er, inevitable results of a long, intimate affair can be hidden within the confines

of a marriage. An unmarried lady does not have the same opportunity."

"Kaspar isn't the smartest man I've ever met," I said. "Perhaps
that inevitable result never occurred to him."

"Not even he could be that ignorant. He strikes me as someone
happy to play with fire and happy to get his hands burned. He
craves excitement. Hence, arranging for his wife and mistress to
attend the same party at his mother-in-law's house. He could easily have told Sigrid to go without him and had a happy spell with
Birgit back in Munich. The fact he didn't choose that course of
action suggests he's in this for a game of titillating pleasure, nothing else."

"What happened after I left the dining room?"

"Very little," he said. "Allerspach exhibited a strangely measured outrage. Brinkmann looked ill. The baroness demanded we
all go on as if nothing had happened, so Max and Liesel started
what they must have hoped would be a lively discussion of Alpine
wildflowers."

"I don't understand Ursula," I said. "If someone murdered one
of our children, I wouldn't be so calm."

"She's likely still in shock."

"What if she's protecting someone?"

"Who?" he asked.

"Consider our suspicion of Gerda and Hans. What if Ursula
knows Kaspar has behaved inappropriately? What if his actions
went further than Gerda let on? What if it's not the first time such a
thing has happened?"

"The baroness might have sympathy for the girl, but I cannot
believe that would extend to protecting the person who killed her
daughter."

"No, I can't either," I said. "I also don't see anything in Gerda's character that suggests she's a murderer. I hate all these unanswered questions."

He was still sitting on the edge of the bed, while I stood in front of him. He reached out, put his arms around my waist, and pulled me onto his lap. "We can't find answers tonight, so let's abandon useful occupation. Byron tells us to *eat, drink, and love; the rest's not worth a fillip.* We've already dined and I don't fancy a drink, so we may as well give ourselves over to amorous pursuits with wild abandon. I shouldn't want to dismiss his advice entirely."

Wild abandon does not generally lead to one being at one's brightest and best the next morning, but on this occasion, the opposite was true. I fairly leapt out of bed, flung open the curtains, and saw that it was still snowing, harder than ever. I tugged at the window sash until it moved, lifted it, and stuck my head outside, closing my eyes and drawing in a deep breath.

"There's nothing like the smell of snow."

Colin flung a pillow over his head and moaned. "Less enthusiasm, my darling girl, I beg you. And do, please, close the window."

I rang the bell and asked to have our breakfast sent up. There was much to be done, but nothing that couldn't wait a little longer. None of us would be going anywhere in the storm. Before a quarter of an hour had passed, I was sitting at the little table in our room, buttering a piece of toast.

Colin sipped his tea, still in bed, propped up by a mound of pillows. "I've been thinking about the message Allerspach received at dinner last night. It's either a valid warning or a diversion. Anyone could've authored it. The baroness's typewriter is in her study and the room is never locked."

"If Kaspar and Birgit are guilty of murder, they'd want us to continue to think he was the intended target of the shot."

"If Hans and Gerda are guilty, would they do the same?" he asked.

I crinkled my brow. "No, I don't think they would. If they're responsible, Sigrid's death was an accident. Why would they want to draw attention to the fact? Better to stay quiet and hope for an opportunity to right the wrong."

He considered my words. "I agree they'd want to stay quiet, but neither of them is a hardened criminal. After realizing they'd killed an innocent woman, they might well have decided to get out of the revenge business."

Someone knocked. As I was modestly attired and Colin was wearing nothing but pajama trousers, I cracked the door open just enough to see who was there.

"Cécile!"

"Let me in, Kallista," she said, her voice a whisper.

I did as she requested, and as soon as Colin realized what was happening, he pushed his tray to the other side of the bed and pulled on a dressing gown.

"Do forgive me," Cécile said. "I would not ordinarily have disturbed you at such a diabolical hour but I felt I had no choice."

"What happened?" I asked.

"Birgit, having no concern for what she might interrupt in the middle of the night, came to my room an hour after we left her. She confided in me that she is with child."

"Allerspach's?" Colin asked.

"*Bien sûr.*"

"That certainly changes things," I said. "She's in an untenable situation and likely desperate. She would've been pressing Kaspar to leave his wife."

"It gives her a profound motive for killing her rival," Colin said. "Does Allerspach know?"

"She claims not to have told him," Cécile said.

"It may be she has told Kaspar and denied doing so to protect him," I said. "They'd both have strong motives and could've planned the attacks on him together. Then, he carried out the murder."

"Far simpler than her doing it," Colin said.

Cécile shook her head. "*Non*, I cannot believe it. If that were the case, why would she tell me? Once her condition is known, her motive is as well, a motive far stronger than that derived simply from her having an affair. If she's cunning enough to be part of such an elaborate plan, she would never admit to me that she's with child."

"I'm inclined to agree." Colin picked up the teacup from his discarded tray and came to the table to refill it. "Would you like some? We can ring for another cup."

"*Non*, monsieur, I had coffee already and that shall fortify me until it's acceptable to switch to champagne."

"We need to ascertain whether Kaspar knows about the baby," I said. "He's not the cleverest of men, so surely it won't be too difficult."

"I'll speak to him as soon as I've dressed," Colin said.

But by the time he was ready, it was too late. After tending to our ablutions, when Colin and I headed downstairs, we found Kaspar lying at the bottom of the steps on the hard marble floor of the villa's entrance hall.

26

Schloss Hohenschwangau
1868

Niels believed, deep in the darkest recesses of his soul, that his melancholy would prove eternal. He expected he'd never again feel joy and was content to wallow in it. Then Ludwig returned from Munich, and it vanished like mountain mist on a bright summer morning. The king hadn't bothered to alert him or Elisabet, or even the servants, of his approach. He liked catching them unaware. His staff was accustomed to his habits and knew they must be on guard at all times. Elisabet, who'd long since given up any pretense of existing to satisfy Ludwig's whims, hardly stirred when he appeared in her studio, Niels with him.

"Your utter disinterest is the primary cause of my profound love for you," the king said. He'd arrived, dusty but energized, only a few minutes earlier. "You're always you, no matter how it makes me feel. I found dear Niels in the *Hohenstaufenzimmer*, singing 'Di quella pira.' You can imagine how horrified he was when he saw me. Verdi, in this house, when he knows of my devotion to Wagner? What would I think? He switched to something from *Lohengrin* almost without drawing an extra breath. I was simultaneously touched and distraught. Can he not be himself around me?"

"Of course I can," Niels sputtered. "Had I known your arrival was imminent—"

"You would have altered your behavior. How many times must I tell you I accept you as you are? Enough of that, though. I've brought some exquisite wine back with me. We'll go to the shores of the Alpsee and picnic."

"It's too cold for a picnic," Elisabet said. "There were snow flurries last night."

"We'll bring fur blankets and build a fire. I'll tell the kitchen what we want to eat. Be ready to leave in half an hour."

By the time the baskets, along with heavy blankets and materials for a fire, were prepared and packed into a wagon that would follow their carriage, the sun had slipped behind the mountains. Frost snapped in the air.

"I'm already half-frozen and we've barely arrived," Elisabet said. "You're a beast to make us do this. I don't know why I agreed to come."

"Because you knew it would be entertaining." Niels passed her a flask of steaming glühwein. "This will keep you warm."

"You can always walk back to the castle if you despise it," Ludwig said.

"Or I could steal the carriage and make you walk."

"I wouldn't mind in the least," the king said. "It's a magnificent night and the cold doesn't trouble me. I'm impervious to such petty discomforts."

Their driver was helping a footman build an enormous bonfire while two maids spread a thick waxed blanket over the ground and then placed platters of food on it. When they'd finished, Ludwig ordered them back to the castle. "I'll drive us myself when we're ready to return."

"I doubt they'll enjoy coming back in the dead of night to clean up after us," Elisabet said.

"Nearly as much as I enjoy going to Munich to tend to my own work," Ludwig said. "We all must shoulder our burdens."

The air was cold, but, wrapped in furs and fortified with hot glühwein, they weren't suffering. Niels melted a hunk of cheese over the fire, and deftly directed it onto thick slices of crusty bread.

"I should like to live in this manner forever," Ludwig said, opening the wine he'd brought from Munich. "There's something about the night, isn't there? It disguises all of man's evils, hiding them in the flickering stars."

The sky was clear and there was no moon. They tilted their heads back and identified constellations. Orion and Taurus, Canis Minor and the Seven Sisters.

"When I grow old and ugly and you've both abandoned me, I'll only come out at night," he continued. "I'll drive through the darkness by the light of the moon."

"Maybe the *Moosleute* will come out and hold up lanterns for you," Niels said. He hadn't thought about the moss people since he was a boy, captivated by the stories of the Brothers Grimm.

"You give me fairy tales but no reassurance that you'll never abandon me. What a tragedy!"

"If I leave you, it will be because you've tired of me," Niels said. "Nothing else could drive me away."

Twelve hours later, Niels's words would be proved a lie.

27

Villa von Düchtel
1906

"He's breathing," I said, crouching next to Kaspar's inert body at the bottom of the stairs.

"This will keep him off his feet for longer than his skiing mishap," Colin said. Kaspar's knee was bent at a terrible angle. "I'll call the doctor in Füssen and ask him what we should do to treat it, as he won't be able to reach us in this storm. Then we can move Allerspach upstairs."

Evidently, no one else in the house was aware of what had happened. I could hear a murmur of voices coming from the direction of the breakfast room, but no one came to us. When Colin returned, he brought a footman with him and together they carried Kaspar to his room. I went back, scrutinized every inch of the staircase, and then hovered in the corridor while they got him situated in bed. He was still unconscious.

"Good morning, Lady Emily," Felix said, emerging from his room. "Are you looking for Kaspar? I think he already went down to breakfast." He noticed that the door was open, peeked inside, and gasped. "What happened?"

"He fell," Colin said.

"How?" Felix asked.

"He tripped on the stairs," I said, holding up a long piece of thin wire. "I found it near the top of the flight, tacked to the wall on one side and, presumably, tied around a baluster on the other."

Colin took it from me. "Tied tightly enough to cause him to lose his balance, but not so tightly that it stayed in place for someone else to do the same."

"Will he be all right?" Felix asked.

"There don't appear to be any broken bones," Colin said. "I've spoken to a doctor who gave me instructions on how to immobilize the leg. His head injury is of more concern."

"I'll say. Look here, I've had enough of all this." The veins on his neck were bulging. "Sigrid's dead and now we know for certain that was a mistake and whoever's behind it won't stop until Kaspar's gone, too. Someone here is responsible. I'd hoped that wasn't the case, but no one from the outside can reach the house right now, not in this weather. So who is trying to kill my closest friend? I want answers, and I want them now."

"We'd all like answers," I said.

Kaspar stirred and moaned.

"Can you hear me?" Colin asked, standing over him.

"Of course I can bloody well hear you. You're shouting in my face."

"I don't think we'll need to worry about his head," I said. "Kaspar, do you remember what happened?"

"I was heading down to breakfast and . . . now I'm here. How that came to pass, I haven't the slightest idea." He grimaced. "My knee."

"I'll immobilize it for you," Colin said.

"Unnecessary," Kaspar said. "It's not that bad. I've had worse."

"If you saw the position it was in after you fell, you might feel otherwise," I said.

"I fell?"

"Down the stairs," I said and held up the wire. "Thanks to this."

"I wish he'd killed me yesterday instead of Sigrid. It's just my luck to be stalked by an incompetent murderer."

"An incompetent murderer who's a guest of your mother-in-law," Felix said.

"Felix, why don't you stay here with your friend now that he's awake. Colin and I will speak to the others."

"I'd like to immobilize the knee first," Colin said.

"And I'd like you to keep your bloody hands off me."

"Don't bother arguing." Colin's tone brooked no nonsense. "It needs to be taken care of or the injury won't heal properly." Kaspar accepted his inevitable defeat, but wasn't happy about it. He gritted his teeth and glared at my husband.

Once Colin had secured Kaspar's knee, we went to each bedroom along the corridor. Most were empty, but Max answered his door immediately. His hair was damp and his clothing freshly pressed.

"I'm just heading down to breakfast," he said. "Is something the matter?"

"Have you left your room yet today?" Colin asked.

"No, why?"

We told him what had happened. His surprise gave every sign of being sincere.

"I'll get straight downstairs. The baroness will be beside herself." Then he gave a wry smile. "Not, mind you, because she'll be full of sympathy for Kaspar, but because her house has been the scene of more violence."

Birgit was the only other person still upstairs. It took her ages to open her door.

"I'm in no state for visitors." She looked exhausted. Her hair resembled a nest made by a deranged bird and she had a filmy dressing gown half wrapped around her.

"Did you just wake up?" I asked.

"Only because you started banging on the door."

"Perhaps you'd like to sit down," Colin said.

"Why would I want to do that?"

"Have you heard anything out of the ordinary overnight or this morning?" I asked.

"I've been asleep, so no." She tapped her foot, impatient.

"Kaspar fell down the stairs and is injured," I said. "It wasn't an accident."

Her eyes widened. "I didn't hear a thing." There was genuine panic in her voice. "Is he all right? He's not—" She stopped and gulped.

"He'll make a full recovery," Colin said. "He's twisted his knee, but will be fine. Think again about last night and this morning. Did you hear anything?"

Her manner changed. Suddenly, she was serious, measured, helpful, even. "Let me think. I was up rather late last night, talking to Frau du Lac. It was at least three o'clock in the morning before I returned to my room." She paused, as if expecting us to inquire as to what they'd discussed. When we didn't, she continued. "I fell asleep almost at once when I got into bed, which was very soon after I got back. I was too tired even to wash my face. After that, I wasn't aware of anything until I heard you knocking on the door."

"I see," Colin said. "Would you please dress quickly and come downstairs?"

"Of course," she said. "I'll be there shortly."

We found Cécile, Ursula, and Liesel seated at the breakfast table, Max standing nearby, anxiety writ on his face.

"I didn't tell them anything," he said when he saw us. "I thought it would be better coming from you."

Colin explained what had happened and asked them each where they had been that morning.

"I came straight here from your room, Kallista," Cécile said. "Ursula and Liesel were already here."

"I had a bit of a lie-in," Liesel said. "It must have been approximately eight thirty when I woke up. I bathed and dressed and came downstairs."

"I met her halfway down the stairs," Ursula said.

"Did any of you hear anything?" I asked. They all replied in the negative.

"The walls in the house are solid concrete," Ursula said. "If he'd shouted as he fell, we might have heard something, but otherwise . . ."

"Given this latest incident we must assume the murderer is still bent on finishing his task," Colin said. "I don't want Allerspach left alone."

"I don't see how that will help," Birgit said, appearing in the doorway. "We don't know who's trying to kill him. If we take turns keeping watch over him, at some point he'll be alone with the murderer."

"I don't intend for everyone to keep watch. I shall stay with him," Colin said. "If, that is, you're all satisfied that I'm not the killer?"

"For all we know, you might be, Herr Hargreaves," Birgit said. "I've heard stories about your work for the Crown. Perhaps you were sent here to assassinate him in order to stop some political intrigue."

"Is Allerspach involved in politics?" Colin asked, a look of disbelief on his face.

"It seems unlikely in the extreme," Birgit said. "He's never shown any interest in it to me, but then I surely don't know him as well as the baroness does." Her tone was more than a little snarky. She turned to Ursula. "Have you any thoughts on the matter?"

"I can't imagine a less diplomatic individual," Ursula said. "Whether that makes him more or less likely to be in politics, I don't know."

"If I were an assassin, I wouldn't have toyed with him for days before missing my shot," Colin said. I could see his patience was wearing thin. Then, he caught himself. "Forgive me, Baroness, I ought not make light of the situation."

"My dear man, I never entertained the idea you were doing any such thing," Ursula said. "Let's take it as read that you didn't kill my daughter. Kaspar shall be safer with you than anyone else."

There was a commotion outside the door.

"Don't talk about me when I'm not there!" It was Kaspar, hobbling along, one arm around Felix's shoulder. "This is unconscionable."

"We were only saying that you need to be protected, Herr Allerspach." Birgit was being suddenly formal with her lover. "As such, Herr Hargreaves has offered to keep by your side day and night."

"Utterly unnecessary," Kaspar said, plopping onto a chair. "I've not yet breakfasted and am famished. There's no need for further discussion. A little knee injury ought not cause this much concern."

"It's not the injury but rather the fact that someone is trying to kill you," I said.

"I wish he'd get on with it. At the present, I don't feel I've much to live for."

The dynamic in the room shifted. Ursula was strangely subdued. Birgit, who I'd expected would consider this a perfect time to faint, took a seat and clasped her hands in front of her on the table. Felix said nothing.

"Herr Allerspach, there is always something to live for," Liesel said. "One must never give up hope. You've suffered a terrible loss, and that's something from which it is difficult to recover. Time is a remarkable thing, however. It renders us capable of recovering from almost anything."

Kaspar's eyes flashed and then he closed them. Finally, he spoke. "I am doing my best to appreciate that you are trying to be helpful, Fräulein Fronberg, but it's not what I need right now."

"What do you need?" Max asked.

"Breakfast first, and then to find out which of you reprobates killed my wife."

Birgit made a strange sound, as if choking back a sob.

"I do not think, monsieur, that you ought to condemn us all as reprobates," Cécile said, arching her eyebrows. "Surely the moniker belongs only to the murderer."

"Frankly, I don't care," Kaspar said. "Now, will someone please fill me a plate? I can't do it myself with this wretched knee."

28

Schloss Hohenschwangau
1868

They didn't return to the castle from their picnic until nearly one o'clock in the morning. Elisabet's observation about the lack of enthusiasm the staff had for going out after that to clean up the remains of the picnic was dead right. There was much grumbling belowstairs, not that the king would ever notice. Unlike the servants, Ludwig and his friends had no commitments the next day, and they all slept past eleven in the morning. Niels woke up first, not because he was ready to, but because his valet roused him.

"Sir, your father is here."

Niels stirred, but didn't open his eyes. He heard the man's voice, but it sounded miles away, as if it were coming from beyond the mountains.

"I'm sorry to disturb you, but he's demanding to see you."

Father. Father. Through the fog in his head, Niels vaguely grasped the meaning of the word. Still, he didn't open his eyes. Then the door to his room slammed violently open.

"Get out of bed at once!"

The harsh gravel of the words had their desired effect. Niels sat bolt upright.

"Would you like me to bring you coffee, sir?" the valet asked.

"Absolutely not," Baron von Schön said. "Leave us."

The valet scurried off.

"Father, I wasn't expecting—"

"You haven't replied to my last six letters and I grew tired of waiting. How many times must I order you back to Munich before you comply?"

"Why is it necessary to have me in Munich?" Niels asked, rising from his bed and pulling on a dressing gown.

"From what I see here, it's more necessary than I previously believed. Still abed this late in the day? What sort of degenerate have you become? It's a disgrace. Put on some clothes and get yourself downstairs. We'll speak in a civilized fashion."

His father charged out of the room, slamming the heavy door behind him. Niels was trembling. He knew what civilized conversations with his father entailed: obsequiousness, self-loathing, and absolute capitulation. He bathed quickly and pulled on his most somber suit.

His father was waiting for him in the *Welfenzimmer,* a cozy, comfortable room with bookcases lining the walls beneath paintings of noble knights and ladies. Today, there was no warmth in the space. It was as if his father had frozen the very air.

"It is unacceptable that it is necessary for me to come here myself and bring you home," the baron said, "but you leave me no choice. You have wasted far too much time playing whatever absurd games it is that His Majesty favors. As monarch, he has license to behave in whatever eccentric fashion he fancies. You do not. You have responsibilities to your family."

"Father, I'm entirely confused," Niels said. "Surely it's an honor to our family that I've become friends with the king—"

"Don't flatter yourself into thinking that's something to brag about. It's time you learn how to run the estate and how to manage our fortune, not to mention to start fulfilling your duties as my heir."

"You're right, of course." Niels did not meet his father's eyes; he knew it would irritate him. "I've been remiss."

"Remiss?" The baron grunted. "Is that what you call it?"

"I beg your forgiveness, sir."

"You'd bloody well better. I've had enough of your antics. We're leaving without delay. Your valet will follow with whatever belonging you have here."

"Father, I can't just—"

"Pardon? I must be mistaken, but it sounds almost as if you're daring to contradict me. We are leaving now."

Niels bowed his head. "May I bid farewell to the king? It would be rude not to thank him for his hospitality."

"He deserves no thanks for keeping you here for such an extended period." He tugged at a bellpull. "But we shall observe the proprieties and see if he's available to hear your goodbyes."

"I don't believe he's risen yet—"

The baron exploded in fury. "I'm not interested in enabling His Majesty's dissolute habits. If he wishes to see you before he leaves, he can. If he can't drag himself from the royal bed, that's for him to choose." His manner turned as soon as Ludwig's butler entered the room. "My son and I must return to Munich at once. We have no desire to disturb the king, but if he's not otherwise engaged, we'd be grateful for the opportunity to take our leave of him."

"I believe he is not yet awake, sir," the butler said. "He was up quite late tending to state business."

"No matter, no matter," the baron said, his manner all ease and grace. "You will pass along our best regards, won't you?"

"Naturally, sir."

And just like that, it was over. The blissful days, the moody nights, the feeling of being accepted and loved. Niels pretended to sleep the entire way back to Munich. He couldn't bear to look at his father's face.

29

Villa von Düchtel
1906

One could not describe being trapped in a house with a murderer as pleasant, so Colin and I invited Cécile to retreat with us to our room, the only place in the villa we could be guaranteed a measure of privacy. I didn't trust any of the others. I voiced this concern and my friend contradicted me.

"*Mais, non,*" she said. "Ursula is utterly trustworthy and she did not murder her daughter."

"If she believes Kaspar did and that he staged the attacks against himself to make him appear innocent, she'd have ample motive to want him dead," I said.

"I can understand that, *oui*." She sighed. "So what are we to do?"

"Someone in the house killed Sigrid," Colin said, "and it's inconceivable that no one saw or heard anything."

"The murder took place outside," I said.

"Yes, but the killer had to leave and get there."

"You have spoken to everyone," Cécile said, "including the servants. What else is there to do?"

"We can't sit around waiting for another murder." Colin was pacing, his voice low and calm, a sure indication of how upset he was. "Birgit and Gerda both have strong motives for wanting Kaspar dead."

"As does Max," I said. "He was having an affair with Sigrid."

"It does not appear that Kaspar is aware Birgit is with child," Cécile said. "If he were, he surely would not have said he has no reason left to live."

"Unless he's being deliberately deceitful or cruel," Colin said.

"I saw her reaction to his words," I said. "She was shocked, more so than she would've been if he knew about the baby."

"If he did, he's got a double motive for killing his wife." Colin crossed his arms. "First, having her out of the way would free him to be with his mistress, and second, he'd be spared the humiliation—and financial consequences—of Sigrid's leaving him in dramatic fashion if she learned about the baby."

"Whoever killed her must be a skilled skier in order to have reached the sleigh," I said. "What if, after sequestering ourselves here for a decent interval, we inform everyone in the house—the staff included—that we've determined the murderer is not one of us. That you've discovered evidence of someone hiding near the site of Sigrid's death. If we concoct a fiction they'll believe, it may put the killer off guard. He won't be concerned with disguising the fact that he slipped out of the house on his murderous deed. Then we can start testing everyone's aptitude for skiing."

"And whoever is the most skilled is guilty?" Cécile asked.

"Not necessarily, but it would enable us to narrow down the field of suspects," Colin said.

"We already know Kaspar and Felix excel at the sport," I said. "You as well, my dear, but we've acknowledged that you're no murderer."

"Surely Birgit would not be capable of such a feat in her condition," Cécile said. "The morning we all went out, she could barely keep upright."

"Neither could Liesel," I said, "but either of them could've been feigning incompetence. Birgit isn't exhibiting any of the usual negative symptoms of pregnancy, so there's no reason to assume she's physically incapable."

"That's an interesting observation, Emily," Colin said. "We have no corroborating evidence to confirm her claim. She might not be with child."

"Why fabricate such a lie?" I asked. "It only gives her stronger motive for wanting Sigrid dead."

"*C'est vrai*," Cécile said, "but the girl is not the most intelligent I've ever met. Perhaps she invented the story because now that Sigrid is dead, she hopes knowledge of her condition may persuade Kaspar to marry her."

"He would become aware eventually that it's a falsehood," Colin said.

Cécile shrugged. "She can claim an unfortunate loss shortly after the wedding."

There were too many unknowns, too many lies, too many people with dodgy credibility. Time was not working in our favor; we had to find the killer before he struck again.

Rather than construct an elaborate fiction, we kept things simple. Colin went out for a ski, without telling any of the others what he was doing. When he returned, he gathered everyone in Ursula's study and announced that he had discovered a snow cave dug into the side of a mountain not two hundred yards from the site of the murder.

"Inside was a multitude of evidence indicating that whomever constructed it spent several nights there." He was leaning against the table Ursula used as a desk. "There were remains of meals, a sleeping pad, and, most significantly, a box of ammunition that matches the sort used in the gun Emily found. I've retrieved it all and locked it away. It's now evident that Sigrid was the victim of a random maniac."

"What about all the attacks on Kaspar?" Felix asked. "They weren't the work of a random maniac."

"No, they weren't," I said, "but given the complicated relationships among the people in this room, it's hardly shocking that someone wants to torment him."

"We can elaborate if you'd like," Colin continued, "but I suspect you'd all prefer that your peccadillos remain private."

I was watching everyone as Colin spoke. Max's entire body relaxed. Birgit chewed on her bottom lip. Ursula narrowed her eyes. Liesel stared at her lap. Kaspar, who'd started using a cane to get around, tapped it on the floor. Felix rose to his feet, unconvinced.

"Are you sure about all this?" he asked. "Why didn't anyone notice this snow cave the day of the murder? It had to be more difficult to find now. It's snowed at least another foot."

"A keen observation," Colin said. "The fresh snow settled differently in the area around the cave. I spotted that and investigated."

"But your wife saw no footprints leading from there to the site of the murder," Felix said.

"The killer must have taken a circuitous route, looping around to the sleigh track."

"But he fired from above," Kaspar said. "I'm certain of that."

"So he climbed a tree." Colin shrugged. "In all the confusion after the shooting, he fled. Given how hard it was snowing, his footprints filled in enough that they weren't visible."

"You're quite sure?" Ursula asked. "It all seems too straightforward."

"Ptolemy said he considered it a good principle to explain phenomena by the simplest hypothesis possible," I said. "It appears that's applicable here. We're faced with a terrible tragedy, but at least it's not compounded by one of us being responsible for Sigrid's death."

"That's something of a relief," Felix said, "but it still doesn't sit quite right with me—"

"What you're feeling tugging at you is caused by the fact that we still don't know who's been tormenting Allerspach," Colin said. "Perhaps whoever is responsible would like to confess so that we can all move on?"

"As no serious physical harm has been done, perhaps Kaspar would be willing to forget the whole thing," Cécile said.

"I suppose it makes no difference," he said, shaking his head and then looking up at the group. "Which of you did it, then?"

No one said a word. After two minutes passed—an eternity when one is sitting and waiting—I spoke.

"It's your choice, Kaspar. Would you like us to interrogate everyone?"

He huffed. "What's the point? It won't bring Sigrid back. I don't really care."

"You should," Birgit said. "How do we know you won't be attacked again?"

"I must agree," Liesel said.

"I have a feeling the individual's motive is no longer pertinent," Colin said. "Let's put it all behind us."

And so they did, with shockingly little effort. Max went off to the music room with his tuba. Kaspar and Felix retired to the sitting room for schnapps and cigars, insisting that Colin join them. Liesel returned to her work in the gallery. Birgit went to her room. Only Ursula remained with Cécile and me.

"I don't believe any of this," she said. "Sigrid was not killed by some wandering madman. You told us all yesterday such a prospect was impossible. What's really going on?"

I hesitated, still not convinced I could trust her. No, I didn't believe she'd murdered her own daughter, but that didn't preclude her involvement with the attacks on Kaspar. While I weighed how to respond, Cécile answered.

"It is of course not true," she said, "but these fools will believe anything so long as it removes them from suspicion. We are giving them rope to hang themselves. Is that the correct expression? They will all relax and reveal sides of themselves they've been trying to hide."

"And you believe that one among them may show us he's a murderer?" The baroness let out a long, tortured sigh. "It's too much to bear. I cannot stand that this criminal is a guest in my house."

An idea suddenly struck me. "Ursula, is it possible that Sigrid was killed to hurt you?"

"No one here bears me a grudge."

"Not even Kaspar?" I asked.

"Especially not Kaspar. We do not and never will enjoy each other's company, but he wouldn't have killed his own wife, particularly as her death brings to an end the generous allowance upon which he relies. He won't be destitute. He'll inherit Sigrid's capital, but that's not enough to live in an extravagant fashion."

"What about the others?" I asked. "The connections between the people in this house are fraught and complicated. Affairs and jealousy, rivalries and betrayal. There might be something, seemingly insignificant or buried so far in the past it appears irrelevant, that connects the killer to you or Sigrid. Tell me the story of your life."

"What good will that do?" she asked.

"I don't know precisely, but my instinct tells me I'm missing something because I'm caught up in the minutiae of the interpersonal relationships of your guests. Perhaps the clue we need lies further in someone's past. We may as well start with yours."

Ursula threw up her arms and went to the tea trolley on the other side of the room that, instead of the trappings of the genial beverage, held a crystal decanter and matching glasses. She filled two of them and pressed one into my hand before sitting on the settee across from us.

"It's kirsch. I can ring for champagne if you'd like, Cécile."

"That is not necessary. Tell your story first."

Ursula took a gulp—not a ladylike sip—before she continued, looking out the window. "I've always loved this land. The mountains and the lakes, the flowers and the forest. Although that's not quite true. Before I came to love it, I hated it with a passion that nearly consumed me. I'd always preferred Munich. Its energy fueled me. My family home was filled with art, but aside from a handful of mediocre landscapes, it was limited to uninspired portraits of dour ancestors. Not that I particularly noticed, at least not until I visited the city's art museums, the Alte Pinakothek and the Neue Pinakothek. Their collections showed me what art could be. I spent hours in them both. Seeing how the works of Dürer and Rubens, Memling and Fragonard contrasted so beautifully with contemporary pieces mesmerized me. It ignited a fuse, a fuse I didn't know I had, and sparked a passion for art of all kinds."

"She is too modest to tell you she studied at the Academy of Art," Cécile said.

"Not officially," Ursula said. "They allowed me to sit in on classes, only because of my family's wealth and influence. I had no talent, only desire, which isn't enough to make a serious artist. I was a fair sculptor, but couldn't sketch to save my life. I realized this soon enough and abandoned the pursuit in favor of collecting. Initially, this amused my parents, who considered it an acceptable way to channel my abundant energy. Before, they'd often expressed a fear that I would follow some fruitless obsession to the point of destruction. Art was genteel enough to soothe their worries."

"Until your mother took you to Paris," Cécile said.

"Yes." Ursula looked into the distance, her eyes unfocused. "Paris had a transcendent effect on me. I fell in love with it as soon as I laid eyes on the Île Saint-Louis. As I gazed at Notre-Dame, I knew I'd found the home of my soul, the place my spirit would be happy, and I refused to return to Munich."

"I do not blame you," Cécile said. "There is no place on earth more *magnifique* than Paris."

"I believe my mother would have once, long ago, agreed with you. She loved the city as well. I'd always had a generous allowance, but within three months, I'd spent a year's worth on paintings, and she began to think I was showing signs of profligacy. She wrote to my father, who ordered us home."

"And you didn't want to go," I said.

"I could imagine nothing worse. My mother pointed out that I was in no position to set up a household in a foreign country and that my budding collection would make a fine addition to my marital home in Munich. I can still picture the expression on her face when she said *marital home*. Until then, I hadn't had even an inkling that there was such a place awaiting me."

"Her father arranged the engagement without first telling even her mother," Cécile said. "I've always thought he feared you might marry a Frenchman if left to your own devices. It is a course I cannot recommend, although my own experience has rather colored my view of husbands, French and otherwise."

"I was infuriated," Ursula said, "and too strong-willed for my own good. I tried to run away, but was stopped by the servants in the house my mother had rented. She canceled the lease and announced that we would leave for Munich the next day, even if she had to tie me up."

"She didn't tie you up, I hope," I said.

"No, she applied a generous dose of chloroform and had a footman put me in the carriage. She gave me more every time I stirred, and I didn't wake up until we'd entered Germany. When we arrived in Munich, my father explained that my allowance was no more and that I would be welcome to live in the house only until my marriage, which was scheduled to take place three days hence."

"To a man she had never met," Cécile said.

"That's outrageous. Why did your father so violently overreact to your passion for Paris? It makes no sense."

Ursula shrugged. "Who could ever understand the motivation of men? Until then, he'd been a kind parent, doting even. Evidently, my desire to move to France was too much for him. He thought I was abandoning him and my heritage. I was meant to meet my fiancé the following day. He and his family arrived for luncheon, but I refused to come down. I believed it was the last time in my life I'd have control over any decision that affected me. This infuriated my father all the more. He didn't speak to me until after the wedding, and then, only in the most perfunctory way. We never had another meaningful conversation."

"I'm so sorry," I said. "How could he treat you that way?"

"In the end, does it matter? My life was ruined. It was then that I learned there is nothing more important than freedom. Without it, one may as well be dead."

30

Munich
1868

When they arrived in Munich, Niels's father stormed into the house without saying a word. His mother was there, just inside the door, hanging back and looking worried, silent until her husband disappeared into his study.

"Niels, my dear boy, forgive your father," she said. "He has the most wonderful news to share with you, but when you didn't answer his letters, he started to despair. Hurt turned into anger, and now here we are."

"He never mentioned news in his letters," Niels said, "only that he wanted me to return home. I'm an adult, Mother, capable of making decisions for myself. There's nothing for me in Munich. I'm happier in the country."

"Yes, yes, of course you are; you always have been." She embraced him. "Come, I've tea waiting for you in my sitting room. I understand you and the king have at last become close. It was always my dearest dream that the two of you would be friends. If only he had a sister for you to marry! Well, it's no matter, of course. Our standing in court will rise regardless."

Niels wanted to shout that he cared nothing for his family's standing in court, but he stopped himself, conscious of the fact that, for the first time in his life, her obsession with royalty might make her a valuable ally. She could help him get back to Hohenschwangau.

"Ludwig remembers you and sends his greetings," he said, lying as if he'd been born to do nothing else. "He recalls a time you were with his mother in the garden of the Residenz here in Munich. You were admiring some roses. He promises to send a cutting from that very plant next spring."

"He's always been so magnanimous. Do you think there's a chance he might appoint you as an advisor? It would be wonderful if you had something to occupy you when you're here in Munich."

"I've no qualifications, so it's unlikely."

"Well, no matter," she said. "We'll all still benefit from his favor and it will be enough for you to manage the family holdings and raise a family."

"Raise a family?"

"Not that you'll do the raising yourself, my dear. That's not what I meant."

He felt the beginnings of a headache creeping up the back of his neck. This was why his father had summoned him home; he'd decided it was time for him to marry. Niels excused himself, ran to his father's study, and burst into the room without knocking.

"I won't play any more of your games," he said. "Tell me what you've done, what you've arranged."

"Whatever makes you think I've arranged something?"

"I'm struggling to understand why you've brought me here, and an arrangement is the only reason I can conjure."

"Does this mean that, at last, you're ready to show some concern for your behavior? Ready to take a measure of responsibility regarding your family's reputation?"

"I've not the slightest notion what you're talking about."

"Your friendship with the king is not appropriate."

"Mother is delighted with it."

"That's because she has no idea what it entails."

"It isn't—"

"I've no interest in any more of your lies. I've been more indulgent than ever was prudent with your singing, your moods, your disinterest in all things worthy. It has all led us to this situation and it stops now. I'm perfectly aware of the king's nature and will not allow him to enchant my son. He's unmarried, dissolute, obsessed with that ridiculous composer, and bankrupting Bavaria with his absurd projects. Proximity to him is not in our family's best interests."

"Mother doesn't agree."

"Your mother doesn't know the first thing about it. I've no intention of allowing you to get further pulled into his orbit, a place that can bring only rumors and ruin. As a result, I have indeed entered into an arrangement. You will marry the daughter of an old friend. From what I gather, she's as unruly and unmanageable as you, but you don't deserve any better. She's all you'll ever be able to get. The wedding will take place Wednesday."

The world was spinning too fast. Niels couldn't focus. Couldn't fathom what was happening. "No, no, Father, I won't marry someone I've never met."

"You'll make her acquaintance tomorrow at lunch with her family."

"No. I won't do it."

"Need I remind you that your lifestyle depends entirely on my goodwill? That I have no tolerance for your whims and strange ideas? You will do as I tell you or you will be out on the street. You know as well as I you've no skills that would enable you to scrape out a living on your own. It's time you take your rightful place in this family and do what is necessary."

Niels's head throbbed. He mouth was dry. His shoulders ached. Then, unexpectedly, a wave of calm washed over him. He was over-reacting. This would be no disaster. He'd always known he'd have to marry eventually. Why should he care who the girl was or when the wedding took place? His father would get what he wanted, and Niels and his wife could set up housekeeping in the country, at the house near Füssen, close to Hohenschwangau.

"Forgive me," he said. "You took me by surprise, that's all. I wasn't expecting this to happen so soon. Of course I will do as you ask. Wednesday is perfectly acceptable. May I know the lady's name?"

His father narrowed his eyes and rose from his seat. He stood in front of Niels, so close he could feel the sickly warmth of his breath on his face.

"You will not trick me," the baron said. "I see what you're angling for and I won't have it. Do you think me a fool? Too old or too stupid to recognize when I'm being manipulated? You'd never capitulate so quickly if you didn't have some scheme in mind. Yes, Wednesday is perfectly acceptable. After the ceremony you and your bride will return here and take up residence with your mother and me. You won't be going back to Füssen."

Niels's breath caught in his throat. "No, of course, I never thought, it's only—"

"Stop babbling and return to your mother. She'll lap up your stories about the king. Perhaps they'll become part of the family lore, something your children will clamor to hear. After you've altered them to make them acceptable to polite company, that is. Your friendship with Ludwig will be no more. Relegate it to the past, for it will never, ever again be part of your future." He grabbed Niels by the wrist and twisted until his son cried out. "You've never liked pain, have you? It's long past time for you to become a man. No more Swan Kings and arias for you. I've half a mind to send you to the army. Cross me again and that's exactly what will happen."

31

Villa von Düchtel
1906

Ursula poured more kirsch into her glass and turned to face the window. The snow was still falling, but just a gentle flurry, large, thick flakes dancing their way to the ground. "It was my refusal to come down to luncheon and meet my betrothed that destroyed my relationship with my father. I'm convinced of it. Until then, he'd indulged me most of the time, rarely reining me in."

"When did you meet the man who would be your husband?" I asked.

"I never laid eyes on him until I stepped into the Frauenkirche the day we were married. We weren't properly introduced until after the ceremony."

"What was he like?" I asked.

"I had no curiosity about him," she said, "and, as he showed equal disinterest in me, our lives remained largely separate. He despised Munich and wanted to live in the country, but his parents insisted that we stay with them in the family home. This pleased me, for it kept me in close proximity to the museums I loved. I began to cultivate a circle of friends from the art world—artists, dealers, other collectors. My in-laws didn't particularly like them, but I didn't particularly care. Their attitude to me changed markedly after Sigrid was born, or rather, my mother-in-law's did. My father-in-law was dead by then. She doted on the child, would deny her nothing."

"And your husband?" I asked.

"He loved his daughter well enough, but his relationship with his mother was rather fraught, so he did everything he could to keep away from her, which meant he kept away from us. We both went about our business and left each other alone, communicating only when it was essential. He died young and left me a fortune and his country estate. I'd only visited it once while he was alive and found it lacking in every regard. It was a dark, masculine place, full of animal heads and displays of swords. I preferred the bustle of Munich. Once it was mine, however, I began to view it as a respite from my husband's family. The more time I spent there, the more I liked it, and before long, I'd fallen in love with the mountains and the forests and began to understand the transcendental appeal of the natural world."

"When did you decide to tear down the old house and build something new?" I asked.

"I was out walking one fine summer day and stopped along the shore of the Alpsee, a large lake not far from here. I sat on a rock and watched a swan swimming away from me," she said.

"If you were a Wagnerian, you would've started singing something from *Lohengrin*," Cécile said.

"A Wagnerian I will never be, but something about the creature moved me, and when he flapped his wings and took flight, I felt a sudden and profound connection to this place and decided to make it my own. I sought out an architect who could design a modern structure purpose-built to house my art collection in a way that linked it to its natural surroundings."

"You've certainly achieved that," I said. Large windows in every room in the house made one feel as if one were nearly outside.

"Now that it's complete, I hardly know what to do with myself. I suppose I'll have to find a new project. Perhaps I'll build another house. This one will forever be associated with Sigrid's death. How could anyone find happiness here after all that has happened?"

Ursula was too drained to talk more, so I went to Birgit's room and tapped softly on the door, not wanting to disturb her if she was asleep. She wasn't. A maid answered the door. Birgit was sitting at the dressing table, her hair arranged in an elaborate coiffure.

"What do you think?" she asked. "If you say anything other than that it's divine, I'll know you're a liar. I never would have dreamed of finding such a skilled girl in the wilds of Bavaria. I was terrified there'd be no one here qualified, but my own maid has lately proved unreliable, so there was no point bringing her."

"Aren't you Bavarian?" I asked.

"Yes, but I've spent most of my life in Berlin."

"What was that like?"

"Far more exciting than I'd expected."

"So how did you wind up here, back in Bavaria?"

She dismissed the maid. "I never talk about anything personal in front of servants. They gossip, you know. It's a terrible habit, something in which I never indulge."

I had the distinct impression that it would take very little to induce Birgit to gossip ferociously. "You were born in Bavaria?"

"Yes, in Munich. My father owns one of the most successful breweries in the city. My mother died when I was ten and he hadn't the slightest idea what to do with a girl, so he sent me to live with my aunt in Berlin. The day after I arrived, she took me and my cousin Gisela—we're nearly the same age—to the zoo. I'd never seen anything like it. All those exotic animals; it was magnificent. It soon became apparent Gisela and I had similar temperaments and interests. We were closer than sisters ever could've been. We harassed our tutors; refused to do our lessons; and, once we were old enough, flirted with our dancing master, who was the handsomest man either of us had ever seen."

"I've heard many tales of irresistible dancing masters," I said. "My mother hired one who was seventy-five if he was a day and refused to teach me to waltz because he insisted it was immoral."

Her eyes widened. "How perfectly dreadful. Gisela and I had a fine time with ours. He danced divinely and taught us the Viennese waltz before we were fourteen. At sixteen, we made our debuts together and were the toast of Berlin."

"But something happened?" I asked. "I can see the furrow in your brow."

"There was a gentleman."

"There's always a gentleman," I said.

She gave a wan smile. "Karl. We both loved him, but he loved her and only her. They were married a little over two years ago. I refused to go to the wedding."

"I'm so sorry."

"She shouldn't have done it. At least that's how I felt at the time. She knew I adored him and I was outraged that she exhibited no empathy for me whatsoever. Furious, I returned to my father's home. Now that I was grown, he was more than happy to have me around, or at least that's what he said. He's always half-crushed by work, so I don't see him all that much, but I don't mind. There's always plenty to do. Balls and parties and that sort of thing."

"Is that how you met Kaspar?" I asked.

Her eyes danced. "I told you I don't approve of gossip, but, yes, that's how I met him. It was at a ball and he was the only gentleman who wouldn't dance. I thought it was due to him being awkward or thinking himself above the society, but then a friend told me it was because he'd been injured climbing the Matterhorn."

"He's climbed the Matterhorn?" I'd heard numerous stories about the peak's dangers from Colin, who'd summited it twice.

"Oh, yes," she said. "Of course, I didn't even know what the Matterhorn was, not then, but the way my friend spoke of it, I could tell it was meant to be quite important, so I marched over to Kaspar, introduced myself, and told him I'd twisted my ankle when I'd climbed it. Well, as you can imagine, that made him laugh like anything. He started asking me questions about routes and ropes and heaven knows what else and exposed me for the fraud I was in a matter of moments, but his manner was so charming as he did it that I was hopeless for him from that day forward."

"When did you learn he was married?"

"I won't stand for any judgment from you or anyone else, Lady Emily. Gisela stole my first love. That gutted me, but after I met Kaspar, I realized I'd never loved Karl. What I'd felt was a sad imitation, a childish infatuation. I forgave my cousin on the spot. Not literally, mind you. She wasn't there, but I decided I'd write to her and beg her forgiveness. It took me a few weeks to get around to it, but I did it eventually. If she loved Karl like I loved Kaspar, of course she had to have him. When two people are made for each other, let no man put them asunder. Or lady."

"Those are marriage vows," I said. "Sacred marriage vows. Gisela didn't lure a husband away from you."

"First off, I didn't lure Kaspar. If anything, it was he who lured me. He was deliciously good at it." A delicate rose tint crept onto her cheeks. "Second, his marriage was anything but sacred. Sigrid didn't even really like him. She was bored to death by all the things he cares about and thought boxing ought to be outlawed. He spent years trying to make her happy, giving her everything she could want, but she'd have none of it. It was never good enough for her. When he saw me, he realized his heart was meant to be somewhere else, and she had long ago reached the same conclusion about hers. She and Max have been embroiled in a disgracefully torrid affair for more years than I can count."

So much for her aversion to gossip. "Was she aware that you and her husband were similarly embroiled?"

"Of course she was. Kaspar told her straightaway. He's very honest, you know. It's one of his many fine qualities. She was hurt at first, not because she wanted him for herself, but because . . . well, no one likes to know her husband has found someone better than her. However, within a few days, she told him she didn't mind in the least."

"Is that so?" I hoped I didn't sound as skeptical as I felt.

She nodded. "Kaspar said that although she'd accepted the situation after hardly any protest, we still ought to be mindful not to flaunt our happiness. That means we can't always spend as much time together as we'd like, but I knew that wouldn't last forever."

"How did you expect it would change?"

"It was all Sigrid's doing. On the sleigh ride, she told Kaspar she'd decided to leave him for Max. She didn't want a divorce, because that would cause a scandal, but that she planned to run off with her lover and live in Odessa."

I raised an eyebrow. "Odessa?"

"Yes, apparently it's miles and miles away. They don't even speak German there, but it's on the sea and Sigrid has always liked the seaside."

"Is that so?"

"Once they left, we'd still need to be discreet, but things would be much better."

"When did they plan to leave?" I asked.

"Next year, after Christmas."

"You didn't mention Odessa when we discussed the sleigh ride before." Neither had Kaspar, but I wasn't about to tell her that.

"I don't like to gossip and Kaspar thought if Sigrid's plans became known it would compromise her reputation. It's not as if it matters anymore."

I felt more than a little sorry for the girl. Kaspar had strung her along in an unconscionable manner. Sigrid and Max were no more likely to flee to Odessa than the inestimable King Edward VII of England, known more familiarly as Bertie, was to be faithful to his long-suffering wife. There could be no doubt; Kaspar had never confessed his affair, nor had he the slightest intention of spending more time with Birgit. He was more than happy to take whatever she gave whenever it was convenient for him and only him.

In service of being thorough, I pulled Max aside later that evening, before we went in to dinner. "I've been meaning to ask you about Odessa," I said. "I understand Sigrid was fascinated by it."

"Sigrid?" He laughed. "She was the most charmingly provincial woman you could ever meet. Hated even the idea of spending time outside Germany and always said she preferred to be landlocked. Insisted one could never be entirely safe in a port city."

"I must have misunderstood."

"I'll say."

"Have you been there?" I asked.

"Odessa? Good heavens, no. Why would anyone want to leave Bavaria?"

While Colin and I had dressed for dinner, I'd shared with him all I'd learned about Ursula and Birgit and how my instinct told me we needed to get to know the rest of the party better. We'd already heard many details of Kaspar and Liesel's lives and agreed we would speak to Felix together that evening. We waited until we'd retired to the sitting room. Ursula, Cécile, Max, and Liesel were playing bridge, while Kaspar and Birgit were sitting in front of the stove, with Felix hovering nearby.

"Brinkmann, when we first met you mentioned a fondness for whisky," Colin said. "I always travel with some of my own and thought you might like to try it."

"I'd be delighted to, thank you."

Colin pulled a flask from his jacket, fetched two glasses from the drinks trolley, and then led Felix to where I was sitting on the other side of the room, as far away as possible from the others.

"Do you spend much time in the country?" Colin asked, filling the glasses.

"Not so much as I'd like, but one can't do everything," Felix said. "Sailing has always been my passion, but I can only indulge it in Bavaria during the summer. Even then, cruising around a lake isn't the same as embarking on an ocean journey, which is what I prefer. Would you care for a cigar?"

"Only if you've got one for me, as well," I said.

"You smoke? I'm astonished."

"It's one of my many dubious habits," I said. "I do it half because I enjoy it and half to horrify my butler. I'm not sure which brings me greater pleasure."

Felix pulled two cigars out of his pocket and passed them to us. "They're not as good as Kaspar's, but they're not bad, either."

Once I'd had a good puff, I smiled at him. "That's delightful. Thank you. Now, tell me, how does someone from Munich become a sailor?"

"My mother's people are from Greece, near Ithaca. They liked to claim they were descended from Odysseus and had the sea in their blood. I spent summers there when I was a boy. It became apparent almost immediately that I shared the family affinity for water; and before long, I was more comfortable on the ocean than solid ground."

"I can understand," Colin said. "I've spent many a pleasant summer of my own sailing through the Greek islands."

"It's a magical place, isn't it?" Felix looked almost wistful. "So easy to close your eyes and imagine you're an ancient hero. Then, just when you're lost in bliss, the wind kicks up and the sea reminds you it has all the power. Doesn't Homer tell us there's no other thing worse than the sea for breaking a man, even though he may be a very strong one?"

This took me aback. I wouldn't have thought him so familiar with Homer. "The *Odyssey*? I'm impressed, Felix."

"I'm a man of hidden depths."

"Rather like the sea you love," I said.

"Quite right, Lady Emily, quite right." He'd taken a seat across from me. "I'm impressed as well. One doesn't expect a lady to know her Homer."

"This lady not only knows it, she reads it in the original Greek."

Colin was standing next to my chair, one hand resting on the back, the other holding his cigar.

"Even more impressive. I've no skill when it comes to languages. I can barely speak German and it's my native tongue."

"How did you come to be friends with Kaspar?" I asked.

He laughed. "You think our relationship is incongruous now that you've discovered I'm familiar with Homer. I can't blame you. Kaspar is a brute, but I won't hide the fact that I am as well. We're neither of us intellectuals and we both love sport."

"When did you meet?"

"Nearly a decade ago at a boxing tournament in Hamburg. We had adjacent seats and started talking while waiting for things to get started. Both of us wanted to prove that we knew more than the other and, as a result, we wound up arguing over who we thought would win the next bout. We bet against each other and kept raising the stakes."

"Who won?" Colin asked.

"Neither of us. The judges declared the fight a draw. We found this hilarious, went to a pub, each admitted that we'd bet so much we would've had to sell our mothers to pay up if we lost, and have been the closest of friends ever since."

"Were you surprised when he married Sigrid?" I asked. "It doesn't seem they had much in common."

"She adored him when they first met and he's rather fond of being worshipped. It didn't last, of course; it never does, does it? But, he was handsome and she was rich. A perfect match so far as they both were concerned."

"And when the infatuation faded?" I asked.

"You've seen that for yourself. I know Birgit told you about our subterfuge."

"It's a lot to ask a friend to feign an affair so one can spend time with his mistress at his mother-in-law's house," Colin said.

"It sounds worse when you say it like that," Felix said, "but I'm always up for a game. Kaspar knows that."

"It was rather cruel to Sigrid," I said, blowing a perfect ring of smoke.

"I can understand why it appears that way, but I knew her well, probably better than her husband did. She was perfectly happy for him to have a distraction so long as she could as well. Hence the arrival of her dear friend Max."

"Yet she was insistent about taking a sleigh ride with Kaspar," I said. "Do you know why?"

He frowned. "That's something I'm keeping well clear of. If you want to know more, you'll have to ask the baroness."

32

Munich
1868

Nothing about the wedding gave the impression of a celebration. The mood was somber, not jubilant. There was no one in the Gothic Frauenkirche but the bride and groom and their parents. And the priest. The archbishop, actually. Niels knew the building well; it was one of the only places in Munich—other than the opera—that he loved. He could still remember when he was barely ten years old and, for the first time, climbed the stairs of the north tower to stare across the city to the Alps, shimmering in the distance like something mystical in a scene from Wagner. Now he stood in the cavernous nave, the ceiling arching high above him, waiting for the woman he'd be bound to for life.

She was at the far end of the aisle, her father holding her by the arm. When they started to walk toward him, he had the impression the man was dragging her along. Her blond hair was so light it was almost silver and set off her bright turquoise eyes. The effect was striking, but not strictly beautiful. When, after what felt like an eternity, they reached the altar and she stood beside him, her height and broad shoulders brought to mind Wagner's Valkyries. From then on, that's how he thought of her, as the Valkyrie.

The archbishop started the service. He read from the Bible. Spoke the Gospel. Gave a sermon. Offered prayers. Vows were given and received. Niels slipped a thin gold band onto the Valkyrie's hand. They took the Eucharist. They prayed. Never once did she meet his eyes.

At the conclusion of the nuptial mass, they all went to the baron's house, the archbishop included, for a wedding lunch. Niels couldn't imagine a sadder little event. The Valkyrie didn't eat. She barely spoke. She didn't look at him once. When at last dessert was cleared away, the happy couple was sent upstairs.

"If you think I'm consummating this marriage, you're wrong," his wife said, her tone defiant. "You should know I was forced into this arrangement."

"As was I," Niels said. "I'm sorry it makes you as unhappy as it makes me."

This seemed to take her aback. She tugged at her lip and looked at him, straight in the face, for the first time. "Do you know anything about me?"

"Only your name."

"Were you looking for a wife?"

"No."

"I want no husband."

"I'll make no demands of you," Niels said. "I know it's awkward that we're being forced to live here with my parents, but my father will have it no other way. I assure you it brings me no pleasure. I dislike Munich and prefer the countryside."

"I despise the country."

"Then you shall be happier than I. I imagine you've a lively group of friends here."

"You don't?"

"They're rarely in town."

She didn't utter another word for hours, until there was a knock on the door. Niels opened it and let in a servant with a large tray.

"Your dinner, sir." He set it on the table in front of the window and left the room.

"You must be hungry," Niels said. "We have an excellent cook. It's the only good thing about this house. Her schnitzel is extraordinary." He uncovered the plates on the tray. "Alas, no schnitzel tonight."

"Cold meat and cheese," the Valkyrie said. "I'm beginning to suspect your parents don't like you any better than mine do me."

"If that's the case, I'm more than sorry for you. At least they gave us wine."

"It would be worse if we were living with mine," she said.

"You can only say that because you've no idea how bad mine are."

She reached for a piece of cheese. "I might not want to be here, but I want to be back home even less. I'll never give you any trouble so long as you respect the fact that I have no interest in a relationship with you."

"Nor do I with you." He knew his father would expect them to have children, but that was a problem for another day. With luck, for another year. "I apologize if that sounds cruel, but it's honest."

"Are you involved with someone else, someone unacceptable?" she asked.

"I was, but I'm not any longer." There was no point lying to her, although he'd never tell her the full truth. "Were you?"

"I was in love with Paris."

"Well, then, I've a wife with a taste for an entire city." He liked her better than he'd expected. In another life, they might have been friends. She reminded him a bit of Elisabet. "I like your spirit." He opened the bottle of Riesling, filled two glasses, passed one to her and raised the other.

"To a marriage that will never exist."

They toasted, and the Valkyrie almost smiled.

33

Villa von Düchtel
1906

Our chat with Felix was pleasanter than I'd expected. I was beginning to understand Cécile's insistence that he was more interesting
than we'd originally suspected. I told her as much—in hushed tones—
after she'd finished her game of bridge.

"*Très, très intéressant,*" she said. "Given that he's not involved with
Birgit, I shall give serious consideration to applying myself to providing for him the education I fear he is so sorely lacking."

"What sort of education is that?" Colin asked, coming up behind me.

"The kind I shall never discuss with you, Monsieur Hargreaves,
because I am confident you are in no need of such a thing."

His eyebrows shot higher than the tumbled curls on his forehead.
"I believe I understand your meaning."

I believed I didn't, but neither of them was paying me the slightest
attention.

"Is that so?" Cécile asked. "I imagine your own tutelage was
expert."

"I shouldn't have tolerated anything less."

She tilted her head. "At Cambridge?"

"Where else?" He grinned. "Emily, darling, shall I fetch you more kirsch?"

"No, no, I'm, actually, er, yes, that would be lovely. Thank you."

When he was gone, I took Cécile by the arm. "What are the two of you talking about?"

"When you are older—decades older, when you achieve the status of at last being a woman of a certain age, I shall tell you, Kallista. Until then, it's best that you remain ignorant."

"It appears I'm not as ignorant as either of us would like."

"Try not to think about it." She paused and pursed her lips. "Or perhaps do think about it. You might find it unexpectedly titillating."

"Now I'm well and truly at sea," I said.

"What's that?" Colin asked, returning with my kirsch.

"I'm teasing your wife," Cécile said.

"So long as you're not tormenting her." His appearance was so charming, his features so perfect, that for a moment I was almost—almost—distracted.

"I've several questions for you," I said.

"Ask him later, *chérie*. I want to hear more about your conversation with Monsieur Brinkmann."

"Right." Colin ran his hand through his thick hair. "We queried him as to why Sigrid was so intent on taking a sleigh ride with her husband. It seemed innocuous enough, but he would have no part of it. Told us if we wanted to know more, we should talk to the baroness."

"I believe I know what you're after," she said. "I spoke with her just before dinner and she mentioned it. She's not hidden the fact that Sigrid had very little capital, and that she and Herr Aller-spach relied on an allowance that she provided. Evidently, Sigrid had decided that they needed more, and had asked her to consider an increase. They discussed it before the party and Ursula decided to give the girl what she wanted."

"And she decided she wouldn't tell her husband until they were sequestered in a private sleigh?" Colin asked. My mind was too full of questions about tutelage to give the discussion my full attention.

"It seems Sigrid was not so sanguine about her husband's affair as he would have us believe," Cécile said. "She was not about to de-mand fidelity, but she planned to insist on more discretion."

"Arranging to have Birgit here was beyond the pale," Colin said.

"Indeed," Cécile said. "Sigrid told Kaspar she had news about a change to their financial situation that she would share with him only if he took her out on the sleigh."

Colin nodded. "To see the waterfall."

"Precisely. It was a matter of control, you see. Sigrid was tired of feeling like she had none. Her husband avoided the conversation as long as he could, most likely because he thought their situation, or rather, his situation, was about to take a turn for the worse. Instead, he learned their allowance would be doubled so long as he started exercising more discretion."

I heard the words, all of them, but hardly computed them. I couldn't stop thinking about Cambridge.

"This makes it difficult to suspect Allerspach killed his wife," Colin said. "If anything, he would've done all he could to keep her safe and improve his lifestyle."

"*Bien sûr*," Cécile said. "I asked Ursula why she didn't tell me this sooner. She confessed it was because she felt it would prove his innocence. She's never liked the man and now that her daughter has been violently murdered, she decided she wasn't going to do anything to wholly exonerate him. She knew it would be wrong to stand by and see him hanged for a crime he hadn't committed, but, on balance, thought it wouldn't be too great a sin to make him squirm, at least until the police can get to the house."

"She told us she didn't believe he was guilty," Colin said.

"*Oui, mais* that was only to ensure she did not take her scheme too far."

"I can't say it's much of a shock to find evidence supporting his innocence, but I am surprised by the details." Colin paused to stop a passing footman so he could refill Cécile's champagne glass. "I wouldn't have thought the baroness would be so generous with a man who clearly does not—did not—love her daughter."

"Ah, Monsieur Hargreaves, in these matters she is almost *française*. Her expectations when it comes to marriage are realistic, not romantic. She knew her daughter was very nearly happy enough. By increasing her allowance, she would give her the control necessary to ensure her a life far more pleasant than Ursula ever had with her own husband."

"I'm sorry to hear that," he said. "Was there no love between them?"

Cécile shrugged. "It was an arrangement. That sort of thing rarely leads to anything but disappointment."

"Emily, are you quite all right?" Colin asked. "You look rather discombobulated."

"No, no," I said, pulling myself back to the present. "It's just that I find myself suddenly full of questions about your time at Cambridge."

Before he could respond, Birgit clapped her hands to get everyone's attention. She announced we must persuade Max to play for us so that we might dance. We all objected. Such a jovial activity this soon after Sigrid's death was inappropriate. There was no dancing, but, eventually, the relief of being freed from the suspicion of guilt flooded Ursula's guests, and the evening proved the most relaxed we'd had since the murder.

"Cambridge?" I asked, when at last Colin and I returned to our room. "What exactly did you do there?"

"You know perfectly well I read Classics."

"And you've nothing further to say on the matter?"

"If the Gods speak, they will surely use the language of the Greeks."

"Isn't that attributed to Cicero? You know I can't abide the man," I said.

"Catullus, then? *Mulier cupido quod dicit amanti / in vento et rapida scribere oportet aqua.* What a woman says to her ardent lover should be written in wind and running water."

He gave me a kiss, fell into bed, and was asleep in practically no time. I did not rest so easily, unable to stop contemplating the full breadth of a Cambridge education.

The next morning, Colin and I, as planned, persuaded the others—Cécile, Kaspar, and Ursula excepted—that we ought to go skiing again. Max protested the most, insisting he was hopeless, that he hated sport, despised being cold, and could hardly stay upright in boots, let alone skis, but I refused to capitulate to him.

"You can't possibly be worse than I am," I said. "We'll keep each other company while the others charge ahead. The views are magnificent and we ought to take advantage of them while we're here."

"I never thought I'd be jealous of Kaspar's injury, but I am." He oozed unhappiness, but eventually, in the face of my relentless insistence, agreed to come. Ordinarily, I wouldn't have pressured him—or anyone—to do something they objected to so strongly, but today, we needed to evaluate who were the best skiers among us.

We set off on the path behind the house, the one Colin had taken the day of the murder. The storm was starting to abate; there were moments I caught a glimpse of blue sky through the thick clouds. Much to my relief, the route was primarily flat. Even so, we hadn't covered much ground before I found myself face down in the snow.

"You'll get it," Colin said, offering his hand to help me up.

"I'm utterly useless."

"You're not." He brushed the snow off me. "Don't try to be fast, focus on letting your muscles get used to the motion. Kick back with one foot and then let yourself glide. Repeat, over and over, until you're either exhausted or you've reached the Austrian border."

"The Austrian border?" I met his eyes. They were twinkling with pleasure and it infuriated me. "That's not remotely amusing."

He grinned. "That's what you say today. If we're trapped here long enough, you'll have practiced so much that you'll be as good as anyone in the world." He swooshed off, but stopped when he reached Birgit. I could see he was giving her the same instructions.

I followed his direction and paid attention to how I moved. Eventually, I was able to gain a certain amount of confidence, at least on flat ground. Hills were another matter altogether.

"Are we permitted to take off our skis and walk?" Liesel asked, calling from the top of a relatively steep incline. In truth, it wasn't steep in the least; but to me, it might as well have been Mount Everest. I lost my balance twice on the way down and sprawled at the bottom.

"It wasn't as bad as I thought," Birgit said, shooting me a look of disdain. She'd gone before me and had stayed on her feet the whole time. "If you can manage not to think about what you're doing and let your legs feel the snow, it's much easier."

"I can't even begin to understand what you mean," Liesel said. "How will my legs feel the snow unless I fall in it?" She unstrapped her bindings, picked up her skis, hoisted them onto her shoulder, took her poles in the other hand, and gingerly inched her way down the slope.

Max came next. While I'd done my best to go as slowly as possible, he took the opposite strategy: barreling forward at breakneck speed. He remained upright almost to the end, but then fell not far from me. He pulled a flask from his coat pocket.

"I didn't have faith that one of those rescue dogs would come in a timely fashion if we needed him, so I brought my own brandy. Would you care for some?"

I took a little swig, located my poles, and put my skis back on. My legs were aching.

"Perhaps now you see the wisdom of my trying to refuse the pleasure of this outing?" The words did not match his countenance. He was smiling, his hazel eyes dancing. He had a tendency to fade into the background, but he was better looking than I'd noticed before, and his temperament was kind and steady. I could understand why Sigrid loved him. However, I had also observed that he was a better skier than he'd let on. He hadn't fallen until the bottom of the hill, and I wondered if that had been deliberate.

Colin, who'd gone ahead with Felix, doubled back to check on us.

"I do hope we're not boring you to death," Max said.

"We're painfully slow," Liesel said.

"You are." Birgit crinkled her nose. "It's not all that hard, especially not after getting your expert instruction, Herr Hargreaves. Is there anything you can't do?"

"Very little, Fräulein, very little."

I knew he was being facetious; but Birgit, having no concept of sarcasm, took his words at face value.

"Capable and confident." She bit her lip and looked up at him through fluttering eyelashes. "A most attractive combination."

"That's what my wife always says." He turned back around, so far as I could tell, by using some sort of magic that enabled him to flip one ski in the opposite direction, placing it perfectly parallel to the other and then bringing that one around. It was an elegant maneuver when executed properly as he naturally had done. If I tried to implement it, I'd wind up more tangled than a Bavarian pretzel.

As we continued on, Birgit managed to keep up with my husband. He was moderating his speed so as not to leave her behind, but their pace was far quicker than that of Liesel, Max, and me. A snail would've found our progress distressingly lethargic. When we eventually caught up to them, it was only because they'd stopped and waited for us.

"Enough, I beg you, enough," Max said as we approached. "Tell me we can turn around! I want glühwein and a roaring fire."

"Yes," Liesel agreed, "after a long bath."

"I've no objection," Colin said.

"Nor do I, so long as we race," Felix said. "Just us gentlemen, of course. I'll wager neither of you can best me."

"What do we get if we do?" Max asked.

"If Hargreaves wins, I'll force Kaspar to give him a dozen cigars. If you, by some miracle, snatch victory from me, I'll arrange an introduction to the director of the Bayreuth Festival so that you might persuade him to allow you to audition for a seat in the orchestra."

"You know the director at Bayreuth?" If Max's eyes had gone any wider, they would've popped out of his head.

"He and my father were at school together."

Max, a dedicated Wagnerian, couldn't resist. He skied fluidly and fast. Not so fast as he would've liked—Colin ended the day with a box of cigars—but fast enough to cast doubt on Max's claim of being a hopeless skier. He was more than capable of having reached the sleigh in plenty of time to fire the shot that killed Sigrid.

34

Munich
1868

That night, Niels slept on the couch in his dressing room, leaving the bed for the Valkyrie. Rather, he didn't sleep on the couch in his dressing room. Morpheus eluded him entirely. He thought about his wife asking whether he was involved with someone else and his answer that he wasn't, not anymore.

Did that have to be strictly true? No, he couldn't return to Hohenschwangau, not now, but that didn't mean he must avoid all contact with Ludwig. His father couldn't control his correspondence. Niels had no paper and didn't want to go into the bedroom and risk disturbing the Valkyrie, so he composed a letter in his head. After the sun came up, he waited until he heard her stir, and then entered the room, sat at his little desk, and wrote down the words he'd memorized.

The Valkyrie watched, but said nothing.

A servant arrived with breakfast. They ate in silence, dressed, and went downstairs, where his wife announced to his parents that she planned to spend the day at one of the city's art museums.

"I will join you, of course," Niels said. Her eyes flashed anger, but he didn't explain until after they'd left the house. "It would've looked bad if I let you go on your own. I've plenty I can do to occupy myself. Let's arrange a time to meet. I'll collect you and no one will notice we've been apart."

She agreed. When the driver dropped them at the Alte Pinakothek, Niels instructed him to collect them again at five o'clock, walked with his wife to the entrance, and stepped inside. When he saw the driver was well out of sight, he went back out and walked to the post office, where he mailed his letter to Hohenschwangau. Then, he was at a loss. How could he fill the day?

He had few acquaintances in town, and none that he particularly liked. This was of no consequence, for he realized he couldn't call on anyone who might tell his father he'd been seen without his wife. He went to a café on Prinzregentenstraße, where he drank coffee and read the newspaper. When he was done, he strolled to the Marienplatz and paused to listen to a military band play. From there, he wandered to the Academy of Science and spent the afternoon browsing their collections. He hadn't expected to find it all that interesting, but it was pleasantly diverting. He learned more than he'd ever wanted to know about minerals and would've sworn that the animal specimens were watching him as he walked by. A gentleman told him one could ask to see the Cabinet of Coins, which contained no fewer than twenty thousand pieces of money from ancient Greece, but Niels denied himself the pleasure, solely because he doubted very much he would consider it even remotely enjoyable.

At the appointed time, he returned to the Alte Pinakothek, found his wife, and after the carriage arrived to collect them helped her into it. When they reached the house, his parents were in the sitting room.

"Wonderful news," his mother said. "We've arranged a wedding trip for you. It will give you the opportunity to get to know each other and for your bond to grow."

The Valkyrie raised her eyebrows at the word *bond*. "How thoughtful," she said. "Where are we to go?"

"England," his father said, "for three months. You'll leave the day after tomorrow. The servants have already begun packing your trunks."

"Three months," Niels said, his mouth suddenly dry. The mail would take longer to reach there, and he couldn't bear the thought of going so long without seeing Ludwig.

"I've a friend who lives in Oxford, an emeritus scholar of medieval history," his father said. "He's agreed to play guide for you, so you won't have to concern yourselves with navigating the country on your own."

"Medieval history?" the Valkyrie asked, then turned to Niels. "Is that a special interest of yours?"

"It is not," he said.

"Then it appears we've both got an education in store for us."

35

Villa von Düchtel
1906

When we reached the house I nearly wept with relief. Every muscle in my body was shrieking with exhaustion. Or rather, would have shrieked if exhaustion hadn't made such an effort impossible. Colin, showing no sign of having exerted himself despite beating Felix in their race, bent over to unbuckle my bindings. He removed my skis, stuck them and my poles upright in a convenient snowbank, then lifted me up and carried me all the way to our room. Once there, he deposited me on the settee, rang for tea, and drew me a bath.

Very few pleasures could match the sensation of sinking into that steaming, rose-scented water. I let him lather my hair with soap and closed my eyes, consumed with bliss, as he massaged my scalp.

"Max has told nothing but lies when it comes to his talent for skiing," he said, "and Birgit has hidden her skills as well. She's not as good as he, but good enough."

"Liesel was as bad as ever, but that could be deliberate. However, given the strength of her alibi, I'm less inclined to suspect her."

"We shan't exclude her from our pool of witnesses; but I agree, it's unlikely she's responsible."

"Birgit's got the strongest motive," I said. "If Kaspar had told her in no uncertain terms that he wouldn't leave his wife, she might have panicked. Her life would've been ruined if she was left unmarried and with his child."

"She might have managed to hide her condition, have the baby somewhere far away, give it up, and return as if nothing had happened," Colin said.

"Theoretically possible, of course, but unlikely in her case. I'm not sure she'd have the wherewithal, let alone the money, to plan such a scheme."

"Her father has a significant fortune."

"Yes, but what is her situation? Is she living off an allowance?"

"Almost certainly."

"Is her father likely to let his daughter run off for months unescorted?"

"Surely she's got a friend who would assist her."

"I highly doubt it," I said. "She's not the sort who appreciates the company of other ladies. She considers them either a threat or beneath her notice. I could theoretically envision her having a maid she trusts. If that were the case, the relationship would be neatly delineated, with her as the superior. However, she told me her maid has recently shown herself to be unreliable."

"Which means she likely has no one who could help her." He was leaning against the wall, very still. "I can imagine her concocting a series of half-botched attempts at harming Kaspar to disguise her true target."

"Could she be a good enough shot to have hit Sigrid?" I asked.

"She's a far more competent skier than we ever would've suspected. It may be that she's a capable marksman as well."

"With Sigrid dead, Kaspar would be free to marry her," I said. "She gives every appearance of believing he adores her and is likely confident he'll propose after a decent interval has passed. It gives her a far stronger motive than Kaspar has for killing his wife."

"Or Max," Colin said. "He loved Sigrid. I cannot accept that, if he'd decided to kill her husband, he would have chosen a method that might have possibly harmed her."

"Unless . . ." I briefly considered another possibility before continuing. "Yes, he adored her, but what if he got tired of playing lover instead of husband? The line between love and hate can be catastrophically thin."

"A valid point."

"There's also Felix," I said. "He admitted he knew Sigrid better than Kaspar did. Don't you find that strange?"

"Are you suggesting he was in love with her, too?"

"If he was, he might have come here, pretending to be attached to Birgit so that he could spend time with Sigrid, not realizing she was involved with Max."

Colin looked skeptical. "If he knew her so well, surely he would've also known about Max."

"Sigrid might have enjoyed the attention that comes from having two gentlemen fawning over her, particularly given that her husband no longer showed anything but superficial interest in her."

"Allerspach told him about the affair when he asked him to come here."

"He told him he needed Felix to pretend to be attached to Birgit so that she could be here to see Kaspar. So far as we know, there was no mention of Max," I said. "There's something we're missing, something that connects one of them to Ursula or this place. I'm certain of it."

"Max has a strong affiliation to the area. He's always lived here. Let's find out more about his history."

We soon settled on a plan. First, Cécile and Ursula recruited Felix and Kaspar into a game of bridge after luncheon. Then, we spent much of the meal telling Birgit and Liesel how tired they appeared and encouraged them to nap. Birgit agreed without argument, but we were not able to get rid of Liesel so easily. Fortunately for us—and unfortunately for her—another headache came on soon after we'd finished eating.

"I can't think of anything much more tedious than watching other people play cards," I said. "Max, Colin, let's go to the gallery."

We spent a pleasant half hour circling the space before we started to coax him into telling us the story of his life. I straightened the Klimt portrait of Cécile—it was hanging crookedly again—and then turned to Max.

"Have you ever had your portrait painted by so lofty an artist?"

"Heavens, no," he said. "My ancestors would've had the means for such things, but the fortune has long since disappeared."

"Were your parents both Bavarian?" I asked.

"My father, yes, but I know very little about my mother. She died when I was four and I have no memories of her. Actually, no, I do have one, of her coming into my bedroom on a cold night and pulling up the blankets all the way to my chin. I can't picture her face or remember her voice, and frankly the image I do have of her in my room is so vague I'm not convinced it's anything but imagination."

"That's sad," I said.

"It would be sadder if I'd been consumed with grief by her loss. I suppose I was too young to be much affected. She and my father were estranged. Until her death, he spent most of his time away, living I don't know where. Everything I heard about her came from my nurse, and she hadn't liked my mother much."

"Why not?" Colin asked.

"I've not the slightest idea," Max said.

"Did your father marry again?" I asked.

"No, he was happy to be left alone. Once she was gone, he moved back into the house. He'd always been a keen musician—it's where my own talent comes from—and liked nothing better than spending the day and half the night singing at his piano. It's how I got my love for opera."

"He must have been glad to share that with you," I said.

"He shared it, but begrudgingly. My father was a solitary man. He didn't ever let me in when he was singing. I only heard him by listening from outside the room. He kept to himself. Did a terrible job managing the family finances and let the house half crumble around us."

"He wasn't sentimental about it?" Colin asked.

"No. It wasn't as if it had been in the family all that long. There was another estate, further away in the valley, that his parents owned, but he refused to ever go there. He didn't explain why. We never shared much beyond superficial conversation. I don't think he liked me much, probably because I reminded him of my mother."

"How long ago did you lose him?" I asked.

"It's been ages. He died when I was away in Berlin. I never understood exactly what happened. A servant found him in his bed and he was buried before I got home." He grunted. "It makes for a terrible story, doesn't it? One disappointment after another, but I never saw it that way. We're all used to our own lives. No matter how bizarre they may seem to someone else, they're perfectly unremarkable to us."

"My father died when I was away as well," Colin said, "and my mother fled to France immediately thereafter. She couldn't bear to be in the house without him. I've always thought that a perfectly ordinary reaction, so I understand exactly what you mean."

"Yes, I believe you do."

"Would you ever leave Bavaria?" I asked.

"Where would I go?" Max smiled. "More pertinent, where would I want to go?"

"Bayreuth?" I suggested.

"That's still in Bavaria, but I doubt I'm the caliber of musician they require."

"You're too modest," Colin said. "I've heard you practicing."

"It doesn't matter," Max said. "I lost the bet, didn't I?"

"Brinkmann will make the introduction regardless," Colin said.

"I wouldn't want to be obligated to him."

"Why not?" I asked. "If he's willing to help, you should let him."

"You're right, of course, but I've always believed it's important to make one's own way in the world."

"You would be making your own way," Colin said. "It's your talent that would win you a seat in the orchestra. An introduction is only the starting point."

"Yes, but a starting point I couldn't earn on my own." Max's face clouded, but not for long. He forced a smile. "I fear I'm destined to live out my days here, playing my tuba for the walls and, now that Sigrid's gone, consoling the baroness. I can hardly abandon her now, can I? We ought to, perhaps, check in on her. Kaspar can be a beast when it comes to cards."

Convinced she was more than capable of handling her son-in-law at a card table, we let him go without us.

"He's an odd bloke," Colin said. "I like him, at least I think I do, but at the same time, I don't know exactly what to make of him."

"He's had a strange upbringing. Perhaps that's why he spent so much time with Sigrid when they were children. She led a more normal existence. He might have craved that."

"He might have envied it."

I raised an eyebrow. "And now he's got Ursula all to himself, the mother he never had? No, I don't believe it. He's exhibiting normal concern for a friend who has suffered a terrible loss."

"That's not quite what I was thinking," Colin said.

"What then?" I asked.

"I wonder what she could tell us about his mother. Or, for that matter, his father. It's as strange a family history as I've ever heard, yet I can't help wondering if there's more to it."

36

Durham, England
1868

Before Niels arrived in England, he'd had no notion rain could fall so hard for so long. This wasn't drizzle or mist but heavy sheets, falling on him constantly from the moment he stepped off the boat in Southampton. It adequately reflected his mood, so he found he didn't altogether object to its presence. It was oddly fitting.

By the time three weeks had passed, they'd toured Westminster Abbey and the Tower of London, stood outside Windsor Castle, and visited so many churches he thought he'd scream if he heard another note of organ music. His father's friend droned on about history with no awareness of whether his charges were paying attention. The man didn't need any audience; the sound of his own voice was enough. They were in another church now, a cathedral. Niels didn't care about the architecture; he didn't care about some fellow called Bede—what kind of a name was that?—who evidently was responsible for inspiring the droning man to his scholarly pursuits.

"Might I have a quiet word with my wife?" From the look on

the man's face, Niels deduced that he'd interrupted him mid-flow. "Forgive me, it's urgent."

The Valkyrie gave him a strange look, but let him take her by the arm and lead her outside.

"Must we stand in the rain?" she asked.

"Must we stay with this awful man? I can't bear it. Wouldn't you rather be in Paris?"

"Paris?" For a fleeting instant, he saw brightness flash in her eyes.

"Why not? We're adults," he said. "He can't force us to stay."

"Perhaps not, but your father can."

"I've got enough money on hand to get us there, but not much further."

She hesitated. "How will we live?"

"I don't know. You could go to whoever it was that drew you there in the first place."

"They'll find us eventually."

"Yes, but . . ." He searched her eyes. "Even if we don't have long, wouldn't it be better than nothing?"

She didn't reply.

"I ought to be clear," he said. "I wouldn't stay in Paris with you. I'd take you there and leave you wherever you'd like."

"And then you'd go to your . . . friend?"

He nodded.

"Paris," she said. "Yes, I'd like it, even if only for a little while."

He sent a telegram to Ludwig from their hotel that night. The next morning, he received a reply. The following day, instead of exploring York, they left their guide wondering why they never appeared at breakfast. That evening, they boarded a ferry in Dover.

The journey brought unintended consequences. As Niels's mother had hoped, he and the Valkyrie started to form a bond between them. She told him about art. He told her about music. They spent hours imagining how their parents had reacted when they'd learned of their disappearance. They were laughing when their train pulled into the Gare du Nord.

The mirth stopped as soon as they stepped onto the platform. Standing at the end of it, fury etched on their faces, were their fathers. They'd only have a few moments until they were spotted.

"It's my fault," the Valkyrie said. "Of course he'd expect to find me here. Paris was too obvious a choice."

"If there hadn't been an obvious choice, they'd have been waiting at the dock in Calais," Niels said. He put his hands on her shoulders and turned her to him. "There's only one way forward. We pretend we're madly in love with each other and tell them we left England because we wanted a more intimate trip, just the two of us."

"They'll never believe it."

"It doesn't matter what they believe, it matters what they do next."

"If you think they're going to let us travel unaccompanied, you're stupider than I thought," she said. "They'll lock us back up in Munich."

There was no more time for talk. The two men were approaching. Niels did the only thing he could think of. He took his wife in his arms and kissed her.

37

Villa von Düchtel
1906

After dinner that night, Colin and I asked Ursula if we could have a private conversation with her. We left the others in the sitting room with their coffee and retired to her study. My muscles were so stiff it required a serious effort to walk all the way there.

"Max told us about his family today," I said, settling on one of the sofas and rejoicing at no longer having to move.

"Ah, yes, his family," she said. "A strange lot, all of them."

"Were you acquainted with his mother?" Colin asked. "He knows almost nothing about her."

"Sadly, that's for the best. She was considerably younger than his father and couldn't be described as enthusiastic about the marriage. Although that's not quite correct. Initially, I believe there was plenty of enthusiasm. He'd been married before, in his youth, but had lost his wife to some sort of disease. I don't know the full story. He was alone for years and then met the lady who would become his second wife at the usual sort of party. She was pretty and charming and incredibly wealthy. They married and had Max. After his birth, his mother became rather unhinged. There was talk of her being a danger to the child. I never heard any details—I don't think anyone outside of the family did—but I do know that when she died, it was a considerable relief to them all."

"How did she die?" I asked.

"In childbirth, when she delivered a stillborn," Ursula said. "Max was never told the truth about what happened. His father was adamant about that."

"Why?" Colin asked.

"I never understood. The strange thing about it was that no one ever noticed she was with child. Admittedly, their house is somewhat isolated, but it always struck me as odd. I didn't know her well, so it's not as if I was in the habit of spending time with her. After her funeral, a group of us ladies started to chat, and we realized none of us knew she was expecting."

"Was she a notably private person?"

"No, but a strange one. She used to wander along the trails by the Alpsee, no one with her but a footman who she required to stay out of sight with a picnic basket at the ready. Whenever she encountered someone else, she'd invite them to dine with her and call for the servant. After it happened to me the second time, I started to avoid the Alpsee altogether."

"What did she talk about during your picnics?" I asked.

"Utter nonsense," Ursula said. "It's too many years ago for me to recall details, but I came away on both occasions wondering if she was quite mad."

"Max seems so amiable," I said.

"And stable," she said. "I'm still relieved when I think of it. Madness can run in families, especially when it comes from both sides."

"His father suffered from it as well?" Colin asked.

"He wasn't like his wife, but he was a difficult man. Always reminded me a bit of Narcissus, from the myth. He was more than a little enamored with himself and, so far as I could tell, cared about no one else."

"Max told us his parents were estranged, and that his father lived somewhere else," I said.

"Yes, that's right. After Max was born, his father spent virtually no time at the house here until his wife's death. Which does make one wonder who was the father of the stillborn child. Not that it matters, I suppose."

"Given the family history, would you have been quite content if your daughter had married him instead of Allerspach?" Colin asked.

"I would've had no reservations about the match," she said. "It's evident Max escaped any tinge of family madness and is a good man, kind and steady, if not the most confident when it comes to himself. Kaspar is the opposite, full of bluster and boast. If she'd married Max, I would've settled more capital upon her. He could be trusted not to squander it."

The wind was howling outside, blowing so hard the windows rattled in their frames. "I thought the storm was over," Colin said.

"Mountain weather does whatever it likes," Ursula said. "Now the police won't be able to get to us for even longer."

"The truth is, if they came now—or had been able to reach us sooner—they would've arrested and charged Allerspach," Colin said, "and I don't think that would serve justice."

"After you all left to go skiing this morning, he thanked me for being willing to increase their allowance so long as he agreed to Sigrid's terms," Ursula said. "That means she told him my intentions, which proves his innocence. He loves money far too much to eliminate his source of income."

"His mistress is with child," I said. "That's a powerful motive for wanting rid of his wife."

"Is she, the little harlot?" Ursula's brow creased and her eyes flashed. "I ought not blame her. She's young and stupid and he would've had no trouble taking advantage of her. I can't help but wonder. In all the years they've been together, Sigrid never conceived a child. Perhaps Birgit is lying to trap him into marrying her now that he's . . . Heavens, do you think she might be the murderer?"

"She's certainly got a strong motive for wanting your daughter out of the way," Colin said.

"She strikes me as wholly incompetent," Ursula said. She tapped a finger against her lips. "Could she have fired the shot?"

"The evidence points to her, but it's all circumstantial," I said.

"So what do you do next?" she asked. "If there's nothing physical to connect her to the crime, how do you catch her?"

"The best way is to manufacture a situation that will make her confess," Colin said.

"That is an excellent plan. Let's do it now," she said.

"It's not time," I said. "Something is still tugging at me, telling me that we haven't yet uncovered the whole story, and until we do, we won't be in a position to confront her or anyone else."

"It sounds to me that there's enough indirect evidence to make a girl like that crumble."

"If she's guilty, I doubt she's as vapid as she'd like us to think. She would've had to bring a gun with her to the house, ski a not inconsequential distance, climb a tree, and kill your daughter from an awkward position with a single shot," Colin said. "That's not the work of a short-witted, unfocused child. It required planning and skill. If she's capable of that, she's capable of standing up to pressure unless the evidence against her is so strong that she cannot deny that the game is up."

"Yet you believe the police would arrest Kaspar without any physical evidence?" she asked.

"At this point, I do," Colin said. "It would've been the simplest thing in the world for him to take a pistol with him on the sleigh ride, kill his wife, and make up the rest of the story. Generally speaking, when a person is murdered, the spouse is guilty more often than not."

"There is another possibility," I said, and told her about Gerda's experience with Kaspar.

"Hans wouldn't have wanted to stand by and see someone who treated her like that get away with it," Ursula said, "but I cannot imagine he would commit murder."

"Why not?" Colin asked.

"He's not that sort of man."

"Murderers rarely seem like they are," I said.

"I'd like to speak to Gerda."

"She didn't want me to tell you any of this," I said. "She's afraid of losing her position."

"I would never let such a thing happen."

"People tend to believe masters over servants," Colin said. "If she knows Emily has betrayed her confidence, she won't trust us again."

"I won't let her know I heard it from you," Ursula said. "I shall summon her, inform her that I'm concerned about Kaspar's behavior, and get her to tell me the whole story."

"That's not a terrible idea," Colin said. "Emily, you should be there as well, to analyze her behavior, ask any questions you think are pertinent, and see if her story has changed at all since you spoke to her."

I worried that would look too suspicious, but in the end, we settled upon a method that, while requiring a bit of fiction, would enable Ursula to bring up the subject without Gerda suspecting I'd told her mistress about it. Colin left the room and Ursula called for the maid. Gerda blanched when she saw me, but I gave her what I hoped was a supportive smile.

"Would you like some coffee?" Ursula asked after telling her to take a seat. Gerda was perched on the edge of one of the settees, looking so uncomfortable she gave the impression it was stuffed with shards of glass.

"No, madam, thank you."

"I need to speak with you about an uncomfortable and awkward subject, one that has been troubling me for some time. I meant to bring it up earlier, but my daughter's death prevented me from doing so. I mentioned it to Lady Emily this morning, who encouraged me to delay no longer.

"It cannot escape anyone's notice that my son-in-law, Herr Allerspach, is not a gentleman, not in the true sense of the word," she continued. "He is a brute and a boor and he thinks he can take whatever he wants. A few months ago, in Munich, we were dining at a friend's house, and I witnessed him trifling with one of the maids. Then, a few weeks later, I heard him boasting to a friend that he makes a habit of such actions. I was horrified, of course, and want to be sure that sort of behavior is not tolerated in this house. Rather than go to the housekeeper, I'd prefer to talk to each of you maids privately. I'm all too aware that some employers blame their servants when such things happen, but to me that's at least as outrageous as the initial harassment."

Gerda looked at the floor and clenched her hands in her lap. Her knuckles were white.

"Has he interfered with you?" Ursula asked.

"He has, madam, but I'm all right and I'd rather not talk about it any further, if it's all the same to you."

"I won't press you for any details you're not comfortable sharing. It's enough to know he's behaving in an unacceptable manner. Has he done the same to other girls in the household?"

"Yes, madam, at least three of them."

"I'm more sorry than I can say. Once this storm passes and the roads are open, I'll fling him out of the house and he will never be welcome here again."

"You'd do that, madam? For us maids?"

"No one should be subjected to such treatment," Ursula said. "Men need to be shown that such behavior will not be allowed. Did you tell anyone else about what happened?"

"Does it matter?"

"I'd like to make sure anyone who knows is aware of my feelings on the matter."

"I told Lady Emily."

Ursula turned to me. "Emily, why didn't you come to me directly?"

"It's my fault, madam. I begged her not to," Gerda said. "I was afraid you might not believe me. I only told her because, well, what with Frau Allerspach being murdered and her husband, who was in the sleigh with her, being so awful . . . it seemed like the sort of thing that had to be mentioned."

"I understand," Ursula said. "Did you tell anyone else? The other maids, who shared their stories with you?"

"Yes, and Hans."

"You two would like to marry soon, wouldn't you?"

"As soon as we've got enough money saved, yes."

"I imagine he would've liked to give Herr Allerspach a whack on the head after what the man did to you," Ursula said.

"Oh, he was right mad, madam, but he's not the sort to lash out. Not like that."

"Surely he wanted to defend your honor?"

"No, madam, he didn't look at it that way. No permanent harm done. We both need our positions and don't want to cause no trouble."

"In the future, please know that I will always believe you when you confide in me," Ursula said. "If anything like this ever happens again, no matter who is the perpetrator, you are to come to me straightaway."

"I will, madam, I promise."

"I'd like to speak to Hans now. Will you send him to me?"

It took nearly a quarter of an hour for the groom to come to the room. He'd been cleaning out stalls in the stables and wanted to make himself more presentable before meeting with his mistress.

"I ought to have spoken with you about all this, madam," he said, "but I didn't think it was my story to tell."

"Isn't it more that you wanted to protect Gerda?" I asked.

"Of course I did, but I see now that I wasn't really succeeding in doing that."

"I can understand why you assumed her position might be at risk," Ursula said, "but had you no desire to protect her from Herr Allerspach?"

Red blotches popped out on his face and neck. "Yes, yes, I did, but what was I to do? Confront a man like that? A boxer?"

"You wanted to fight him?" I asked.

"Wouldn't you? If you were a gentleman, that is, madam," he said.

"I would want to," I said, "in fact, I do."

"I feel the same, of course, but he's got more money than I could ever count and he's a boxer and, if you'll excuse me, Baroness, he's your son-in-law and you're likely to believe him over me. There wasn't no good that could come from going after him."

"None at all?" I met his eyes.

"Well . . . if I can be candid?"

"Please do so," I said.

"I would've felt a great deal of satisfaction if I could've punched him in the face, even just once."

"Personally, I would've wanted two or three good blows at least," Ursula said. She assured him, as she had Gerda, that Kaspar would no longer be welcome in the house, then dismissed him.

As he made to leave the room, I stopped him. "What happened to your face?" I asked. "However did you get that bruise?"

"A mishap with a horse. It looks worse than it feels."

"What sort of mishap?" Ursula asked.

"I got caught between him and the wall of his stall."

"I'm glad you weren't more badly injured," she said.

"Thank you, madam, I am as well." He gave a little bow and left.

"Do you believe him?" I asked.

"About the bruise? I do," Ursula said. "He's always been a hard worker and has never given me cause to doubt his honesty."

"And the rest? Was his manner as you expected?"

"I expected him to have been a bit more nervous," she said, "but he clearly has the courage of his convictions."

"Colin had much the same impression when he initially interviewed him," I said.

"So is he no longer a suspect?"

"He had both motive and opportunity," I said. "He's bound to be a capable skier, could've left the stables at any time that morning without drawing attention to himself, and has a bruise that could've been caused by recoil from the pistol."

"I hadn't thought of that." She sighed. "What now?"

"Colin and I will interrogate everyone in the house—servants and guests—again. Someone had to have seen something they don't consider significant. I won't give up until I've discovered what it is."

38

Munich
1868

The kiss hadn't made much of an impression on anyone. Not their fathers, not the Valkyrie, not Niels himself. Without comment, he and his wife had been marched straight from the platform in the Gare du Nord to another in the Gare de l'Est, where they boarded a train to Munich. Niels expected his father would lecture him the entire length of the trip, but he didn't speak to his son at all, only read the same newspaper over and over until they pulled into the station in his home city. The Valkyrie and her father were in a separate compartment. He wondered if she was getting the same treatment.

The experience taught Niels that silence was a harsher punishment than censure. It left you waiting, anxious, and kept every bit of your body on edge. It filled the space fuller than any words could and left no room for even a modicum of relief.

And then, they were home, sitting with their mothers in the drawing room, being peppered with questions about the English countryside, as if nothing out of the ordinary had occurred. The next evening, they dined at the Valkyrie's parents' house. No one mentioned anything about them having fled from Durham.

"It's like being trapped in the most bizarre sort of dream," his wife said, after they'd returned home at the end of the evening. "Whatever can they mean by it?"

"They're sending the message that, no matter what we do, our circumstances will never change."

"We're married, so that's no shock," she said. "It was foolish of us to run. We're bound together by the church. If we wanted to avoid that, we would've had to have acted before the ceremony."

"You tried," Niels said. "You refused to see me when I came to meet you."

"It wasn't much of an effort, and now we're stuck. Their insistence on pretending nothing happened is making me half-mad with fury."

"I'd rather they rail at us and tell us to behave."

Her mouth drooped. "They don't have to. What's done is done. How we feel about it is irrelevant. I think their motivation for sending us away was pure. They thought it might bring us together."

"I do like you better now than I did before. Not that I knew much about you before."

"I still don't want to be your wife."

The words didn't wound him, not in the slightest. He didn't want to be her husband, but they were going to have to find a way to coexist. It would be simpler if they had a house of their own, but his father, convinced that much freedom would provide him opportunities to see Ludwig, would never allow that.

"They believe we've acted like disobedient children," he said. "In my case, not only regarding this situation but because of the way I was living my life before our wedding. It's why my father forced me to marry. You're right that we can't change the situation, but we can, perhaps, negotiate a truce between ourselves. If we're to spend our lives as partners—"

"I'm not your partner and never will be, not in any meaningful emotional way. I'm going to tell your parents we want more space, a sitting room and two bedrooms. You can do as you please, and I will do whatever is necessary to fulfill the role of wife. I'll live in this house, because I have no choice. I'll be civil to your parents, because that's polite. I'll try not to resent you, because you didn't want this any more than I did." Her voice was listless, as if she had no more spirit with which to fight.

When his father had accused him of acquiescing too quickly to his marriage plans, he'd been right. Niels had known that a good wife would give him the cover he needed to eventually return to Ludwig. As a respectable married man, he would not be judged in the same light he might have been before. He would do whatever he could to keep the Valkyrie reasonably content, but it would be preferable if there was some way for her to find a measure of happiness.

"Is there anything I can do to improve your situation?" he asked. "Is there someone you'd like to, er, spend time with? Perhaps your friend from Paris? If so, I could make a show of being friends with him and he'd then be free to come here as often as he likes. No one need know he was spending time with you instead of me."

"There's nothing left for me. I might as well die here, in this house. My life is as good as over."

39

Villa von Düchtel
1906

The next day, Colin and I met again with all the servants, again using the butler's room. This time, we explicitly focused on little details from the day of the murder. Had anyone staying in the house surprised them? Been where they hadn't expected them? Were any of the servants missing, even briefly, from their posts? Had any of their tasks been derailed? We asked every question we could think of, but no one had anything different to tell us from what they'd said before, until we spoke with the laundress, who admitted to having washed a knitted wool hat the day of the murder.

"What was odd about it is that it was crusty. There were bits of tree in it. When I washed it, the water turned red. The hat's a kind of rusty color and I figured the dye must be running. That's why I didn't mention it before. But now you're here once more so I thought, I might as well say something. Maybe it was red because of blood."

"Do you still have the hat?" Colin asked.

She pulled a wadded mass of wool out of her apron pocket. "The trouble is, I'm good at my job. If it was blood, there's none on it now."

Given the specifics of the attack on Sigrid, it made no sense that the killer's clothing would've been spattered with blood. When we finished speaking to the rest of the servants, none of whom admitted to recognizing the hat, we took it upstairs and showed it to Cécile and Ursula in the gallery.

"It is obviously not mine," Cécile said. "It is hideous and shapeless. Please remove it from my sight."

"It's too small for a man's head," Ursula said, examining it. "I can't say I remember seeing anyone wear it. It looks as if it's more likely to belong to one of the servants than to one of us."

"If I were a murderer, I would dress in servants' clothes to do my evil deed," Cécile said. "Anyone might have taken this from one of their rooms in order to cast suspicions elsewhere."

"If I were a murderer, I wouldn't have bothered with servants' clothes." Ursula flung the hat onto the settee next to her. "You'd be more likely to draw attention to yourself by going belowstairs than by staying away. If the hat had blood on it, why not just burn it?"

"That's an interesting thought, Baroness," Colin said. He motioned for me to join him and started for the stairs. I followed, stopping only to straighten the Klimt portrait of Cécile, which was once again hanging at an angle.

"Where are we going?" I asked, catching up to him.

"I'm not sure how—or if—the hat is significant, but Ursula's comment makes me want to examine the fireplace grates in the bedrooms."

"If the killer fired from a tree, his clothes wouldn't have been covered with blood," I said.

"No, but if he was being careful, he'd be worried someone might have seen him and, after returning to the house, might have burned whatever he'd worn when he fired the shot."

"An overcoat is awfully bulky," I said.

"A skilled skier doesn't need a heavy overcoat, only a light sweater."

"It's been days since the murder and cold as anything. The fires will all have been burning constantly."

"It's a long shot, but perhaps there's a shard of something left behind."

I knew, then, that he was becoming frustrated. We had evidence against Birgit, Kaspar, and Hans, yet nothing incontrovertible, nothing that could prove beyond doubt who had killed Sigrid. Colin wanted to find something solid. A button, a fastener, a brooch. Something that could point to the identity of the guilty party.

We went from room to room, poking at the fires, starting in ours, where we discovered two small pieces of a German newspaper had escaped the flames and were lodged at the edge of the hearth.

"That's not something we brought with us," I said.

Colin frowned. "Anyone could have come in and used the fireplace to destroy evidence." The bedroom doors had locks, but they were flimsy at best and could easily be opened with a set of simple picks.

We went to Birgit's room next, where we found a scrap of ribbon wedged in the side of the tiled firebox. All of the hearths were long, like those found in old Norman houses, large enough to contain a Yule log, but the grates that held the wood were narrower and placed in the center. As a result, the far edges remained relatively cool, even when a fire was burning.

"She might have used it to tie together her letters from Kaspar," I said. "Once Sigrid was dead, she was afraid they could prove a liability."

"You sound suddenly convinced of her innocence," Colin said.

"I wouldn't go that far."

There were bits of sheet music in Max's fireplace; a small, industrial, oval metal ring with an opening and a metal nail in Liesel's; a glass bottle in Ursula's; a key in Cécile's; more nails in Kaspar's and Birgit's; and a pen in Felix's.

"Who burns a pen?" I asked.

"The more pertinent question is *why?*"

Felix was in the sitting room with Kaspar, Max, and Birgit, playing *Schafkopf,* a Bavarian card game whose rules I did not fully understand. The best I could tell, they varied widely based on who was playing.

"Brinkmann, might I have a quick word?" Colin asked. Felix followed us into the corridor. "Did you have a reason for burning this pen?" He held up the charred remains of the instrument.

"Ought I to? I don't even recognize it."

"It was in the fireplace in your room," I said.

He took it from Colin. "It looks perfectly ordinary to me, other than it's having been burnt to a crisp. There's nothing special about it. It might've been in there for ages."

"Not quite," Colin said. "This house party is the first time the residence has been fully occupied since it was built."

"One of the servants could have found it on the floor and tossed it in the fire instead of putting it away," he said.

"Wouldn't it have been easier to put it on the desk?" I asked.

"Look, it's not mine, that's all I can tell you," he said. He pulled his brows together and looked at it again. "I guess that's not true, but it's not exactly false, either. It could be mine. Or, rather, it could've been in the room when I got there. I haven't written anything since I arrived, but there must have been at least one pen on the desk.

Does it matter? It's not as if Sigrid was killed with it. The pen is not, it appears, mightier than the pistol."

We pulled Max aside next and showed him the bit of sheet music. He beetled his brows. "It's mine, from 'Einzug der Gäste'—the Entrance of the Guests—in *Tannhäuser*. I wondered what had happened to it. I couldn't find it the other day."

"Do you remember exactly when you were looking for it?" I asked.

He crinkled his brow. "Actually, it was last night, just before dinner."

Next, we checked with the housekeeper, who confirmed there ought to be a pen on the desk in each room, and showed Ursula and Cécile, who were chatting in the former's study, what we'd found.

"The key is to one of the bedrooms," the baroness said, picking it up and examining it. Colin took it upstairs and returned a few minutes later.

"It's to Brinkmann's."

Cécile laughed. "I assure you I don't need a key to get in his room, and if I did, I certainly wouldn't have tossed it in the fire when I'd finished with it."

"Have you been in his room?" Colin asked.

"Monsieur Hargreaves, you know better than to ask a lady a question like that."

"I apologize," he said. "That's not what I was driving at, however. If you've been in his room, whoever left the key might have noticed and, as a result, picked your fire to deposit it in."

"Fair enough," Cécile said.

"I recognize the bottle," Ursula said. "It's laudanum. I keep some in my room but promise you I didn't use it to drug Kaspar's coffee the night before the murder."

"Has it gone missing?" I asked.

She rushed upstairs and checked. "No, it's still there."

"The nails and the metal ring could be left from the construction of the house," Colin said, "and could've wound up in the fireplaces by accident. The newspaper in our room might have been used by one of the maids to light the fire. The bottle, the pen, the key, and the sheet music, however, are not so easily explained."

"It's important, all of it," I said. "We're getting closer now, I can feel it. Our murderer is not quite so clever as he thinks."

40

Munich
1869

Niels did his best to improve his wife's disposition, but nothing made her happy. In the end, he convinced his father to give her an allowance of her own, so she could continue to collect art. That brought her joy.

"We could try to be friends, you know," he said one day after she'd come home with a canvas by Manet, depicting a nude woman picnicking with clothed friends.

"Then tell me what you think of my new painting."

"It's compelling," he said. "I know so little about art, I've no idea how to properly discuss it, but I like it, especially the way the woman in the foreground is sitting there, clearly without a concern in the world, despite being naked. I'd like to have a long conversation with her. Perhaps she could teach me how to leave my own concerns behind."

"It's a study for a larger work, a work that the Académie des Beaux-Arts refused to display in its Salon six years ago. Instead, it was put in the Salon des Refusés with other rejects, and a critic commented that it looked as if it had been painted with a mop."

"That's simply absurd. The man must have never seen a mop in his life. Perhaps we should send him one."

This made the Valkyrie laugh.

"Perhaps we can be friends," she said.

And so, just like that, they were. They welcomed each other's company. They dined privately in their rooms. As months went by, they both started to believe their lives might not be quite so untenable as they'd feared.

At least that's what his wife told Niels. He wasn't convinced, but he didn't disabuse her of the notion that he, too, could live like this for the rest of his life. Given her feelings, she wouldn't be able to accept the truth: that he could never be happy so long as he was separated from Ludwig.

The king had never replied to any of Niels's letters. Or rather, Niels had never received any of his replies. He never believed, or even entertained the possibility, that Ludwig hadn't written to him, but Niels had no trouble imagining his father intercepting the letters and destroying them. Elisabet wrote frequently, and his parents, knowing nothing about her, saw no reason to divert her correspondence from him. Through her, he was able to keep up with what his friends were doing, but it caused him only sorrow.

The sorrow didn't consume him, however, because now he had the Valkyrie to distract him. Their friendship blossomed. There would never be a romantic spark between them, but that they cared about each other was undeniable. His wife was no longer sullen and detached. Her face lit up when she saw him. She was eager to share the details of her day. She made an effort to be kind to him. She genuinely enjoyed his company. He should have remembered Ludwig's story about Sophie. About how he recognized she loved him. About how he acted deliberately to avoid hurting her. But Niels was not thinking about any of that. It never occurred to him that he should.

And then, fate intervened, and for the third time, his life changed in an instant. On a cold, gray autumn day, his father developed a cough. Two weeks later, he was dead from pneumonia, freeing his son to at last live his life however he saw fit.

"We don't have to stay here anymore," he said to his wife, the morning of the funeral. "We can live wherever we like. You could go to Paris."

"There's nothing left for me there," she said. "I've thought about it since our fathers intercepted us at the Gare du Nord. It would be foolish to try to recapture the past."

"Then come to the countryside with me. You may find you like it."

"I couldn't bear to live outside of a city, but I know you love it, so I can hardly refuse to see the place."

Niels should have noticed she was doing this specially for him. That she had fully accepted him as someone who would always be essential in her life. She had no money of her own, and her parents shunned her more often than they welcomed her. Her friends never seemed to be around. She'd realized he was all she had. Niels never considered her situation. There was room for nothing in his mind but the idea of seeing Ludwig again.

Niels started to pack even before he'd buried his father. His mother didn't object to the trip, not when she believed proximity to the king would increase her standing at court once she was out of mourning. He arranged for her sister to come for an indefinite stay. The day she and her husband arrived, he and the Valkyrie set off for Füssen.

"The mountains here are like nothing else," he said, as the carriage approached the gates of Schloss Hohenschwangau. "Have you ever before laid eyes on such beauty?"

"They're . . . well . . . I suppose they're very tall," she said, "and, beautiful, yes."

Ludwig and Elisabet were expecting them. Waiting for them, outside the castle, both equally excited. When the carriage stopped, Ludwig opened the door and helped the Valkyrie exit. He looked even more vigorous, more handsome—and somehow, inexplicably, taller—than Niels remembered. His eyes were shining as he grinned.

"At last, my Lohengrin returns." The king embraced Niels and they walked inside, arm in arm, not saying a word to either of the ladies. The only thing that would ever matter again was them being together.

41

Villa von Düchtel
1906

Colin and I left Cécile and Ursula in the study, went upstairs, and searched each bedroom again, not entirely sure what we were looking for. Nothing stood out as unusual, so we returned to the gallery and sat on a settee in the center of the room.

"A bottle of laudanum. A pen. A key. Sheet music," I said. "I cannot for the life of me think of what they mean."

"The baroness. Brinkmann. Cécile. Max." Colin tapped the fingers on his hands together. "Only Cécile had no particular connection to Sigrid."

"Cécile's her mother's closest friend."

"And Brinkmann was her husband's closest friend."

"Cécile has a connection to him," I said. I stood up and started to wander through the room, hoping I might find inspiration in something from Ursula's collection. Or rather, that letting the art occupy the front of my brain would leave the rest of it free to try to figure out what was going on. "She has an extraordinary selection of small objects, doesn't she? Look at this Renaissance jewelry. Who would've thought to pair it with a Greek vase?"

"The level of detail on both is exquisite," Colin said, coming up behind me. "They complement each other."

"I hadn't noticed this before. Look how its rough form contrasts with the perfection of its neighbor." I pointed to a wax figure of the Erinyes—the Furies from Greek mythology, goddesses of vengeance—next to the most perfect portrait miniature I'd ever seen. It depicted a young lady in sixteenth-century dress, the lace on her stiff, tall collar so realistic I could hardly believe it was only two-dimensional.

"I hadn't either," Colin said. "The juxtaposition is profound. Sometimes the baroness places things from different eras close together to remind us of their similarities, but here it's as if she's asking us to contrast the level of detail in each work."

"Precisely. It's what's so brilliant about her method of curation. She keeps you thinking, no matter where you look. Just when you begin to believe you've cracked the code of her method, you stumble upon something that tears your theory to shreds."

"I wouldn't have thought that—"

"Wait," I said. "We're getting carried away."

"Art has always had that effect on us."

"This is different." I picked up the Erinyes. "I would have noticed this the night of the party, but I'm certain it wasn't here."

"How can you be sure? You couldn't have looked at every single object in the room. There are too many."

"I specifically remember seeing the portrait miniature. I had the same reaction to the lace then that I just had now. Given my interest in Greek mythology, I would never have missed a sculpture of the

Erinyes so close to it. Further, I didn't notice it when I was here with Cécile and Ursula the other day."

I picked up the wax sculpture, carried it to the study, and asked Ursula about its provenance.

"How odd," she said. "I've never seen it before." I'd set it on the table she used for a desk. She crouched down in front of it, her eyes level with the piece. "It's not bad, but it's not entirely worthwhile either, is it? The figures are recognizable as the Furies, but the detail on their faces is rather clumsily done as are the folds in their clothing. I'd be no more likely to purchase it than Cécile would be to wear that dreadful wool hat."

"Let's ask Liesel what she makes of it," Colin said and went to fetch her.

Like Ursula, she knelt down to examine it. "Do you have a magnifying glass, Baroness?" she asked. Ursula pulled one from a cabinet drawer and handed it to her. "It was molded, which is rather strange. It would make better sense—and lead to a more impressive result—to use metal tools. It's more precise."

"And a sculptor would surely have them on hand," Ursula said.

"It's definitely not ancient," Liesel said. "The Greeks and Romans did use wax, I believe primarily for funeral offerings, but this bears no resemblance to what I'd expect from something thousands of years old."

"Would it be likely to have survived so long?" Colin asked.

"Possible, I imagine, but not likely," Liesel said. "Look at their hair. It's a style that was in favor probably twenty years ago."

"I should've noticed that," I said.

"It's definitely a modern work," Liesel said. "Where did it come from?"

"We were hoping you could enlighten us on that point," I said.

"Me? I wouldn't want to hazard a guess. It wouldn't have been in a gallery, though. More like a souvenir stand near the Parthenon."

"Do you remember cataloging it?" I asked.

She closed her eyes and paused. "Let's see . . . where did you say it was? On the east wall near a portrait miniature? I know I've completed that area, but I can't say I recall seeing this in particular. Forgive me, Baroness—you have so many exquisite things, it's not possible to remember every single one. May I run upstairs and get my work? We can check whether I noted down its presence."

She came back ever so quickly, panting. "No, it's not in my ledger, which means it was not there at the time. I was cataloging that section the morning of Frau Allerspach's death. You'd asked me the night before, Baroness, if I'd be willing to take on the project, and I wanted to get started right away."

"So it likely wasn't there until after the murder," I said.

"It's so strange," Liesel said. "I would've thought I'd have noticed it—"

I didn't stay to hear the rest of her sentence. I had an idea. I collected the nails and the metal ring from my room and went down to the kitchen.

"Welcome, Lady Emily," the cook said. "I do hope poor Fräulein Fronberg doesn't have another headache and that you're here for more tea?"

"No, fortunately she does not. I've come with a question for you."

"Oh dear, not more about the murder, I hope. I've told you everything I can remember."

"Were any of your pots missing that day?" I asked.

"My pots?" She scrunched her lips and her nose. "Not that I recall."

"Do you recognize these?" I held out the ring and nails on the palm of my hand.

"They're ordinary nails, aren't they? The kind I use to hang my pots and pans. Oh, I see." She took the ring out of my hand. "It's identical to the ones on their handles." She walked to the wall where they hung, looked at each of them, pulled one down, and handed it to me.

"There's a new ring on it," I said. It was shinier than the others.

She shouted for one of the kitchen maids. "Who fixed this?"

"Well, that was me, Cook," the girl said. She turned to me and bobbed a curtsy. "I was drying the dishes and putting them away and the ring was gone, so I couldn't hang it up. The opening on the handle isn't large enough to go over the head of the nail."

"When was this?" I asked.

"The night Frau Allerspach died. Most everyone else was already in bed, but I could tell I wouldn't be able to sleep, not with a ghost in the place. They wander, you know, those who've died violently. It's not as if I didn't like Frau Allerspach well enough when she was alive, but I don't fancy the idea of running into her ghost. At any rate, I got another ring out, put it on, and closed it the best I could."

"Probably not very securely, given that the previous one fell off," the cook said.

"Did you wash the dishes as well as dry them?" I asked.

"Yes."

"Do you remember what had been cooked in this pot?"

"Well . . . not really, no," she said. "Maybe cheese or something. Yes, that was it. I remember it was ever so hard to get out."

"I didn't prepare anything with melted cheese that day," the cook said. "Think harder. It had to be something else."

The girl shook her head. "I can't imagine what, but it might be I just don't remember. A lot happened that day, after all."

"Could it have been wax?" I asked.

"Wax? Who would ever eat that?" She pulled a face. "I guess it could've been, though."

She'd scrubbed the pot well. There was no sign of wax or anything else in it. I thanked them both and went back upstairs. Colin was waiting for me in the corridor.

"Did you learn what you hoped to?" he asked.

"I did. I'm reasonably certain I know what happened, but I haven't the slightest idea of what the killer's motive was and—given that there's still hardly any physical evidence—without it, don't have a strong case."

"Do you want to talk it through? We might be able to figure it out together."

"We might, but hard evidence is always better, isn't it? There's something I want to check. I have an idea."

I took him by the hand and led him back to the gallery. "Take that down from the wall." I pointed to Klimt's portrait of Cécile. He did as I asked. The frame was unexpectedly light. He lowered it to the ground, keeping it balanced upright. I went around to the back. There, tucked in between the canvas and the frame, was a large envelope, stuffed almost to the point of bursting. "This may give us our answers."

"How did you know to look there?" he asked.

"The painting was constantly hanging off-kilter. I straightened it more times than I can count. It occurred to me that something must be causing that to happen. The packet is so thick it pushed one side out from the wall and that must have been enough to keep it out of balance."

He pulled out a penknife from his pocket and handed it to me so I could slice open the envelope. I pulled out a sheaf of papers and read the one on top. My heart caught in my throat. "I can't say it's something I'd ever have suspected," I said, handing it to him, "but at least now we know."

42

Schloss Hohenschwangau
1869

It didn't take long after arriving at Hohenschwangau for Niels's wife to understand that, although he'd started treating her as a friend, the husband who'd been forced upon her had very little interest in any kind of meaningful relationship with her. She couldn't begin to understand the connection between Niels and the king, but there was no denying they shared a bond. When she asked Ludwig about the art in the castle, he had no interest in talking to her about it. Instead, he'd pull Niels outside for a walk. They'd disappear for hours and when they returned there was something off about the both of them. She couldn't determine what precisely, but it was something almost familiar.

She took to spending her time with Elisabet, but was reluctant to bring up the subject. In the end, she didn't need to; Elisabet did instead.

"It's quite a relief to have you here," Elisabet said. "You can't imagine what it's like when there's no one around but the two of them. They were always focused entirely on each other, but it's all the more noticeable since they've been separated for so long. Before, I could almost believe we were the Three Musketeers. We had heaps of fun together. Perhaps things will go back to normal after a few months."

"Months? Surely we won't be here that long," the Valkyrie said. "What am I meant to do?"

"Whatever you'd like." Elisabet looked at her through narrowed eyes. "You're not madly in love with him are you?"

"With my husband? Heavens, no, but I'd come to believe we were friends who would make a life together."

"If you're not in love with him, you're in a brilliant position. Travel. Take a lover. Now that you're out from under the thumb of your father-in-law, the world is offering you endless possibilities."

"You make it sound so easy."

"It is, once you throw off the mantle of obligation," Elisabet said. "Do you see me living as a slave to my husband?"

"You're married?"

"I am."

"And Herr Ney doesn't mind you living here at the palace, without him?"

"He's Dr. Montgomery, if you must know," she said. "Most of the time I don't even tell people I'm married. What business is it of theirs, after all?"

"You didn't take his name?"

"Why should I have? I've got an identity of my own. I don't need his."

The Valkyrie had not the slightest idea how to respond to that. When she retired to bed that evening, she stayed awake, listening for Niels to open the door to his bedroom on the other side of the corridor. He and Ludwig had decided to go for a midnight walk under the full moon, but he didn't return until luncheon the next day.

"Where have you been hiding?" she asked, pulling him aside when he and Ludwig came into the dining room.

"Forgive me, I've been a beast. The night was so beautiful we stayed out until the sun started to rise. I fell asleep as soon as I got to my room and only just awakened. What have you done this morning?"

"Nothing except wait for you."

"You have all the resources of this magnificent place at your fingertips. You don't need me to take advantage of them."

She realized that once again, she was on her own, destined to never be happy, not unless she took the only action she could think of that would make a positive change in her life.

43

Villa von Düchtel
1906

Taking the stack of papers with us, Colin and I headed back toward the study, detouring first to telephone the police. The snow had stopped overnight and the sun had been shining all morning. The roads were bound to be passable soon, if they weren't already.

"You two look rather serious," Ursula said when we entered the room. "We're having quite a laugh over the Furies. I think I may keep them after all."

"You admitted to me that you have some skill as a sculptor, didn't you?" I asked.

"Yes, when Cécile told you I'd studied at the academy in Munich."

"Yet the talent didn't pass on to your daughter," I said.

"My daughter? Good heavens, no, but then Sigrid never had any interest in art. I hired a drawing master for her when she was twelve, but he told me she was hopeless before the end of the first day and refused to return to the house."

"I didn't mean Sigrid," I said, "rather your other daughter, Liesel."

263

"Liesel?" She balked, but her face turned a dark shade of red. "You're very confused, Emily, if you think that—"

Liesel shot toward the door, but Colin stepped in front of her, took her by the shoulders, and brought her back to us. "Don't try it again," he said. "I'll physically restrain you if necessary."

"It's not necessary," Liesel said, taking a seat. She clasped her hands in her lap and focused her eyes on the floor in front of her feet.

"Do you remember this document?" I asked, passing Ursula the first of the papers I'd found behind the painting.

"Good heavens." She was trembling. "I never thought I'd see this again. I—" She looked at Liesel. "Are you really her?"

"The child you abandoned? I always have been, since the day of my birth in Paris."

"I'm overwhelmed." Ursula dropped onto a chair. "Not a day has gone by that I haven't wondered what happened to you. I knew your father would take care of you, but to have had no details, for all these decades, was a tremendous source of . . . well, it would've been worse for you than me. Is Hugo . . ." Her voice trailed and she swallowed, hard.

"My father?" Liesel asked. "He's dead."

Ursula closed her eyes. "It was too much to hope."

"Too much to hope? Too much to hope?" Liesel's voice reached a painful pitch. "What did you think? That he was still in love with you? Carrying a flame for you all these years? That he was waiting for you in Paris?"

"*Arrêtez*, both of you," Cécile said. "Start at the beginning. You cannot open the book of someone's life in the middle and expect it to make sense."

"She's the only one who can tell it from the start." Liesel spat the words.

264

"That's correct." Ursula sighed and looked at Cécile, rather than her daughter, as she spoke. "You know I was unhappy as a young woman."

"*Oui*, the story is infamous. Your mother took you to Paris, where your senses were lit on fire, but your father insisted you return to Munich and forced you to marry a man you did not know."

"That's all true, but it's not complete. After I started collecting art, I met a sculptor from Mainz called Hugo Kratzl. He'd come to Munich to exhibit some of his work in a gallery I knew well. His talent was—"

"Mediocre at best," Liesel said.

"Yes, that is true," Ursula said, "but everything else about him was magnificent. He was intelligent and curious and handsome and I fell in love with him before I'd known him for five minutes. Most of my friends were passionate about the idea of a bohemian lifestyle, but I was the only one of us daring enough to adopt it. Hugo and I became lovers and before long, I found myself with child."

"Hardly surprising," Liesel said.

"No, it shouldn't have been, but in those days, such things weren't discussed. I had a vague notion of how it all worked, but no knowledge of the specifics. I knew I was doing something I shouldn't, but it never occurred to me what might come next. My naïveté was painful. Hugo wanted to marry me, and I was prepared to run away with him. I would've given anything up for him."

"Yet you chose not to," Liesel said. There was anger in her voice, but an equal measure of pain.

"We made plans to elope. He needed to go back to Mainz and I was to accompany him. We'd be married there and raise our family. When the night came that we were to go, I slipped out of my bedroom with only a small valise containing some clothes and the few pieces of jewelry I owned. It was nothing valuable, all that belonged to the family and was in my mother's possession, but it would bring us some money. By then, I was so enamored with Hugo, I was convinced we could live on the proceeds of his art."

"The stupidity is astonishing," Liesel said.

"Yes, it is, but it's also beautiful to love someone so much you have infinite faith in him," Ursula said.

"You never got to Mainz," Cécile said.

"No, I didn't. My father was waiting for me at the bottom of the stairs. My maid, whom I'd foolishly believed to be my confidante, had told him of my plans. He ordered Hugo away, making it clear he would never see me again. I was desperate, furious, and terrified, but Hugo had the presence of mind to remain calm. He agreed to leave and to make no fuss, but only if my father would let him have the baby after it was born. My mother came down when she heard the commotion—my father hadn't bothered to tell her what was happening—and when she heard the whole story, agreed that Hugo should raise the child. It would be immoral, she argued, to keep an infant from his father. Neither of them had the slightest concern for its mother.

"They concocted a plan," she continued. "My mother would notify Hugo when the child was born and tell him where to come to collect it. My father wanted me to spend my confinement in the French countryside, where his sister lived, but my mother objected. She didn't want anyone else to know what I'd done. My reputation— and that of the family—would be destroyed. So instead, she insisted on Paris. It's far easier to be anonymous in a large city. Once we arrived there, I wasn't permitted to leave the rooms we'd rented. I was being punished, after all.

"When my labor started, a midwife tended to me, and took the baby away as soon as she was born." She looked at Liesel. "I wasn't even allowed to see you."

"Why should you have been? I was obviously of no value to you."

"I understand why you feel like that, but at the time, I had no power over my own life. Had the elopement succeeded, things would've been different; but because it didn't, there was nothing I could do. I'd already taken the only action I could to try to protect you."

"This letter," I said, holding it up.

"Yes." Ursula's eyes swam with tears. "Hugo agreed to my parents' stipulations that he would raise the child without me and never tell her who I was. She'd never know my name and I would never know hers. I wanted him to have some sort of insurance, something to guarantee that if he died before she was grown, she wouldn't be left a penniless orphan."

"So by then you'd abandoned your faith in him and decided he'd never be able to support himself through the sales of his art?" Liesel asked.

"By then, I only cared about providing for you should it become necessary."

"Necessary. How generous of you. How magnanimous. My sister grew up in luxury while I shivered in an attic apartment; but because I wasn't a penniless orphan, that was all right."

"I wish I'd had a way to do more," Ursula said. "A few days before you were born, when my mother had gone out for the afternoon, I wrote that letter, explicitly stating that I was your mother and that you were being remanded into the care of your father. I convinced the maid who worked for us to summon a notary so that the document would be official. If you ever needed to prove your identity, it would be possible."

"But you didn't know the baby's name," I said.

"The notary assured me that the detail I provided, along with a birth certificate, which her father would have, would be enough."

"That's here as well." I pulled it out from the papers. "*Liesel Kratzl was born at 4:32 p.m. at her grandmother's residence* . . . Hugo Kratzl and Ursula von Düchtel are listed as the parents. It's signed by Hugo and the mayor of the arrondissement. I thought von Düchtel was your married name?"

"A friend—a sculptor—who refused to take her husband's name inspired me to return to the identity I was born with," Ursula said. "I made the switch before Sigrid was born, so she never found it unusual."

"How considerate." Liesel crossed her arms. "My father changed his name as well, to Fronberg, because your parents insisted on it so you would have a harder time should you ever try to find him."

"I cannot adequately apologize for having given you up," Ursula said. "I honestly saw no other way forward. I had neither money nor power."

"You could've tried to find my father."

"I did. Less than a week after your birth, my mother and I were summoned back to Munich, where my father announced that I would be married a few days later. The match was a disaster, but it made it possible for me to write to your father. I sent scores of letters to Mainz. Hugo never answered any of them. After my father-in-law died and my husband was focused on his own interests, I went to Mainz to look for Hugo. His friends told me he'd married and gone to New York. This broke my heart, but I could hardly blame him."

"They were lying," Liesel said. "He went to Berlin, where he did marry, so that I'd have a mother."

"The letters are here, Ursula," I said, holding the envelope. "They were tied together with twine and on top is a note signed by Hugo, explaining that he had his landlady in Mainz forward everything to him. She promised she would never provide the address to anyone who inquired after it."

"He had loyal friends," Ursula said.

"He wrote that he saved them for Liesel so that she'd know you loved her, tried to make contact, and always wanted the best for her," I said.

"Yes, wasn't that sweet?" Liesel smirked. "Do you feel absolved now?"

"I'll never feel absolved," Ursula said. "I don't deserve your forgiveness. But Sigrid . . . what did she ever do to you? I can understand you wanting me dead, but her?"

"The day before my father died, when he knew the end wasn't far off, he told me that, once he was gone, I would find something important inside a sculpture of his," Liesel said. "It was one of his favorite pieces, a stylized bust of a woman. I'd always assumed it was my mother. My real mother, that is, not you."

"I would never suggest I have a right to that title," Ursula said.

"I'd also always assumed it was made from stone, but I'd never picked it up until the morning after his death. He kept it on a high shelf in his studio. It was apparent at once that it was hollow and made from plaster. There was no way to open it except by breaking it, so I did. Inside was everything you found today, Lady Emily. My birth certificate, the letters the baroness wrote to my father, her notarized letter, and a thick stack of correspondence between the two of them from before he was forced to leave Munich."

"After my father ordered Hugo away, I sent the ones he'd written to me back to him in Mainz," Ursula said. "I knew my parents would search my room—which they did—and I didn't want them destroyed."

"He organized them in chronological order," Liesel said. "It disgusted me, finding them, because when I saw how carefully he'd kept them, I knew then that he'd never really loved the woman I thought was my mother. It was always you. You've robbed me of what I believed was a happy childhood. All of it was a lie."

"I'm sorry, so very sorry—"

"I'm not interested in your worthless apologies," Liesel said. "If you hadn't been confronted by any of this, you never would've thought about it again. I was furious for a while, but then I calmed down. I recognized your name. You've a stellar reputation among art dealers. I knew you were wealthy and I soon discovered that you had another daughter. I've always lived with uncertainty. There's never enough money. My gallery is successful, relatively speaking, but there are many months each year where I'm hard-pressed to cover my expenses. My childhood had been much the same, and I was tired of it. Tired of scrimping and saving. Tired of having the dull ache of constant worry in the back of my mind."

"If you'd asked me, I would've—"

"Yes, you would've given me an allowance," Liesel said. "You owe me more than that, much more, and I didn't want a relationship with you, the woman who abandoned me. I have heard of the English game of cricket and understand some call it the long game. Is that correct?"

"It can run extremely long," Colin said.

"I decided I could play a long game," Liesel continued. "As your daughter, I have a legal right to my inheritance. While I bore no particular grudge against my sister, I had no affection for her. So far as I'm concerned, she's already had her share of your fortune, and she stood between me and the rest. Once she started talking about the sleigh ride, I knew it would provide me the opportunity I needed. That day, I skied to a spot the sleigh would pass, switched my boots for a pair of Kaspar's that I'd taken from his room, so no one would notice a second set of footprints, climbed a tree, and waited. I'm an excellent shot and an excellent skier, so getting it done was no trouble at all. I dropped the gun so that I couldn't be found with it. With Sigrid gone, I would be the baroness's sole remaining heir." She turned to Ursula. "After you died, I would come forward, prove my identity, and collect my birthright. I was very careful to check the details of all the pertinent laws. Your fortune would be mine."

The coldness in her voice was terrifying. There was no hint of remorse or regret or even a desire that things might have been different.

"I took tea to your room," I said, "and saw you sleeping."

"When I traveled here, I brought with me a wax bust and a wig that matched my hair color," she said. "The drapes were closed. With the room dark and a mountain of blankets, it was simple to create the illusion that I was in bed. When I returned to the house, I went back upstairs and slipped into my room, careful to avoid running into anyone, and melted the wax over my fire in a pot I'd taken from the kitchen in the middle of the night. I'd crafted a wooden mold of the Erinyes—a fitting choice, don't you think?—and poured the wax into it. When it was hard, I removed it and burned the mold and the wig."

"You didn't notice that the ring fell off the pot," Colin said.

"No, I didn't, but was aware that after burning so much, something might be noticed in my fireplace, so I tossed a few things in and near the rest of them, so anything in mine wouldn't stand out."

"I expect you would've killed me next?" Ursula asked.

"Oh, no, I can be patient. Violence is only justified when it's necessary. I could tolerate the anxiety around my financial state so long as I knew it would eventually come to an end. I'm not evil, after all."

"Why the attacks on Kaspar?" I asked.

"To make everyone think he was the target," she said. "Then, when Sigrid died, you'd all start to wonder if the clumsy attempts against him were meant to cover up the fact that he wanted his wife dead. Spouses are usually the guilty parties in these sorts of cases, I understand. Frankly, I'm shocked anyone looked further than that."

"The police likely wouldn't have," Colin said. "You'd have stood by and let him hang?"

Liesel shrugged. "I'm not accountable if the courts find an innocent man guilty in the absence of physical evidence. His death would be on their hands." Her coldness was astonishing.

"Why did you hide the papers behind the painting of Cécile?"

"I wanted them found in Ursula's possession," Liesel said. "After her death, if they weren't discovered in the natural course of things, I would've arranged for them to be. I could have offered to value the collection or make a new inventory or something of the sort. I'd have brought in other curators as well and made sure one of them dealt with the Klimt. Then, when it all came out, I'd be overwhelmed with emotion and point out what would seem obvious: that the baroness had brought me here in the first place because she knew who I was and wanted to get to know me. No one would ever remember that it was I who asked a dealer friend in Paris to tell the Baroness von Düchtel about my gallery in Berlin. It all worked a charm."

"Did it?" I asked, cocking my head. "A woman is dead and you'll be hanged for her murder."

"Not here, I won't," Liesel said. "Germany abandoned hanging centuries ago. It will be the axe for me. Perhaps I'll emulate Anne Boleyn and ask for a French swordsman instead. It would be much more elegant."

44

Schloss Hohenschwangau
1874

"A child?" Ludwig's head snapped around. "You have a child? How is that possible?"

"I believe you're familiar with the general mechanisms," Niels said.

"I was under the impression that you're not intimate with your wife."

"I'm not, not usually. You know how difficult it's been. When she left here, all those years ago, she was in something of a rage. She fled to Mainz and then returned to Munich, where she set up housekeeping outside the family home."

"She should do whatever she wants within reason," Ludwig said. "Keep her happy, so she'll leave us be."

"That's exactly what I've done. When I saw her and my mother at Christmas she told me she wanted a child."

"I said within reason. A child doesn't meet that qualification."

"She told me a heartbreaking story about something that happened before we married. She'd had a lover and lost their child."

"Well, that's most careless of her. She should've hired a nurse to look after it."

"Don't be obtuse," Niels said. "She wasn't allowed even to see the infant after its birth. It was taken from her and sent away. Shortly thereafter, our marriage was arranged. I always thought she'd been in love with someone her family considered unsuitable and assumed— hoped, rather—that their connection might be rekindled after our wedding, but he's nowhere to be found."

"That's hardly our problem."

"No, but we do need to keep her content. It's the right thing, to let her have a family. It is expected, after all."

"It's expected of me as well, you know, but I haven't given in to the pressure."

"You're a king. I'm not."

"You're a baron and I'm your feudal lord." He smiled and Niels breathed a sigh of relief. He'd been dreading this conversation since he'd opened the Valkyrie's letter announcing their daughter's birth. She'd named the infant Sigrid and explained that this time it was Lohengrin who was guilty of betrayal, not his wife.

Niels paid little attention to his wife's censure. Instead, he resigned himself to compartmentalizing the bits of his life, shutting away those that brought him no joy. Sigrid did not fall into that category. He adored their child, but the rift in his marriage meant having scant time with her. Most of the time, he accepted this as the cost of sharing the king's world. Was the choice a wise one? Over the years he questioned the decision, for although he had a piece of Ludwig's heart, he'd never have it all. There were months of loneliness, times when he was cast aside, subject to his lover's whims and increasingly erratic moods. He'd remember Elisabet's warnings and wish he'd taken heed. Until Ludwig returned to him. Then, for a while, doubt would vanish, but not forever. Tying his happiness to the king guaranteed stretches of bliss, but they would always be interspersed with searing pain.

45

Villa von Düchtel
1906

The police managed to reach Ursula's house later that day and took Liesel away. We spoke to Kaspar privately and told him the details of the crime.

His shoulders drooped. "It feels more real now, knowing what happened," he said. "I've been a bit numb. I never suspected Liesel. She was so innocuous."

"She was unemotional and calculating, which made it easy for her to keep her guard up and evade suspicion," Colin said.

"I can't begin to comprehend that it's possible to spend days in the presence of a murderer and not have the slightest idea."

Ursula and Cécile came into the room. "I understand how you feel. I can't begin to comprehend that it's possible to spend years in the presence of a man who harasses women and not have the slightest idea."

"What are you talking about?" Kaspar said.

"I know what you've done and shan't tolerate it in my household.

There's a train that leaves Füssen in three hours. That gives you plenty of time to pack and get to the station."

"Baroness, I don't understand. There must be some kind of misunderstanding. I would never behave in an inappropriate manner in your house or elsewhere. Please, you must listen to me, I—"

"In fact, Herr Allerspach, there is no cause for me to listen to you. I'm ashamed that I hadn't given my servants cause to have enough faith in me that they might have come forward earlier. Begone. I don't want to see you again."

He sputtered but didn't speak and left the room.

"It is good to be rid of him," Cécile said. Ursula sat down, tears in her eyes.

"I can't believe it's all come to this," she said. "What a mess I've caused. I should've tried harder to find Liesel. I was broken, physically and emotionally, after her birth. I walked like a ghost into my marriage; and when I realized my husband didn't even care to be my friend, I was crushed."

"Crushed?" Cécile asked. "Why, given that you hadn't wanted to marry him in the first place?"

"I was young and heartbroken when we married, but after a few months, I started to heal and I decided to open my heart to him. I wasn't looking for romantic love, but I understood the need for a partner in life. We took an abbreviated wedding trip, and on the way home from it, I came to see that he was the sort of man I could befriend. I respected him. We were honest with each other, neither promising more than we could give. At least that's what I thought.

"At the time, I didn't know why his father was so insistent on him marrying. I assumed that Niels—that was his name—preferred the life of a bachelor, with no commitments, and that his parents wanted him to provide the family with an heir."

"An ordinary enough situation," I said.

"Yes," Ursula said. "I didn't realize how wrong I was until after his father died. Once he became baron, Niels had control over the family fortune. He could live however he wanted, and he told me I could, too. I didn't think anything of it at first, not until we came into the country together."

"To the old house that stood here?" Colin asked.

"No, to Schloss Hohenschwangau, to stay with the king, Ludwig the Second. My husband had an intimate friendship with him and within a few days, I saw that I would never have a partner in my marriage. Like a fool, I'd walked into another kind of heartbreak. This time, I wasn't being wrenched away from the only man I would ever love; instead, I was losing what I believed was my last chance for a normal life. I wasn't asking for passion or adoration, only understanding and companionship, but Niels would never be able to give either to me. His entire being was engaged elsewhere. Perhaps my expectations were unreasonable, but his betrayal wounded me deeply."

"Why would he withhold friendship?" Cécile asked.

"He didn't do it consciously. He'd have been quite content for me to live in the old house that stood here. He would've asked no questions should I ever have sought comfort elsewhere and would've expected the same from me, but those weeks at Hohenschwangau showed me that I never would have been content with that. I wanted more. So I returned to Munich and never lived with him again."

"But Sigrid . . ." My voice trailed.

"Yes, Sigrid. I was lonely and I wanted someone who would always be mine. Ridiculous, isn't it, to believe that's what a child is? I thought she would fill the hole in my heart. She did for many years, but now she, too, is gone, like everyone else I've loved."

"Was she close to her father?" Colin asked.

"Close enough. She inherited his love for Wagner and for *der Märchenkönig*. I never was able to fully escape Ludwig. I should've been more sympathetic to Niels. In a way, I tried to do the same thing to him that my father had done to me: keep him away from a love of which I didn't approve. Now I'm ashamed of myself."

"What happened to Niels?" I asked.

"Ludwig's life did not come to a happy end," Ursula said. "He'd all but bankrupted himself building castles and his eccentricities consumed him entirely. He started coming out only at night and would sleep all day. He'd take long sleigh rides in the moonlight. He was rarely in Munich and many people in the government believed he was no longer capable of performing his royal duties."

"He was declared mad," Colin said.

"Yes, although it's a diagnosis I never could accept," Ursula said. "Much though I hated him, my feelings were due to his standing in the way of my getting what I wanted. His ministers likely shared a similar point of view. There was madness in Ludwig's family and it was easy enough for those with power behind the scenes to get what they wanted. He was declared unfit to rule and deposed."

"He died shortly thereafter, if I recall," Colin said.

"Three days later. The official account says that he killed his doctor and then drowned himself while they were walking along the shores of the Würmsee near Schloss Berg. The idea is preposterous. The man was far too full of self-importance to ever have done such a thing. Further, he was an excellent swimmer. I met the doctor who conducted his autopsy. He told me there was no water in Ludwig's lungs."

"So he didn't drown," I said.

"No. There have been all kinds of stories. People who heard gunshots. A boatman who claims the king asked him to help him escape that day. There's a woman I know in possession of a coat that she claims Ludwig was wearing when he died; it has bullet holes in it."

"Yet the official cause of death remains suicide?" I asked.

Ursula shrugged. "Many people prefer to avoid uncomfortable truths, and, in the end, those in power got what they wanted."

"And Niels?" Cécile asked.

"He wasn't at Berg that day. When they took the king into custody, Niels retreated to his old house here. When the news came that Ludwig was dead, he walked to the shore of the Alpsee and shot himself in the head."

"How terrible," I said.

"I often wonder what would've happened if he'd possessed the strength to go on. If I'd been more kind, more willing to meet him halfway, it might have been different. Perhaps we could have found ourselves friends. But one can't go back." She gave herself a little shake. "There's no point dwelling on such morbid things."

"It's all so tragic," I said.

"It's why I can't stand the sight of Neuschwanstein," Ursula said. "Its construction led to nothing but infinite sadness."

Dinner was a somber affair that night, but the wine was excellent and by the time we'd all retired to the music room and were listening to Max play the piano, the mood had already begun to shift. Birgit looked very much alone, but Max convinced her to sing with him. Her voice, untrained and pure, was lovely. She told me she had no intention of ever seeing Kaspar again, but the next morning, he sent a sleigh to collect her and she left, giggling. She was the only one of us who didn't attend Sigrid's funeral.

Felix arranged for Max to meet the director at Bayreuth and, soon thereafter, he and his Wagner tuba earned a seat in the orchestra. Ursula convinced Felix and Cécile to stay on with her in Bavaria until spring came.

"I still don't understand why she'd want Felix with her as well," I said once Colin and I were settled into our compartment on the train out of Munich.

"Because she knew Cécile wouldn't stay if he left," he said.

"Cécile may have indulged in a flirtation with him, but she's hardly attached to the man. She never would've abandoned her grieving friend in favor of him."

"Of course not, but, like Cécile, Ursula respects the value of tutelage. She wouldn't interfere in such a thing."

"Tutelage, again with the tutelage. Whatever do you mean by it? I'm not naïve enough to believe you're referring to your university education."

"It would be better, perhaps, if I showed you. Lengthy explanations can be so dry. Tedious, really. Dare I say *boring beyond belief*?" He looked deep into my eyes. "We've something of a history when it comes to train compartments."

"Some of my favorite memories are connected with them."

"Intimately connected, if I recall," he said, pulling me close, "particularly on the Orient Express en route to Constantinople. Even so, I'm not certain we could claim exhaustive schooling when it comes to taking full advantage of them. How long until we arrive in Bremen?"

"Not long enough, but we'll have the boat after that. Perhaps by the time we disembark in Southampton, I'll have a better understanding of what you mean by tutelage, at least when it comes to confined spaces."

"Rest assured, my dear, by then, you will be an expert."

Author's Note

I became interested in Ludwig II during a stop at Schloss Neuschwanstein while on a road trip through Europe. The view of the castle against the backdrop of the Alps is spectacular, but touring the inside left me with myriad questions about its builder. Here was a cultured, misunderstood man who ran through his fortune in a quest to create a world—inspired by the works of Richard Wagner—in which he would feel comfortable living. His death remains something of a mystery. The public has never been satisfied by the official explanation that he killed his doctor and then himself after he was declared insane and removed from the throne. The doctor's body showed signs of a struggle; the king's did not. The members of the search party who found the corpses were forced to take an oath that they would never speak about what they saw. One of them, a fisherman called Jakob Lidl, wrote about it in his diary, claiming Ludwig had engaged him to help him escape from the castle at Berg. After they boarded Lidl's boat, a shot to the back felled the king. The fisherman, afraid he'd be killed as well, shoved the body into the lake and fled.

The countess Wrnba-Kaunitz claimed to have owned the coat Ludwig was wearing at the time of his death. It had two bullet holes in it. Dr. Rudolf Magg, who lived in the area, examined the king's body shortly after it was found. Magg's daughter's physician claims to have read a confession of sorts Magg left behind, admitting that his official report was false. The king died not by drowning, but from shots to the back.

There are more stories about sketches done at the scene that show blood coming from Ludwig's mouth and a note written by his personal physician that makes a direct accusation of murder based on what he witnessed at Lake Starnberg. The trouble is, all the physical evidence has vanished. A handwriting expert authenticated the writing in Lidl's diary, but it disappeared after his death. There are, however, extant photographs of the key pages. No one has ever found Magg's supposed confession, and the countess's coat was never seen again after she and her husband died in a fire.

It's unlikely we'll ever know the details of Ludwig's death. Instead, we're left with tantalizing clues that point to conspiracy. This, in turn, feeds the public's long-running obsession with the Mad King. The human brain craves a good story, one that makes sense, even in the absence of demonstrable facts.

After my visit to Neuschwanstein, I felt a great sympathy for Ludwig. As I started reading biographies of him, I began to see how complicated he was. He treated servants cruelly, hated everything ugly, and could be rather vicious. His diaries reveal that, as a devout Catholic, he struggled with his homosexuality. His friendship with Elisabet Ney provided him with much-needed support. In a letter to him, she wrote, "God has made you as you are. You did not create yourself . . . therefore you may freely admit what you are."

Even so, he struggled to find personal happiness, alternating between throwing himself into passionate relationships with men and then chastising himself for them. He never married and never provided an heir. Could this, along with his focusing more on building projects than the difficult political situations of the time, have motivated the powers that be to have wanted him gone? Possibly not just dethroned, but dead? Whatever happened on that tragic day, Ludwig remains very much in the present-day consciousness.

Sources

Baedeker, Karl. *Southern Germany: Wurtemberg and Bavaria*. 10th ed. Leipzig: Baedeker, 1910.

Bertram, Werner. *A Royal Recluse: Memories of Ludwig II of Bavaria*. Munich: Martin Herpich & Son, Engravers and Publishers, 1936.

Cutrer, Emily Fourmy. *The Art of the Woman: The Life and Work of Elisabet Ney*. College Station: Texas A&M University Press, 1988.

"Elisabet Ney Biography." n.d. The Official Website of the City of Austin. Accessed May 6, 2023. https://www.austintexas.gov /sites/default/files/files/Parks/Ney/Elisabet_Ney_Bio.pdf.

Geretsegger, Heinz, Max Peintner, and Walter Pichler. *Otto Wagner 1841–1918: The Expanding City, the Beginning of Modern Architecture*. New York: Rizzoli, 1979.

Jervis, Simon, and Gerhard Hojer. *Designs for the Dream King: The Castles and Palaces of Ludwig II of Bavaria*. London: Debrett's Peerage Ltd, 1978.

King, Greg. *The Mad King*. Secaucus, NJ: Birch Lane Press, 1996.

Kühler, Michael, and Ernst Wrba. *The Castles of King Ludwig II.* Translated by Ruth Chitty. Würzburg: Verlagshaus Würzburg GmbH & Co. KG, 2008.

Sarnitz, August. *Otto Wagner: 1841–1981: Forerunner of Modern Architecture.* Köln: Taschen, 2005.

Schiff, Gert, and Stephan Waetzoldt. *German Masters of the Nineteenth Century.* New York: Metropolitan Museum of Art, 1981.

Symons, Susan. *Schloss in Bavaria.* St. Just-in-Roseland, Cornwall: Roseland Books, 2017.

Wagner, Otto, and Harry Francis Mallgrave. *Modern Architecture: A Guidebook for His Students to This Field of Art.* Santa Monica, CA: The Getty Center for the History of Art and the Humanities, 1990.

Acknowledgments

Myriad thanks to . . . Charlie Spicer, dream editor.

Hannah Pierdolla, Andy Martin, Sarah Melnyk, and David Rotstein.

Anne Hawkins, agent extraordinaire.

Claudia Panzer and Andreas Brieke, for ensuring my Bavarians sound like Bavarians.

Brett Battles, Laura Bradford, Rob Browne, Bill Cameron, Christina Chen, Jon Clinch, Jane Grant, Nick Hawkins, Elizabeth Letts, Lara Matthys, Carrie Medders, Erica Ruth Neubauer, Missy Rightley, Renee Rosen, Martha Schwartz, and Lauren Willig. Much love.

Alexander, Katie, and Jess.

My parents.

Andrew, who has proved over many years to truly be my soul's far better part.

About the Author

Charles Osgood

TASHA ALEXANDER, is the author of the *New York Times* bestselling Lady Emily Mystery series. The daughter of two philosophy professors, she studied English literature and medieval history at the University of Notre Dame. She and her husband, novelist Andrew Child, live on a ranch in southeastern Wyoming.